It Had To Be You

Lisa Marie McKay

Acknowledgments

The amazing Cherry Adair has mentored writers in her own inimitable fashion. Every year, she issues the "Finish The Damn Book" challenge and this book was the result of that challenge in my life. Cherry, saying "thank you" can never be enough.

Endless gratitude to Erik and Kristen Schubach. You know what you've done. Don't try to deny it.

My heartfelt thanks to Maureen Fazzio, Jennifer Smith, Jenna Riley and Connie Hoag for your careful reading and input. And, you know, sorry. I'm possibly the world's worst typist.

And as usual, thanks to my roommate and the little sister of my heart, Jennifer Smith. I would never be able to find anything in the refrigerator without you.

To Mikael.

No matter what you say, you are a hero.

Chapter One

Hope glared out over her steering wheel and snapped loudly enough that the crappy I-5 traffic and a crappier phone headset couldn't hide her words or her irritation. "I'm returning his Wonder Mixer accessory kit, Miriam, because I'm a nice person. Hell, I'm a freaking peach."

Her best friend and sister-in-law snorted. "Tch! A cream puff, perhaps. When are you going to grow a spine? You're driving to Gold Bar, Hope. Gold Bar. You know, I do not think I even know where this Gold Bar is."

"Oh, you do, too. You're just being dramatic."

Miriam's answering screech and brief torrent of Norwegian were almost enough to make Hope rip out her earpiece. "I'm dramatic? I am?"

"Case in point." Hope snarled as a BMW cut her off. "Nice move, buddy! No, why don't you take the whole road?"

"Excuse me? Still talking here."

Hope sighed and glanced at her oil gauge again. Managing the upscale Home Again building supply store had its benefits, but replacing her aging Toyota truck wasn't one of them. At least, not while she was having her own little nest remodeled. The guy at the Lightning Lube place had told her last month that the oil spot on her driveway meant nothing and this car would run forever. At least that's what he'd told her breasts.

"--Letting some man take advantage of you! You must quit this...this being a--"

"A decent human being? Is that what you were going to say?" Hope shoved a stubborn wisp of dark blonde hair out of her mouth. She just couldn't get herself to cut it short enough to keep it from doing that, but the baby-fine strands were getting closer. Miriam once teased her that the worse her love life was, the shorter her hair was cut. If that had been true, she'd be bald by now.

"You are a decent human being, Hope, darling. Stupid, but decent."

"Thank you very much." A teenager in a bucket of rust veered over into her lane and she leaned on the horn. "Oh, yeah? Same to you, buddy!"

"Quit yelling at traffic and listen to me. You are a nice woman. You need to find a nice man and forget about these losers. I don't know why it's so hard for you. When I was single, I knew lots of nice, single men."

"No, really?" Before marrying Hope's brother, Miriam had been a lingerie model. Even after three children, she was still tall and lithe and an exotic golden color all over. The Norwegian accent that was just sweet on Hope's grandparents turned sultry when Miriam spoke, and on top of all of this, she had that certain something men loved. She simply oozed that *I-know-what-you're-thinking-and-if-you're-very-good-I-might-let-you-try-it* attitude. Some days, it was all Hope could do not to hate her.

Evidently, Miriam wasn't finished torturing her yet. "I don't understand why you settle. These guys are such losers! Why can't you just treat this like one of your little projects?"

Hope turned on her signal and eased off the highway. According to her computer-generated directions, this was the fastest way to Brian's house in Gold Bar, but looking at the snarls of traffic surrounding her, she doubted it. What would this trip be like during rush hour? She shuddered.

"Are you even listening to me, Hope?"

"Yes, I'm listening. Guys. Losers. Projects. None of it makes sense, but I'm listening."

Her sister-in-law sighed. "If you treat it like a project, you'll be more successful at it. What's the thing you always tell me when we're fixing up the house?"

"Start with quality materials."

"That's it, quality materials. None of these are quality materials."

That was it. Her gorgeous friend and sister-in-law had hit the nail on the head. "I think you're right, Miriam."

"You do?"

"Yes, I do." Hope would have laughed at the doubt and suspicion in Miriam's voice if she hadn't been so close to tears. Tears, of all things! "You're absolutely right."

"I am? Of course, I am! Now, if--"

"But you're missing one important part. There are no good men left. The last one got married two years ago and I was a bridesmaid for the blessed event." Even now, the shame and pain of that day was enough to scald her from the inside out. She blinked hard and scowled at another driver who was trying to merge into her lane.

"Terrence was the wrong man for you."

Hope laughed without humor. "And evidently, so was Brian."

"I never trusted Brian."

"And James."

"He had beady eyes."

"Tony?"

"Was not a tiger."

"True enough. And then there was Doug."

There was silence on the line for a moment. "Which one was Doug, again?" Miriam asked.

"Mama's boy."

"Narrow it down a little more."

"Ponytail, earring, grew his own herbs."

"I got nothing."

"Rode a mountain bike everywhere."

"Oh, that's right! The one with the really small... um... kickstand, right?"

"Miriam!"

"Well, you shouldn't have told me, then. Although it seems to me that all that time on a bike seat couldn't have helped him much. Starting with a deficit like he did, yes? He must have known--"

Hope waited for the rest of Miriam's assessment but heard nothing.

"Known what? Hello?" Hope tapped her earpiece, then glanced at the display on her dash-mounted cell phone. Dead. How could it be dead?

A pothole jolted her attention back to the road and the flash of a blinking red light on the dash caught her eye.

"Oh, perfect. Just perfect."

Hope pulled off the road and stared for a moment at the oil warning light before switching off the engine. The March sky glowered down on her, but the rain didn't worry her nearly as much as the lack of signal on her cell phone. She had barely made it past hard-core suburbia; how could she be out of signal range? She even had the tiny phone plugged into the car charger, as she always did when she drove.

"Sitting here isn't getting anything done, Hope Lindstrom. Get your bottom moving." A mean-spirited wind pushed back at the door when she opened it, and she shivered. The denim jacket had seemed like a good idea two hours ago, but now, she was flat-out chilled. And not an espresso stand in sight? Surely that was illegal.

The car hood popped right up. "Is this a good sign?" Hope muttered. Maybe there was an obvious restart button, or a shoelace left untied or…. "Shoot."

She'd just dropped her keys.

In the way of all dropped keys, they were nowhere in sight. Hope peered under the bumper, praying they'd be right there. Aha! Her keys! Only a couple feet back and handily situated next to a brown puddle. A growing brown puddle.

"No. Please, no."

A slow but steady drip of oil plopped from the underside of her truck into the small pool. As she laid there on her belly in the dirt and gravel on the side of the road, she took a slow deep breath and tried to remember what her Nana always told her. "When it's as bad as it can be, at least it won't get any worse."

That's when the rain started.

"Why is it no one will just shoot me and put me out of my misery?" she wondered out loud.

"Well, mostly because it's illegal," a deep, resonant voice answered.

Hope shrieked and started up, slamming her head against the undercarriage of her truck, then collapsed into the dirt again. She was still moaning when strong hands pulled her out and turned her over. None too gently, Hope felt those hands run over her abused skull and she yelped again when they found a tender spot.

"Lady, are you okay? Open your eyes. Can you open your eyes?"

Of course, she could. She was opening them now, wasn't she? Or nearly.

"Listen, if you don't open your eyes--"

"I am, I am. Get off me, already." Hope pried open one eyelid and looked up into the most beautiful face she'd ever seen. She didn't know who he was, but if he'd been sporting a set of angel wings, she wouldn't have been surprised. Thick blonde hair, perfectly cut and adorably mussed, glacier-blue eyes and mouth to weep for. He looked like he'd stolen his cheekbones from a Viking warrior and when he smiled--why was he smiling?--a dimple appeared in his left cheek. Hope rubbed her eyes and felt the grit from the road scratch into her skin. "Great. Just great."

"You're going to have a hell of a knot back here."

"Oh, good. Santa got my letter, then." Hope opened one eye again and glared. "You really shouldn't sneak up on people like that."

Thor, the Viking God lifted one eyebrow. "Really? Sneak? I pulled my car over, got out, shut the door and walked over gravel. I had no idea I was so stealthy."

"Yeah, you and Batman. Or should I say Odin?" Hope caught his quizzical look and sighed. "Never mind."

"Okay. Want to try sitting up?" The man grasped her hand, and at Hope's nod, pulled her upright. When the world spun around her, she moaned and squeezed her eyes shut and heard the Viking say, "Uh oh."

And then she was violently sick. She felt his hand against her forehead and heard murmurs, but all that she could focus on was the sudden pain in her head. Something scratchy was bundled under her cheek and a soft cloth swiped across her mouth, and again, she heard his voice. *When did sounds start hurting?* She wondered as the roar of a passing semi pummeled her and the diesel fumes pinched at her brain. The nausea rose up again until a sudden, blessed darkness made it all go away.

Sounds woke her. She heard the hubbub around her and wondered why there was a small army in her bedroom. Maybe Miriam brought over the kids, she thought, and moaned. Kids. That's what she needed right now. Her niece and nephews on top of what felt like the worst hangover in her life.

"Hey, you're back."

Hope pried open one eye and looked at the twelve-year-old leaning over her. Red hair, blue eyes and freckles. All he needed was a fishing pole, overalls and a sandwich made by Aunt Bea. She could almost hear the theme song for *The Andy Griffith Show*. "Don't you have to go to school?" she asked.

The colorized version of Opie Griffith blinked. "Excuse me?"

"It's a school day. Go to school. Let Auntie Hope go back to sleep, Opie."

A ripple of laughter ran around the room and jumped on Hope's head. She moaned again.

"Your name's Hope?" Opie flicked a penlight out. Evidently Mayberry fishing wasn't what it used to be since Opie's new hobby was apparently searing out eyeballs with innocent looking penlights. Sheriff Andy Griffith was going to hear about this. "What's your last name, Auntie Hope?"

"Lindstrom." She yelped when he ran his hands over her skull. "Ow! Why? Why did you do that?"

"Do you know what year it is?"

"If I give you a cookie, will you go away?"

A woman with smooth cocoa-colored skin appeared beside the redheaded boy. "I told you, you need to grow a beard or something until you lose that baby face."

"And the last time I tried to grow a beard, every nurse in the ER tried to wipe the smudge of dirt off my chin." Opie looked seriously depressed by this.

Poor Opie, Hope thought.

"You shouldn't worry about it." Hope patted his hand, trying to pull those probing fingers away from her sore head. "By the time you hit sixteen, you'll have as much beard as any of the other boys."

Opie rolled his eyes, and pointedly ignored the snickering woman next to him. "Ms. Lindstrom, my name is Dr. Evans. You're in the emergency room at Evergreen Memorial. Do you remember how you got hurt?"

"Banged my head when Thor scared me. Wait a minute. You're a doctor? But, you're what…twelve?" Hope peered closer at him. Even with a screaming headache, she knew he was way too young to be a doctor.

Dr. Opie—oops, Evans—picked up a folder and scrawled some quick notes, scowling. "Go to medical school, they said. Get treated with respect, they said. The women'll go nuts. Ha! I should get a refund."

The woman standing next to Hope's bed laughed. "Hope, I'm Terry, one of the nurses here. Please excuse Dr. Evans. He's a little sensitive."

"That's okay." Hope looked over at the muttering young man and whispered to Terry. "He's really a doctor?"

The nurse nodded.

Hope looked around the room. It *looked* like an emergency room, all sterile and ugly, with scary looking equipment and lights. "And he's not some child prodigy or something?"

Terry shook her head no.

"Oh man, I am so old." Hope let her eyes drift shut.

"You're old? Girl, I could've birthed him. Talk to me about old."

The infant doctor walked over then. "Okay, Ms. Lindstrom, I'm going to need to get some imaging on you. Any chance you're pregnant?"

She snorted.

"I'll take that as a no." He marked something else on the folder in front of him.

"Why do I need imaging? Is that an x-ray?" Hope asked.

"To make sure your concussion isn't going to kill you." Dr. Evans turned to Terry. "Let's get a head CT."

"Wait a minute, seriously? Kill me? I bonked my head!"

The redheaded doctor sat on a rolling stool next to her bed. "Subdural hematoma. A bruise, essentially, on your brain. Bonk your head, break a blood vessel…voila. Blood floods your skull and you die. We don't like it when that happens."

"No kidding."

"Nope. Way too many forms to fill out. And they take away my PlayStation." He clicked his pen and tucked it into his pocket.

"The bastards."

"Yup. See you in a few minutes."

A young woman in a white coat swept into the room, and in a few deft moves, had Hope up off the uncomfortable emergency room bed and into the equally bad wheelchair. She murmured something that didn't quite penetrate the pain that was screaming through Hope's skull and whisked her out the door and down the hall.

The doctor called after her. "Don't worry, Hope, I'll have the front desk contact your...."

They'd call Miriam, she thought. Good. Without turning, Hope waved her hand in thanks.

Ninety frustrating minutes later, Hope was back in the questionable privacy of her emergency room cubicle. Eyes closed, stomach churning again, she wondered how much worse the day was going to get.

"Hey, Hope. You okay?"

She groaned and opened her eyes. Brian. Her ex...what had he been to her, exactly? A lover? A companion? A possible future? Yeah, for about five minutes, he'd been all those things.

"What are you doing here, Brian?"

He shifted his feet a bit and stuffed workman's hands into the pockets of his faded jeans. At one point, she'd found that gesture endearing and sexy. The way it stretched the flannel shirt over broad shoulders, tightened denim over…well, other parts. Now, it just pissed her off.

"They called me and said you'd had an accident. I was working near the hospital anyway, so it wasn't a problem for me to come by."

Hope closed her eyes. "Well. How convenient. How did they get your number?"

"I was going to ask you the same thing."

Was it her imagination, or did Brian sound accusing? Hope opened her eyes again, and sure enough, he was watching her like she was acting, waiting for her to break character any second. The throbbing in her head escalated to pounding in tandem with her temper.

"Well, I didn't tell anyone to call you. I don't know who —" Her eyes fell to the cardboard box half covered by her purse, sitting on chair beside her. The cardboard box that had been inside her car. The cardboard box that had Brian's name, Brian's address and, yes, there it was, Brian's phone number right on the label. "I think I figured it out." Hope pointed at the box.

"Huh?" Brian glanced at the label, then blank-faced, turned back to her. Hope sighed. He had never been the sharpest pencil in the box.

"Your phone number's on the mailing label. On the box. See?" Hope closed her eyes again. "Maybe whoever took me to the hospital grabbed it and brought it in."

Hope could hear him walk over to the box and pick it up. "My accessory kit! Where was this?"

"Hall closet. I guess you forgot it, in your rush to leave." It was bitchy. She knew it was bitchy. But dammit, she still didn't have any idea what had happened between them. She was allowed to be a little bitchy. "Since the label had your address, I was bringing it back to you. You did say that you were moving back to your old house, didn't you?"

"You went to my house? Please tell me you didn't go to my house."

Hope opened her eyes again, and sure enough, he looked as panicked as he'd sounded. "No, I didn't make it all the way there. Between my car breaking down and this pesky little concussion, my plans changed. Why?"

"Well...I...I just don't...um...."

"Brian. Why don't you want me near your house? We broke up. I got it. Do you think I'd do something to your home?" She peered at him as he shifted his feet. "What's going on here?"

Moving her purse from the chair to the floor, Brian sat down and set the box beside him. He studied his hands as if looking for the answers to her questions, then sighed. "I don't think my wife would've liked it."

"Excuse me?"

"I said, I don't think—"

"I heard what you said! What the hell do you mean, your wife? We've been broken up for two and a half weeks, and you went out and got married?"

"Hope, you've got it all wrong."

"Really? We broke up, now you're married, and I'm wrong?" Hope pressed the heels of her hands to her eyes. "Enlighten me, please. How am I wrong?"

"I didn't just get married." Brian cleared his throat. "I've been married. For about three years."

"What?" It should have been a scream, Hope thought. She should be screaming. But the words froze under what felt like a chunk of ice in her throat. "You…you moved in with me."

"I know. We'd decided on a trial separation and I moved into a furnished place for a month and then when I met you, and I went over to your place that night, well, it was just so much more comfortable."

"More comfortable." She lowered her hands and stared at him.

"Yeah." He brightened a bit. "It's a great house and you've really made it…I don't know…."

"Great?"

"Yeah! I mean, I know it's got a ways to go, but the house itself is terrific."

Hope opened her mouth but only a strangled sound escaped. Brian continued as if he'd said nothing surprising.

"I really thought that we might be good together, but Marianne thought counseling was a good idea and this way, we won't have to sell the house and everything."

Hope leaned her head back and stared at the acoustic tile on the ceiling. "So you lied to me, moved in with me while you were still married and then left me, not only for another woman, but another woman who happens to be the wife you didn't mention. And a house?"

Brian hunched his shoulders and looked sheepish. "I know I should have told you—"

"You think?"

"But I didn't really lie about it."

"YOU TOLD ME YOU WERE DIVORCED!!"

"Well…I was going to be, so it's the same thing."

"Since you returned home and you're back with your wife without any silly little legal issues to deal with, OBVIOUSLY this is not true!" The volume of her own voice made her wince, but she didn't look away from Brian. Brian, now indelibly labeled as The Weasel. He'd weaseled his way into her home and her body. He'd weaseled his way out. And even now, he was trying to weasel out of admitting what he'd done.

"Listen, Hope, I know you're upset, but I hope we can still be friends." Brian stood and taking the cardboard box he'd set down earlier, turned toward the door to go.

A new voice, rich with disdain and sprinkled with a hint of Norwegian iceberg resounded from the doorway. "Friends? You want to be friends, you…you…!"

"Weasel?" Hope offered.

"Not even close!" Miriam stormed into the room, her leather duster flaring out behind her, swirling around her knee-high boots, slim-cut black pants and ruby red bustier. Hope wondered briefly if Miriam thought the ensemble was appropriate for hospital visits, or if she was simply planning on fighting evil computers and robots later that day.

Brian, however, was unimpressed both with the ensemble and with Miriam. He'd been impressed the first time they met, oh sure. Hope had never really figured out what had happened. "Stay out of it, Miriam. This is none of your business."

"Oh, God." Hope sighed. "Miriam…."

"None of my business? *None* of my business?" Miriam's accent thickened and she waved off Hope's attempt to calm her. "My family is my business, you filthy rat dropping! Now get your worthless ass out of my sight! And Brian?"

He paused in the doorway, held by the venom in the voice of a beautiful woman.

"If you ever bother Hope again—if you ever so much as glance in her direction—they will not be able to identify you with dental records."

He left, and without a backward glance.

"Wow. Good one, Miriam." Hope leaned back.

"Thank you, darling. I have been saving it up." She tossed back a mane of hair that was a thousand shades of gold and considered her manicure. "So. Now you are rid of that one, once and for all. And you can stop whinging about it, can't you, and move on to greener pastures. The children have a new dentist, and I think he's single--"

"No."

"I haven't asked him, so I don't know for sure--"

"No, Miriam."

"But he's definitely cute, and his office looks decent, so he must be doing well--"

"Miriam, for the sweet love of God, listen to me." Hope grabbed her sister-in-law's hand. "Are you listening?"

"Okay, yah. I'm listening." Miriam's amber-colored eyes widened at the fierce look on Hope's face.

"I'm done. I'm done with all of them."

Miriam's perfect brow wrinkled. "Pardon?"

"I'm through with men, Miriam. Every last one of them. Don't set me up, don't arrange casual encounters at dinner parties, and for God's sake, stop leaving applications for singles groups lying around!" Hope took a deep breath and willed Miriam to understand. "I'm never going through this again. I'm done."

For once, Miriam was silent as Hope closed her eyes and waited for this nightmare of a day to be over.

Chapter Two

T. Erik Yoriksson eased his new, gleaming BMW into his reserved parking space and gave the sleek black dash a loving and proprietary pat. His parents were still giving him and his new baby disapproving looks, his sister Tilda was calling it his penis extender and his insurance agent nearly burst into tears, but Erik…Erik was in love.

Besides, after four years in the Army and six years spent getting his Bachelor's and MBA –and spent was the operative word there – he was due a little indulgence. God knew he'd worked for it. Being the youngest vice president of Western Telecomm hadn't just been handed to him.

Grabbing the sports bag off the passenger seat and hitting the lock command on his keyless remote, Erik headed to the stairwell. His space in the condominium's garage was three levels underground and his condo sat on the fourteenth floor. Erik slung the leather strap of his bag across his chest and set the timer on his watch. Before one minute had ticked off, he was at ground level and still moving steadily. When he slid his key card over the pad outside the door of his floor, he glanced at his watch. Six minutes and fifty-three seconds.

"Damn."

Shrugging off the pathetic time – he'd do better tomorrow – Erik started toward his condo before a sound behind him had him glancing over his shoulder, then stopping in his tracks.

"Marty! You sneaky bastard!" A grin nearly split his face as a young man in uniform approached.

"If you paid attention, poor Yorik, no one could sneak up on you." Jasper Martin held out his right hand and after shaking it, Erik pulled him for a quick, hard hug.

"How the hell are you, man?" Erik skimmed over the pressed fatigues and dully gleaming boots to latch onto the small animal carrier in Marty's left hand. "And who is this?"

Excited scrabbling rocked the carrier and Erik spotted white and black fur surrounding gleaming eyes.

"This is Ruger."

"Ruger. Nice. Hey, come on in. Want coffee?" Unlocking his door, Erik looped the bag onto the hook by the hall closet and motioned Marty inside.

"Yeah, coffee'd be good." Marty rested the carrier against his leg and popped the latch. Without missing a beat, he caught a small white bundle of fluff as it shot out of the carrier like a bullet.

Erik chuckled as he stepped into the gleaming white kitchen, flipping the switch on the streamlined machine, dropping one of coffee pod into its slot. "How are you, man? And how's…" He pawed through his memory. He could picture Marty's girlfriend, in all of her dyed and fluffed glory, but couldn't pull out her name.

"Amanda."

"Amanda, that's right. How is she?"

Marty looked down at the pup he held and rubbed a furry ear. Closing its eyes, the small dog leaned into the hand that dwarfed its head and sighed. "She's just fine."

"Good."

"Yeah. Thanks." Accepting the mug Erik held out to him, the soldier walked over to the living room and lowered himself onto the sleek black leather of the couch. "Okay if he's on the couch with me?"

Bringing over his own oversized mug, Erik sat on the arm of the matching chair. "Sure. He pees, though, you're cleaning it up. It's good to see you, man."

"Been a while." Marty looked over the rim of his cup and smirked. "Not since you moved into this high-rise. Eight months?"

"Yeah, about that. What's new with you? Still with K-9 at Lewis?"

Joint Base Lewis-McCord, the military facility south of Seattle, had been Jasper Martin's home base since shortly after Erik finished his tour of duty six years before. It had been Marty who'd encouraged Erik to join the K-9 unit, and Marty who'd signed his papers when Erik resigned.

"Still hanging with the dogs, yeah, but I'm being deployed. Afghanistan."

"Again? Fun." Both men shrugged. "Well, it'll be different than Iraq, at least."

"Well..." Marty cleared his throat. "That's kind of why I'm here." He set the coffee mug down on the chrome and glass end table, positioning carefully on a granite coaster.

Erik watched him fidget and felt a trickle of unease go down his back. "What's going on, Marty?"

"You know Amanda and I were living together, right?"

Erik winced. "Were?"

Marty nodded. "Yeah. She wasn't too thrilled about my deployment. And…oh, hell. You and I both know she wasn't a lifer."

"No, she wasn't. I didn't know you knew it, though." Erik moved to sit in the chair and cupped his mug in his hands. "I know nobody wanted to say anything."

"Nobody had to. I'm not stupid, Erik."

Erik shook his head. "That you're not. But women can mess a guy up, Marty."

The other man laughed. "Yeah. True. She had me coming and going often enough. Like with this guy." Marty looked down at the sleeping puppy on his chest.

"How's that?"

"Well, it started because I wanted a dog. A pet, not a work dog. But no way could I convince her that a rottie or a shepherd would be the way to go. She wouldn't hear it. So I did some research and got a small dog with a big attitude. This, my friend, is a wire hair fox terrier."

"Okay. I thought he was a little bit of a departure for you."

Marty laughed again, and this time he sounded like he meant it. "Don't let him fool you, man. He's not just a lapdog. Quick, smart. I've trained a dozen dogs for all kinds of purposes and this one might have me beat."

"Sounds like you got a good one."

Marty rubbed his eyebrow and squinted at Erik. "He could be. He will be, I think."

"Amanda's going to train him while you're gone? I know some good training places; my parents swear by one--"

"No. She's not. It's part of the reason she threw me out. She never handled the fact that I traveled. I thought she was taking him to classes already and crate training him while I was gone. Turns out, she was treating him like a toy. Ignoring him when she felt like it. And then he got a hold of her high heels—Timmy Chews--"

"Jimmy Choos."

"Yeah, whatever. She just *freaked*, man."

Erik shrugged, thinking about his sister's reaction to the demise of one of her favorite pairs. "They're expensive."

"How do you know this shit?"

"I got a mom and a sister."

"And any woman you want in a fifty-mile radius."

Erik smirked over the rim of his mug. "Please. Only fifty miles?"

Marty laughed. "You asshole."

"There you go. So what's the plan for him? Ruger, right?"

"Ruger." He looked down at the puppy again. "It's Ruger. Unless you want to change it."

"Change it? Why would I...oh, no. No. Marty, you can't--"

"Erik, I got no choice. It's you or the pound. I can't get in touch with the breeder to return him and I can't take him to the pound. It'll be just for the deployment." Marty shifted the puppy and held him out. "You were one of the best K-9 handlers I ever trained. If anyone can take this dog and make him into what he's supposed to be, it's you."

Erik stared at the ball of fur that had been shoved into his hands. With a yawn that showed a long, curled tongue, pink against black lips, the puppy opened its button-black eyes and focused on him. Erik sighed. "You sneaky bastard."

"I will not cry. I will not knuckle under. I am a strong, capable, determined woman."

Opening her eyes, Hope pulled the key from the ignition of her rented car and swung open its door. She caught it just before it bashed into the shiny silver BMW parked next to her and eased out of the car, clutching the handle to her. After dealing with her insurance agency, the car rental place in town, the legal staff at the corporate office for the oil change place and her slightly hysterical mother, Hope was ready for her final hurdle of the day. Western Telecomm.

It wasn't that she wanted something for nothing, she reasoned to herself, marshalling her arguments as she approached the steel and glass building in the heart of downtown Seattle. The guys at the oil change place had damaged her car; it was the right thing that the company pay for the repairs and the rental she'd have to drive until it was fixed. And frankly, her insurance company was paid very well to handle just these sorts of problems. That's why she got the extras on her policy, after all. And as for her mother…well, what was to be done there? Mom was Mom, and woe betide the fool who thought he, or she, could stop or change that force of nature.

If she could just deal with the phone people.

She'd called the customer service line from her office at Home Again, and stopped by the store next door to hers, but all she'd gotten was nonsense and a run-around. Her cell phone was as dead as a guy wearing a red shirt on Star Trek, and by God, she wanted it fixed or replaced. She wanted an assurance that this wouldn't happen again. She wanted her freaking phone list. And schedule. And the pictures of her nieces and nephews!

"Strong. Determined. Capable." Hope walked into the lobby and scanned the building directory until she found her quarry. Western Telecomm, watch out.

Stuffing herself into the nearest elevator gave her the first inkling that the people she planned to see might be more than she bargained for. Designer suits, high heels, smooth leather briefcases all vied for space in the tiny area and everyone, but everyone looked terribly important and awfully busy.

Hope escaped into a large, plush lobby and squared her shoulders. Her work shirt under her blazer wasn't creased, she noted, and she didn't need those stupid high heels. Five feet, five inches of strong determined woman. She could handle this.

"Excuse me." Hope waited for the twenty-something redhead seated behind the reception desk to look at her before she continued. Flies and honey, Hope, she reminded herself silently. "I need to speak to someone about my phone."

Red blinked slowly, her heavily mascaraed lashes wafting in front of her face by an inch or two. Hope wondered if she could actually feel the breeze from them, or if her imagination was in overdrive again. "Your phone?"

"Yes. My cell phone. I have a problem with it and the people at your mall store seem to think that it's not Western Telecomm's responsibility."

Bubblegum pink lips opened and closed like her nephew's beta fish, and Hope could almost see the spinning wheels in Red's head. "But…we don't deal with phones here."

Widening her eyes, Hope did her own version of fish lips. "Really? You don't? How strange, given that this is a wireless communication corporation. You know, cell phones?"

"Well, yes, but ma'am, we don't deal with that *here*." The young woman flapped her hands to indicate the lobby, the building. Hell, for all Hope knew, she was including the whole state in that gesture.

"Well, someone is going to deal with it *here*, because I'm done with getting the runaround, helpless act everywhere else." Hope folded her arms and leveled the fiercest weapon in her polite arsenal: her mother's smile.

As if on cue, the young woman paled beneath her blusher. Hope could almost feel sorry for her, knowing how that smile had been used against her entire life. Almost. Not quite.

"But...but...but I can't do anything about phones. And there's no one here who does that, either. I--"

"I understand." Hope smiled again and leaned in a bit. "You're not in charge of that."

The young woman blew out a breath. "No, I'm not. I'm new, actually, and I--"

Hope held up her hand to stop the deluge of information she knew was headed her way. "All you need to do is direct me to someone who can fix this."

"At this level, ma'am, I'm not sure that's possible." The young woman looked around the desk area for help. "Um, Misty? This lady needs to talk to someone about her phone."

Misty pulled the second chair at the reception desk out and slid into it. Unlike the fiery looks of the first young woman, she was tiny and dark and as beautiful as an Asian sculpture. Her long, black hair was a perfect waterfall down her back and as she sat next to the redhead, they made a portrait of contrasting loveliness.

Right then, Hope hated them both.

"Her phone? Like, she wants us to call maintenance?" Misty blinked at Red.

Red shook back her curls. "No, her cell phone."

"Her cell phone?" Misty's perfect brow furrowed. "We don't do that."

Hope took in a slow deep breath. "Misty, you work for a cell phone company."

The young woman curled her lip. "Yeah, I know."

Patience, Hope reminded herself. "Therefore, someone in your company must actually deal with your products."

Misty used a tone that had gotten three of Hope's employees fired in the past year. "Uh, *yeah*. But this is the corporate office." She and Red exchanged smirks.

The red Hope saw was no longer in the receptionist's hair. "Then I would suggest, young lady, that you find someone corporate who can actually deal with problems, instead of just sitting at a reception desk, looking decorative. Or better yet, I will." Hope started past the desk to the nearest hallway of offices.

"You can't go back there!" Alarmed now, Misty and Red stood up and rushed toward her.

"Really? Why not? Because the solution to my valid customer concerns are being addressed out here?" Hope stormed down the hallway.

"Call security, Terra!" Misty grabbed at Hope's arm. "Listen--"

Hope looked at the petite manicured hand on her arm and turned slowly to face Misty, who loosened her grip and stepped back, eyes wide. "You did not just touch me. Did you?"

Misty's chin went up. "You can't go back here."

"And you can't tell me what to do when you can't even be bothered to provide customer service," Hope retorted. "Do you know what that means? Customer service?"

A deep voice answered behind her. "I know what customer service means. May I help you?"

Hope froze. She knew that voice, she *knew* it. Telling herself there was no way for such a coincidence to happen, she turned slowly.

Thor, God of Thunder, was back and stood behind her. Strangely, he was wearing a suit. She stared into glacier-blue eyes and watched a huge grin cover his perfect face.

"Hey! It's you!" Thor looked honestly pleased to see her, weird as that was. He continued, his deep voice rubbing along her nerves like dark brown velvet. "How are you doing? How's the head?"

Hope sighed. So much for Thor being a concussion-induced hallucination.

Erik shifted Ruger's carrier and smiled at the pretty blonde from the side of the road. Her color was back, he noted, pleased to see the greenish shade gone from her face. When she was barfing, she'd looked a little like the Wicked Witch of the West. His smile faded as he realized, color or no color, she looked a little sick as he'd spoken to her.

"Do you need to sit down?" Erik flicked a glance at his least-favorite receptionist. "Misty, will you bring the lady some water, please?"

The young woman protested. "But Erik, she shoved her way back here and--"

"Misty. Water. Now. Thank you."

Misty stomped off in her high heels and Erik focused on the woman in front of him. "Is your head still hurting? The EMTs were kind of worried about you. Can I call someone for you?"

"No. No, thank you."

Erik smiled at Misty when she handed him the small bottle of chilled water. "Great. I'll take it from here; you can head back up front. Thanks for your help, Misty."

After giving the blonde a quick, nasty look, Misty smiled back at Erik. "Sure. I'm happy to help...anytime."

Swallowing a chuckle as the blonde rolled her eyes, he nodded solemnly. "And you're a big help. We'd be lost without you here."

Looking mollified, Misty sauntered away, casting a last, sultry glance over her shoulder. At least Erik thought it was supposed to be sultry. Well, he thought, despite all that, she can't be a complete loss. She's young yet. She could grow up. He doubted it, but it could happen.

Turning back to the woman in front of him, he took a moment to enjoy the view. Her eyes were gray, he realized, cool and sharp, in contrast to the soft warmth of her dark honey hair and peachy skin. She looked crisp and official and more than a little irritated. Time to stop thinking about her eyes, Yoriksson, he told himself silently.

"If you'll step this way, Ms…" Erik indicated his office at the end of the hallway.

"Lindstrom."

"Ms. Lindstrom. Or is it Mrs.?" Erik paused in front of the open door and waited for her to enter. She could have sat on one of the comfortable club chairs, she could have chosen the couch that took up the space along the wall of his office. She didn't.

"It's Ms."

Ms. Lindstrom of the cool eyes and warm skin and oh, yes…perfect heart-shaped butt, he noted as she walked past him, sat down in the least comfortable chair in the room, right in front of his desk and set her bag on the floor next to her feet. Erik got the message. This was not a social visit.

Erik closed the door and set down the dog carrier next to his desk. "Ms. Lindstrom, I'm sure we can find a solution for the customer service issue you're having. If you'll just give me a moment?" He tried a smile on her, but the cool eyes turned positively frosty.

O-kay.

Going to the closet door next to his private bathroom, he pulled out a duffle bag and unzipped it. In short order, he had a small dog bed, several toys and an unpleasantly aromatic treat set up beside his desk. Scrabbling sounds emitted from the carrier.

"Hang on, buddy."

Erik unclipped the latch and caught Ruger as he lunged at one of the puppy's favorite things: a new person in his world. One disadvantage of having an insanely cute pup was the complete lack of boundaries the animal learned. No one seemed to mind that the little dog jumped all over them. No one said anything to discourage Ruger. And, as Erik was quickly learning, no one had bothered to teach the little dog the most basic of manners.

He didn't blame Marty so much. He'd seen the way his friend had trained dogs for service. Though he shied away from thinking about Magnus directly, he knew the time and effort it had taken to get a dog to the level of skill and performance that all of Marty's dogs achieved. Whether it was sniffing out drugs or locating bombs, his friend had boundless patience, an ocean of kindness and the bone-deep stubbornness of a mule that had produced the best dogs in the K-9 units in the Army. On top of all of that, Erik knew how often Marty had been required to travel for his work. He didn't blame Marty. He did, however, blame Marty's ex.

Amanda.

Lovely, in a plastic, Barbie-doll sort of way, Amanda was as spoiled an urban princess as Erik had ever had the misfortune to meet. The only thing that surprised him about the demise of his friend's relationship with Amanda was that it had lasted as long as it did. She had the talent, an unmistakable gift, for turning everything she touched into crap, and it looked like she'd done a number on this dog.

As he restrained the corkscrewing antics of the dog, he glanced up at the cool and lovely Ms. Lindstrom and caught the horror and dismay on her face.

"What is that?" she asked, staring at Ruger.

Erik laughed, pleased to see a sense of humor emerging in her. "It's a dog, of course."

"What's wrong with it?"

He looked up and realized she hadn't been joking. "Nothing's wrong with him. He's a puppy."

Ms. Lindstrom shook her head. "I think it's having a seizure."

"No, he's just excited. Very common for the breed, or so I'm told." Distracting the pup with the chewy treat, Erik coaxed him onto the dog bed. Fortunately, the treat worked its magic and Ruger was instantly, utterly, blissfully engrossed in chewing it into nothingness. With luck, he'd work himself into exhaustion like he had the night before.

"All right. If you say so. Listen…" she paused, brow crinkling.

"Erik. Yoriksson. Hi." Erik held out his hand and she shook it, almost gingerly.

"Mr. Yoriksson, I really--"

"Oh, please. Call me Erik."

"Fine. Erik. I don't have a lot of time— oh my God. What is that stench?" She covered her nose and mouth with her hand and looked around his office.

Erik sniffed, hoping it wasn't him. "Oh, that's the bully stick you're smelling."

"The what?"

"Bully stick. Dog treat. I haven't found a dog yet that doesn't love them."

"What is it? That has to be one of the worst smells in the world." She flapped a hand in front of her face as if to disperse the smell.

"You don't want to know."

She lifted her head and narrowed her eyes at him. "Excuse me?"

"Trust me, Ms. Lindstrom. You don't want to know. Think of it as a smelly dog biscuit," Erik laughed.

She sat straighter in her chair, if that were possible, and glared at him. "If I ask a question, it's because I want an answer."

"You really want to know?"

"Did I not just say so?"

"Bull's penis."

Her mouth dropped open. "Excuse me?" she asked again.

"It's a bull's penis. Cured and treated, but essentially, that's all it is. Dogs really love them. You can get all different lengths and thicknesses. You can even get braided bully sticks. Better for larger dogs; it takes them a while to chew through those."

She closed her eyes. "I didn't want to know that."

Erik shrugged and spread his hands.

"Yes, you told me so." She glared at him as if he'd uttered the words. "Try not to be so smug about it."

"Hey!" Erik drew back. "I didn't say--"

"No, but you thought it." Gray eyes that were no longer cool and watchful snapped at him and he couldn't find it in himself to argue the point. He had, after all, been thinking exactly that.

"Not that it matters; I'm not here to discuss you or your…dog, or its questionable taste in food."

Erik shook his head. "He's not mine, I'm just watching him for a friend. And it's not really food, it's more of a treat for—but you're not here to discuss that. Got it. What are you here to discuss, Ms. Lindstrom?"

"This." The woman pulled out a small phone that sported Western Telecomm's logo and set it on his desk.

"Your cell phone. Okay." Erik studied her a moment. "I'm guessing there's a problem with it."

"It died on Saturday, right before my car…trouble. Even if I'd been in any shape to call for help, I couldn't have."

"Hmm." Erik leaned back in his chair. "It was lucky that I stopped, then."

She stared at him as if he'd lost his mind. "Oh, absolutely. The fact that you scared the bejesus out of me and I got a concussion when I hit my head on my car was a stroke of luck, all right."

O-kay. Erik smiled at her again, not particularly giving a rat's fuzzy butt if it made her hackles rise. "I assume you're looking to replace your phone. You do realize that this is the corporate office and we don't carry stock here? I'm going to have to send you to one of our retail locations to handle this."

Color stained her cheeks and she pressed her deliciously full lips together. "And this is why I'm here now. I do understand that you don't carry phones here. I get that. But your retail store employees refused to help me."

Now she had his attention. "Really." Erik turned to his computer and tapped a few keys. "Which location was this?"

"The one near Home Again, in the Magnolia neighborhood."

Erik typed a bit more. "On Condon Way?"

"Yes."

Erik located the store manager name and reached for his desk phone. "Tim, exactly the man I wanted. This is Erik Yoriksson at corporate--" Erik paused as the man babbled in reply, his voice filled with desperate enthusiasm. "No, that's fine. I need your help with something, Tim. I have a customer here who said she wasn't helped at your store. A Ms. Lindstrom. Ring any bells?"

Holding the phone away from his ear, he let the agitated employee respond. Evidently, Ms. Lindstrom had made quite the impression. Erik looked up at her with wide eyes and she flushed and looked away from him, folding her arms.

"Uh huh. Uh huh. Really…" He reached across his desk and picked up the small phone. In a few deft movements, he had the cover off and the battery exposed. "Okay, I see it. And did you show this to the customer?"

There was a beat of silence and Erik continued.

"This is the type of communication I've referred to, Tim, in the company notes. You're up on that, right. Good. I imagine I'll get a full accounting of the incident in your weekly? Great. No, I'll take care of it from here. Uh huh. Make sure you talk to your staff, Tim. It breaks up my day if I have to go to individual stores outside of the scheduled inspections. Good. I look forward to talking with you again, then."

Erik replaced the handset in its cradle and sighed. As unpleasant as his last conversation was, he disliked the one to come even more. When was he going to get used to this?

"Okay. Ms. Lindstrom, let me show something on your phone." Erik stood and walked around the desk, the pieces of the phone in his hands. "Do you see how the battery fits into its spot there? When I pull it out..." He removed the small piece from the phone and held out the blackened shell. "The battery shorted out, or something like that, and it pretty much killed your phone."

The woman cradled the phone in her hands and looked up at him. "Okay. Fine. And why didn't the people at the store tell me that? Why didn't they just replace it? Why did I have to go through all of this rigamarole?"

Erik put his hands in his pockets and studied the ground for a moment. "They said nothing about this?"

"They said--" she stopped. "They said something, and then there was yelling."

He nodded, not looking at her.

She sighed. "Look. I'm sorry. But I have a whole lot going on, and I missed work to take care of this. I'm a little short on time and a lot short on patience. Can you just replace my phone? Please?"

Erik nodded. "You bet. We can do that. There are some good phones on sale right now, so--"

Ms. Lindstrom held up her hand. "Hang on. I pay extra for insurance on this thing. If something goes wrong with it, it's supposed to be replaced."

"And that's true, so long as you use Western Telecomm approved batteries in the phone. Otherwise, the warranty is voided." Erik held up the burned out battery between his fingers. "This is not a Western Telecomm battery. It's not even a competitor's battery—it's a cheap knock-off. This is the reason your phone is destroyed. You're lucky you weren't injured. The heat this produced…your face or your ear should be burned."

"I wasn't holding it. It was--" She shook her head. "You're not going to replace my phone."

"We will replace your phone. We just won't do it for free." Erik moved behind the desk again and pulled up a different program on his computer. "Let me see if you're due for an upgrade. What's your first name, Ms. Lindstrom?"

"Hope."

He tapped a few keys. "And your mobile number?" When she told him, he pulled up her account. "This is good. You are eligible for a phone upgrade and whichever retail store you choose can take care of that for you. We have one in this building, on the street level."

"What about my schedule and my phone list and the pictures?" She leaned forward. "Can they put them on the new phone?"

"No, but you can go online and get all of that from the Backup Manager."

She blinked. "Pardon?"

"Backup Manager. It's the thing on your phone that records your contact list and pictures and everything, online. You just type in your account name--" Erik watched her raise her eyes to the left. "You didn't sign up for Backup Manager, did you?"

"No."

She looked so forlorn that he didn't have the heart to say more. It would just be rubbing her nose in it. "The person who helps you today will be able to set up your phone so it saves your information automatically."

She nodded and said nothing.

"Hey." Erik rested his arms on the desk and leaned toward her. "It's not so bad, is it? You get a new phone, you'll get a huge discount on it. And if you want, I can go with you, walk you through the selection process. It's been awhile since I've been on the sales floor, but I get to see all the new stuff first. I can help you with this."

Then he smiled at her.

And she narrowed her eyes at him.

Emotions spun across her face like a kaleidoscope. The sadness fell first to incredulity and then to anger. She drew a deep breath in through her nose and, Erik noticed, her nostrils actually flared.

This can't be a good sign, he thought.

"Mr. Yorkson--"

"It's Yoriksson, actually. A mouthful, but easier than some of my cousins' names, especially the family who's still in Sweden. But please, call me Erik."

"Mr. Yoriksson."

Uh oh.

"I'm sure many...people are delighted by you and your helpful attitude." She looked him over briefly and made a little laughing sound. "But I think I can manage to buy a new phone all by myself. Thank you. But no. I'll just let you get back to...whatever it is that you do."

Ms. Lindstrom – Hope, though he hadn't been invited to call her that – stood and picked up her bag, giving him one more frosty look before slinging the strap over her shoulder.

Both of them froze as the contents of her bag clattered to the floor of his office. A hairbrush, a small paperback, a brown leather wallet mixed in with the usual detritus of a woman's purse rained down around her feet, narrowly missing...

Ruger.

With red threads and leather piping hanging from his mouth, the pup looked up at the mixture of Ms. Lindstrom's belongings falling from the newly formed hole in the bottom of her bag. Her leather-trimmed, bright red bag. Delighted with the new toys descending from heaven, he spat out a scrap of fabric and leapt at the falling papers. He'd just snapped up a thick permanent marker when Erik lunged.

"Ruger! No. No. Leave it!" Grabbing the pup, Erik pried the marker out of his mouth and handed it to the open-mouthed woman in front of him. "That's it. If you're going to act like that, you're going back in your kennel. And no biscuit! Bad dog. No biscuit."

By the time Erik had wrestled the puppy into the carrier and latched the door, Ms. Lindstrom had gathered her belongings and was cradling them in the remains of her purse.

"I'm really sorry about that. He--"

She held up one hand to stop him from talking and nearly dropped her purse and its contents again. With a low growling sound that stopped him in his tracks as he was about to help with her things, she turned and walked out of his office.

"That went well," Erik said out loud.

Chapter Three

"Paul! If you kill your little brother, I shall be very angry with you, young man!"

Miriam's dulcet tones drifted to Hope as she strode across damp grass to a wooden bench. It was always so easy to locate Miriam and the kids at the park. All she ever had to do was listen. Or look for the mushroom cloud.

"Hey." She flopped down on the bench and watched her youngest nephew try to bean his sister with a plastic bat. "I think Sebastian's trying to hit a homer."

"Sebastian! How many times do I have to tell you not to decapitate your siblings?" Miriam stood and stomped over to the sandbox where her daughter, Lene, was attempting to build a small city. "Give me that bat. No, right this instant."

Miriam was a constant source of amazement. Not only did she actively parent her children when all of her friends and neighbors shuffled their spawn over to a nanny's care, but she managed to do so without sinking through sand and sod in four inch stiletto heeled thigh high boots.

But really, what else could she wear with that strapless snakeskin-print mini dress and cropped jacket?

Hope smoothed her blue chambray work shirt and sighed. Sometimes she had to remind herself that she loved Miriam like the sister she'd never had.

Waggling the bat triumphantly, Miriam walked back to the bench and dropped the toy into the largest purse Hope had ever seen. "What is that, a suitcase? How long were you planning on being at the park?" Hope asked.

Her sister in law rolled her eyes. "It's a Bottega Veneta, darling. Isn't it fabulous?"

"Fabulous." Hope nodded. "How much did that thing cost you? I mean, how much do you have to spend to get 'fabulous?'"

Miriam raised an eyebrow and smiled. "How much did you spend on your sink and faucet in your bathroom?"

The women stared at each other for a moment until Hope pursed her lips. "Fair enough. Good call. You're right, I don't really need to know."

Flipping golden hair back over her shoulder, Miriam chuckled. "Worried I'll send your brother to the poorhouse?"

"No." Hope shook her head. "I'm worried you'll bankrupt him and the family will be homeless and you'll show up at my door."

The other woman trilled laughter, causing two joggers to look over, lose their footing and stumble into each other, nearly causing a head-on collision with a couple rollerblading down the path. Miriam, Hope thought, should come with a warning label.

"Relax, it's not a Gadino. It's not even a Birkin. And we'll be coming to your house soon enough."

Alarm bells rang in Hope's head. "Excuse me?"

"In two weeks." Miriam idly studied the joggers as they argued with one another and the skaters looked on. "The fifteenth. You remember?"

"No."

"A party. At your house. Ringing the bell?"

"No."

"We talked about it."

"No, we didn't."

"You put it in your calendar."

Hope pressed the heels of her hands to her temples. "The one in my phone?"

"Of course," Miriam wrinkled her perfect brow. "You pulled it out and did something. And you set a...oh, what is it? The thing. You know, the thing."

"A reminder?"

"Yes, that."

Hope leaned back against the bench and studied the uncertain spring sky. "Well, I'd love to argue the point with you, but I can't. I have no way to disprove what you're saying."

"I have witnesses."

Hope chortled. "Daniel doesn't count! He'd say you built the Ark if you asked him to."

Miriam merely smiled and shrugged. As sounds of shouting from the joggers escalated, both women leaned forward to get a better look. "Look at those idiots. What are they thinking? And in front of children." She clucked her tongue then turned to face Hope. "You can't argue? *You*? Why not? Are you sick?"

"No, I'm not--" Hope snorted. "I don't argue that much."

Miriam just rolled her eyes.

"*Anyway*. I can't *discuss* this with any knowledge because my phone died."

"When was this?"

Hope stared at her sister in law. "Friday? While I was on my way to Gold Bar? I was talking to you? Remember?"

Miriam stretched out a booted leg and studied the leather on her razor-sharp heel. "Oh, when you hung up on me."

"I didn't hang up on you! My phone died!" Hope dragged out the shopping bag from the phone store and produced her new phone. "And this is what sucked up my entire freaking day,"

"Ooo!" Miriam grabbed the phone and cooed. "Look at the pretty color. Like a box from Tiffany's."

Stroking the phone's aquamarine case cover, Miriam turned the phone back and forth. Hope sighed.

"It better be pretty. It cost enough."

Startled, Miriam nearly dropped the phone. "You *bought* a new phone? Even though the other broke? You have insurance on everything."

"I had insurance on this, too, but after climbing the crap ladder all the way to the corporate offices of my phone company, Thor said my bargain battery voided the warranty. Schmuck." Hope retrieved the cell phone from Miriam and studied it glumly.

Miriam folded her arms and frowned. "The Viking god of thunder is involved in a cell phone company?"

"I'm not sure I can even make a call on this."

"Was it a slow day in Valhalla?" A smile flirted with the corner of Miriam's mouth.

"What? No, don't be silly. It wasn't actually Thor, it was just some guy who looked like him." Hope pressed a few of the buttons, trying to remember what the salesperson had told her.

"You're going to break it. And how do you know what Thor looks like?" Miriam took the phone again. "Huh. Are there instructions?"

"Imagine what Thor would look like." Hope paused as her sister-in-law tilted her head and got a dreamy expression on her face. "Exactly. That's what this guy looked like."

"Hot?"

"Oh, yeah. And believe me, he knew it, too." Even thinking about Thor made Hope's blood boil again. Or Erik. Whatever. "He tried to do that smiling thing, you know, the smiling thing? The 'I'm so unbelievably gorgeous, you'll let me get away with murder' thing? As if my knees would just give out and he'd be able to walk all over me. Well, I don't think so, buddy. Hmph!"

"Mmmm. Yum. Single?"

"Miriam!" Hope glared at her and pulled out the inch-thick owner's manual for her new phone from the shopping bag.

"Sorry, darling. Habit."

"Break it. Here." Hope thumped the tome onto the bench between them and took the phone again. "You look up how to make a call, I'll try to work it out this way."

Miriam looked at the book the way most women study bugs. "Watch the children, Hope. I'll be right back."

"Watch them do what?" Hope looked up from her phone. "Lene! Stop eating the sand! Stop that right now. I will tell your mother!"

Satisfied that none of the children were in imminent danger, she went back to the mysteries of her new phone, until she heard Miriam's voice.

"—Right over here. I knew someone would be able to help."

A pimple-faced teenager stood next to Miriam, his mouth open slightly as he nodded. "I can help." Miriam beamed at him and Hope could swear the boy swallowed his own tongue.

"Here, Hope. Give him the phone."

"What? Why? Who is this?" Hope demanded.

"This is…" Miriam turned to the teen.

"Tommy. It's Tommy. I'm Tommy."

"Tommy." Miriam's smile did to Tommy what Thor thought his would do to Hope. "This is Hope, my sister-in-law. Can you show us how to use her new phone?"

"Sure, what—oh, man! You got the Covet III!"

Hope blinked then checked the cover of the instruction manual. "Yes. That's what I got."

As Tommy launched into phone-related gibberish until Hope held up her hand to stop it.

"Tommy. I need to make calls, receive calls and keep my schedule straight. Just…show me that, please."

"Oh, man." The boy looked at the phone in his hand. "And all the stuff this baby can do…."

"Yeah, I'm a philistine."

"Huh?" He tore his attention away from the phone to stare blankly at her, glancing to Miriam for help.

"Never mind, Toby," Miriam said.

"Tommy."

"Of course. If you could just show Hope the basics?" Miriam patted the boy's shoulder and he quivered.

The next fifteen minutes gave Hope more knowledge about cell phones and teenage slang than she thought possible to know.

"Well. Thank you, Tommy. You've been very helpful." Hope looked at the boy with new respect.

Miriam winked at him and he swallowed hard. "I always say, if you have problems with computers or phones, get an expert. Get a teenager." She reached into her bag and pressed and folded bill in his hand, then leaned in and kissed his cheek.

Hope watched him stumble back to his friends, who'd gathered a short distance away to watch the proceedings. "I really hope that kid doesn't drive. You know better than to kiss them."

Miriam shrugged and sat next to her on the bench again, crossing her legs. The group of boys turned to stare and she waved.

"Although," Hope mused, "you could have just kissed him and not tipped him. Saved yourself the money. How much did you give him, anyway?"

"Twenty."

"Miriam!"

"What?" Miriam tossed her hair. "It was worth every--"

Both women froze as Hope's phone erupted with sound and strains of Wagner's "Flight of the Valkyries" filled the air. Miriam burst out laughing.

"What," she gasped, "is that?"

Hope scowled at the display. "That's a salesman with a twisted sense of humor. How do I shut this off?"

"Twisted—what?"

Hope jabbed at a few buttons and the music grew louder. "Oh, jeeze louise! How—oh, finally. I guess I was still mad at Thor and was saying something."

"Bitching."

Hope glowered. "And he picked that for my ringtone. Little smart ass."

Miriam smiled. "Better than being a dumbass."

"My line."

"I know. I stole it." Miriam reached over and turned Hope's watch to see the time, then stood. "Kids, let's go. Time to head home."

Three dirty children raced past the women and Hope shook her head. "You're going to have to hose them down."

"Well, it's Monday, isn't it?" Miriam swung her suitcase-purse onto her shoulder and started after the kids. "Now this Thor. Does he have a real name?"

"Miriam."

"I'm not matchmaking; I'm curious. Did you call him Thor?" She blinked innocently as Hope frowned at her.

"Erik."

"Just Erik? Like Madonna or Cher?"

Hope chuckled. "No, he had a last name. What was it... York. No, that's not right. Yoriksson. That's it. But he kept saying, 'Oh no, call me Erik.'"

Miriam put an arm around her shoulders and squeezed. "He's a jerk and we hate him."

Hope grimaced. "Actually, I was probably the jerk. He just made me so mad. All smooth and sure of himself."

"Well, we can still hate him, then." Miriam hummed a little under her breath. "Erik...Yoriksson, you say? Hmm."

"What?"

"That name rings a bell for me." Miriam pondered a moment. "How do I know that name?"

"Ex-boyfriend?"

Miriam laughed. "No, silly."

Hope smiled. "All other men ceased to exist when you met Daniel, I know, I know."

Miriam hummed again. "But I know that name. How do I know that name?"

"Maybe you know his annoying little dog."

Miriam stopped. "How do you know he has a dog?"

"Because it was in the office with him. And it ate my purse." The memory made Hope's jaw ache from the clenching of her teeth.

"Oh," Miriam breathed.

Hope's eyes widened and she stopped walking. "Miriam. No. No!!"

Miriam's smile bloomed. "Oh, yes. Yes! We're going purse shopping! Children, you get to go see Gamma!"

Hope groaned.

Erik set the pet carrier on the granite counter of his kitchen and opened the door. For once, Ruger didn't shoot out of the opening but blinked sleepily at him.

"Well, the dog park did the trick, didn't it?" Erik commented as he scooped the small dog out of the carrier. "And wow, do you stink! Nothing like dead fish to roll in, huh?"

They'd romped and played for two hours with dogs of every size and shape on the shore of Puget Sound; the enclosed dog park made it possible for Ruger to be off leash as he played. It also made it possible for him to do every other disgusting dog antic he wished.

Like roll in the remains of a dead, rotting fish.

Holding the puppy away from himself, Erik carried Ruger into the bathroom and shut the door. He set the small dog into the large soaker tub and stripped off his suit jacket and shirt.

Warm, earth tones and smooth granite abounded in the bathroom, the sinks and deep soaking tub standing out in creamy contrast. The ebony and espresso tones of the cabinetry gleamed over the marble tiled floor and brushed pewter gave off a subtle glow, repeated in the sleek lighting. Ruger whined from the depths of the tub and tried to jump out of the smooth-sided prison. When this failed, he yapped and skittered toward the gleaming faucet.

"I swear to God, you scratch that tub…" he warned the suddenly agitated dog. Ruger paused and looked up at him, then sat. Erik blinked.

"Well. Would you look at that. You sat."

Ruger wagged his tail then scooted to the edge of the tub.

"No. You just wait right there."

With a sigh, the little dog laid down and rested his head on his paws. Erik chuckled and opened one of the sleek ebony cabinets and pulled out the puppy shampoo that was part of the grocery bag of stuff Marty left with Ruger. Crouching next to the tub, he grasped the pup by the scruff of the neck and turned on the water.

Ruger transformed from one second to the next into a terrified, yelping, squealing whirlwind, desperate to escape. Stinking, dirty water sprayed the glass tiles that surrounded the tub and Erik struggled to keep his grip on eight pounds of absolute panic. "Hey! Settle down, buddy. You're okay."

The little dog continued to flail his entire body in an effort to get free and finally, Erik kicked off his shoes and climbed into the tub, socks, work slacks and all. Holding the small trembling dog, he took the spray nozzle and gently wet his fur before working soap into the dirt and mats. "Little idiot." Erik kept his voice low and calm and felt the trembling ease a bit. "You played in Puget Sound. You were fine then. And a bath freaks you out? Where's the tough guy? You'd never make it in the Army like--"

What he was about to say, even think, stopped him cold. It took him another moment to realize that his sudden tension had transferred to the puppy, who was shaking like a leaf again. Murmurs and scratches didn't make it stop, either, and finally, Erik fell back on his old standby. He sang.

The melody was simple enough, one his mother sang to him from babyhood, in the language of her homeland. As he sang to Ruger, the little dog calmed and stared up at him.

"Sov gott, vackra delfin, Sov gott, jag vita varg. Vi har kärlek för varandra. För varandra. För alltid...."

Erik studied the small face inches from his and sighed. At least the dog was clean. He didn't hold out as much hope for his trousers. Climbing out of the tub, he snagged a snowy white towel from the table between the shower and tub and dried Ruger quickly, then put another clean, dry towel on the floor. The puppy sniffed the towel and after a few half-hearted scratches turned once in a circle and laid down. Erik didn't even fight the grin. "Rough day, huh, little guy?"

As he was about to strip off the rest of his clothing when his cell phone rang, vibrating the cloth of the suit jacket hanging on the hook by the door.

"This is Erik."

"Erik. Daniel."

"Hey, man, what's up?" Erik stepped over Ruger to reach the sink and pulled out some cleaning supplies and swiftly wiped down the big mess the little dog made.

"Not much. Wanted to see if you're up for having your ass handed to you again tomorrow."

Erik laughed. Daniel Lindstrom was a relatively new acquaintance, but one he already enjoyed.

"Is that the way you remember it?" he asked. "You were the one crying for your mama."

Daniel's anatomically impossible suggestion made Erik laugh harder. "Yeah, yeah. Heard it all before. Like when I beat you in racquetball last week."

"You're delusional. Hey, meeting some of the guys at Tom's for brewskies tonight. You in? We're forming a softball team at work. We could use you."

Erik thought about it for a moment, studying the sleeping puppy at his feet. With luck, Ruger would wake up only long enough to eat his dinner and climb into his kennel. "I'm there. When? Got it. Later."

He set the phone safely away from the sink and started the shower. With a little bit more of that luck, he'd have enough time to change and take the dog on a short walk before meeting with Daniel and his friends.

Stepping into the glass enclosure of the granite steam shower, Erik sluiced off dirt and sweat quickly, then let the steam work a little magic on tired, aching muscles. He'd gone to the gym that morning and worked out with one of the trainers to keep up on his fitness levels. Working out alone, it was just too easy to get complacent, and Erik was determined to find ways to be challenged. So this trainer was a sadist, so what? It was worth every second of pain to feel like he'd kept his edge.

Erik used the top of the shower to stretch then stepped out onto the bathmat. Ruger was still asleep on the towel, so he stepped over the puppy and pulled out his shaving kit. Maybe there'd be someone new at the bar that night. Sure, it was a sports bar, but women liked sports, right? He'd be fine never dating another one like Hockey Freak, but a nice girl who liked baseball…would that be so hard to find? Maybe with dark blonde hair. Crisp, cool gray eyes. A butt that could make a grown man — he stopped. What was he doing, thinking about Angry Chick now? Tonight was going to be a boys' night, he decided. And if someone hot and interested stumbled onto his path, well, he'd just have to make sure to break her fall.

Humming a little, he sped through shaving, brushing his teeth and combing his hair, then turned and scooped up the dirty clothes off the floor.

And saw Ruger, contentedly chewing on the lowest bathroom cabinet.

"No! Ruger! No chew! Leave it!"

The little dog scrambled away and left behind a nub that had once been the drawer pull. He folded his ears back and gazed up at Erik beseechingly.

Erik sighed. "Bad dog."

"I kid you not, it was five freaking minutes. And this handle thing is like solid wood and metal." Erik laughed shortly and tipped his beer back to drain the bottle. "The designer who did the place was always finding weird crap to 'incorporate into the space.' Whatever the hell that means."

Daniel Lindstrom grinned and slapped him on the back. His geek-made-good glasses shone in the dim light and the sympathy he pretended to offer rang patently false. "It means you got hosed by some fancy piece in stupid shoes."

Erik grabbed a handful of pretzels from the basket in front of them. "Nah, she was my ex. She was really nice about the fees. Gave me a lot of it at cost."

"Uh huh. All of this, over a dog. I thought you were the single guy, the beacon of hope for us poor married slobs and a dog wasn't in the books for you."

"It's not actually my dog. And did I say that?" Erik shook his head as the server scooped up his empty bottle and waggled it in question. With a wink and a smile, she sauntered away, swaying her hips hard enough to make the glass on her tray clink. She was hot enough, but her blonde hair was too blonde and even in this light, he recognized the vacuous gleam in her baby-blue eyes.

No, thank you.

"Yes, you said that."

"When?"

"When Sarah hit on you at the gym."

Erik shrugged. "I didn't want to give her false expectations."

Daniel threw back his head and laughed. For a skinny guy, he could shut up a room with his voice. "Sarah? Are you kidding? She's been with every guy who'll have her in the gym. She's not exactly looking to settle down, either."

Erik shrugged again. He wasn't going to argue with Daniel about it, but he'd seen the loneliness and desperation in Sarah, the need that had translated into sleeping with anyone who wanted her. No way was he going to add to that damage.

"I had to say something. Besides, you were the one going on and on about how cool it is to be married."

Daniel looked smug. "It is cool being married…to my wife. The rest of you poor suckers are out of luck."

Erik laughed and shook his head and thought again about the furious and frustrated woman in his office. Dammit. Maybe that waitress was still around....

"Hey, there they are." Daniel elbowed Erik and raised his beer to signal the men entering the bar. "Nice of you to show up, ladies. Thought you got lost."

The good-natured razzing continued for a bit and eventually conversation turned to softball. Practice times were discussed, sponsors named and positions decided, all within a single round of beer and buffalo wings.

"Oh, before I forget," Daniel cut off the third baseman who was pontificating on the Mariners' chances for year and wiped his fingers on a grubby paper napkin. "Here. Take this."

Erik took the slightly sticky business card and held it up in the dim light. "Home Again?"

Daniel nodded. "My sister manages the place. It's pricey, but if you need that drawer pull replaced, she'll find it for you."

Erik looked at the card. The rest of the print was too small to read in the bad lighting, but he could see the address well enough. "I think this is where the ex got a lot of the stuff for my condo. Green bags, right?"

Daniel's brow wrinkled. "I think so."

"Yeah, I remember. I remember this logo." Erik tapped the card. "This is the place. Thanks, man."

"No problem. Now, if you think for a second that the Pirates are going all the way this year...."

Erik tucked the card into his pocket.

Chapter Four

Erik pulled out the mangled remains of the business card from his pocket and peered at the address. Buffalo wing sauce from Daniel's hand had smeared the edge of the card and Ruger had zeroed in on it like a heat-seeking missile. He'd gotten the card away from the puppy, but not before it had been well and truly gnawed.

Home Again looked like a successful enough business. The grounds were beautifully landscaped around the nearly Georgian facade of the store, the paint on its exterior was bright and the parking lot was remarkably tidy. Erik glanced around, unable to name what was wrong with this picture.

"All right, shorty." Erik opened the car windows a crack and looked into the backseat where Ruger sat in his carrier. "You have to stay here. Get your rest. There's a lot of the condo left to destroy when we get home tonight."

Walking across the nearly pristine parking lot, it hit him. The parking lot was nearly empty, and it was — Erik checked his watch — only six-thirty. How could this business be doing so well without customers?

He strode in through the sliding glass doors, barely noting the 'exit only' sign, nodding to the couple he passed. A cluster of employees stood near the front counter.

The staff of Home Again appeared to be having a good time, he noticed. All clad in blue chambray shirts and tan pants, they laughed and chatted. All of them except the one wearing a ball cap, who busily made notes on a clipboard.

Erik waited, but no one seemed to realize he was standing there. He cleared his throat.

When she lifted her head, it took him a moment to recognize the cool gray eyes of Angry Chick.

"What are you doing here?" she demanded.

In the sudden silence, Erik saw the widened eyes and dropped jaws of the other staff members. So Angry Chick wasn't always angry. "I'm here for a drawer pull."

Now her jaw dropped. It was like looking at a school of denim-clad codfish, he thought. *And here I stand, without fries.* Angry Chick looked at her watch and turned to the young brunette next to her.

"Caitlin, did you lock the doors?"

"I did, right at six-thirty."

Angry Chick then turned to a young man who'd just joined the group. "Kyle. Exit doors locked?"

"Yeah. Well, just now, Hope. I had to check out the last customers."

Hope, Erik thought. That was her name. He'd forgotten when he nicknamed her Angry Chick. Then it dawned.

Hope Lindstrom.

"Hey, you're Daniel's sister! He was the one who told me to come here." Erik's grin faded a little as he saw Hope's left eyebrow arch.

"Daniel. Great. Did Daniel mention the store hours?"

Erik pulled out the tattered card squinted at what was left of the print. "He gave me one of your cards. The dog got to it and I couldn't read the hours."

"Imagine that."

"It wasn't really his fault. There was sauce on it." Erik tried smiling again. Caitlin, the little brunette in charge of locking doors, sighed and smiled back. "Am I too late?"

Her eyes narrowed. He could almost hear her teeth grind, but she smiled, too. It was a hard, professional smile completely devoid of warmth, but it was there.

"No, that's fine. I'm sure everyone won't mind pushing back the store meeting."

"Oh, I didn't realize--" he began.

She turned to the young man on her right. "Kyle. Is your till still up?"

"Yes, ma'am. I locked it, but I haven't counted it yet."

She nodded and huffed out a breath. "Make sure it's up and ready to go. Let's get the rest of the tills counted down and be sure the store is set to open."

The staff scattered. Hope stopped two of them before they made their escape. "Aaron, Nick. Take Thor to aisle seven so he can find his drawer pull."

"What did you just call me?" Erik felt the skin on his face tighten.

"Pardon?" she looked up him, her face blank and cool. Nearly a foot difference in their height didn't seem to register at all to her.

"Did you just call me Thor?" Erik breathed in through his nose and out his mouth. "My name is Erik."

Hope held his gaze for a moment, unwavering, then checked her watch again. Another small, false smile bent her lips and avoided her eyes as she lifted her head. "I won't keep you. Erik."

She strode away, calling out instruction to a few people unlucky enough not to be as busy as she deemed necessary. Through a faintly red haze, he heard one of the young men ask the other, "Is it really Thor?"

The other lisped back, "Well, it hurth a little."

They giggled like school girls and Erik closed his eyes.

The day really wasn't getting any better yet.

Erik hooked his keychain on the wall-mounted holder and set the Home Again bag on the credenza in the entryway. He unlatched the carrier and Ruger skittered out, dancing around his feet.

"Little rat." Erik studied the small dog racing between him and the kitchen, then back again. "Yeah, yeah. I'm coming. Not that you deserve any dinner."

By the time the puppy had made his fourth circuit, Erik was in the kitchen, scooping kibble into a bowl. Ruger yipped and danced and dove at the kibble Erik put on the floor like he hadn't been fed in days. Leaving him to enjoy his meal, Erik walked into the bathroom, scooping up the drawer pull on his way.

The gnawed handle was attached with a simple screw. It was easy enough to remove it and replace it with the new one he'd just bought, although, he admitted silently, he might have done better to listen to Heckle and Jeckle and get an actual screwdriver with the new knob. The Swiss Army knife screwdriver worked just fine, but a slightly longer handle on a real tool might have made the job a little easier.

Erik was just finishing when the puppy trotted into the bathroom and plopped down next to him as he sat on the tiled floor. "Returning to the scene of the crime?" he asked Ruger.

Ruger belched.

"Nice one."

He slid the cabinet drawer closed and stood, pleased with himself for the handling the simple repair with a minimum of fuss. Well, mostly. The trip to Home Again had been enough fussing for a lifetime.

What was with Angry Chick, anyway? Hope, he corrected himself. He had to remember to call her Hope. If he had to guess, Erik didn't think Daniel was the kind of person who'd appreciate the nickname he'd given the man's sister.

So he'd gone into the store a little late. So what? He was a customer and the customer was always right.

The memory of Angry Ch—*Hope* sitting in his office surfaced again and he winced. She'd been his customer and he hadn't let her be right. And Erik knew that when a customer crossed the line, like by going into a store after it had closed, that person needed to be stopped. Gently, but stopped all the same.

Folding the screwdriver back into the handle of the knife, he thought about the meeting he'd interrupted. What would he have done, he wondered, if someone had pulled that crap on him?

He wouldn't have called that person Thor, that was for damn sure.

Ruger got up and sniffed the new handle. "Don't even think about it, buddy," Erik warned him. "After everything I went through tonight, I never want to buy another one of those again. And I definitely never want to see Angry Chick Hope again."

The puppy sat right in front of the cabinet and looked up at him, then looked at the drawer pull again. Standing a few feet away from the gleaming ebony, Erik saw that the new handle was completely different from the others. At first glance, it was similar but the longer he looked at it, the more apparent the differences became.

Some people would be fine with it, he thought. *I could be fine with it.*

"I'm not going to be fine with it."

Ruger looked back at the sound of his voice.

Erik groaned. "This will drive me right up a freaking wall."

The handle would have to go. It would have to be returned. It would have to be exchanged.

At Home Again.

"Shit."

Ruger barked and wagged his tail. Erik scowled at him. "Sure, easy for you to say."

"Thor's back."

Hope looked up from the mountain of tax forms she'd just compiled for the accountant. April fifteenth loomed on the horizon and this was the last of the paperwork she needed to complete. "Pardon me?" she frowned at Aaron.

"Thor. Your friend. He's back." The young man stuck his hands in his pockets and leaned against the door jamb of her office.

"He's not my friend. Why is he back?" Hope fastened the top sheet to the paperwork with an enormous binder clip and slid it into the file folder. "And why are you telling me this? He's a customer. Go help him." *Help him leave my store*, she added silently.

"I think you should take care of him."

She stacked the file folders together, and brought the schedule chart on her freshly cleared desk. May was going to be a nightmare for staffing. "And why is that?" she asked absently.

"He's an HW."

"You can handle that." Memorial Day, Hope thought. Nobody better want it off. There would be Hws –

Handyman Wannabes – wandering through Home Again by the truckload that weekend.

"Hope."

"What, Aaron?" Hope glared up at one of favorite sales associates.

"He has a book."

"Oh, God." Hope closed her eyes.

"And a list." Aaron sounded sympathetic, but she couldn't see him. The rotten kid could have been laughing at her for all she knew.

"Of course he does."

"And…." Aaron shifted his feet and Hope looked at him. Shuffling meant trouble with this young man.

"What else?"

He cleared his throat. "I think I saw a flow chart. And a schematic drawing."

"I do not need this today, Aaron. I don't this or this… this *guy*."

He laughed. "C'mon, boss. He's a pretty good guy, all around. A little clueless here, but he doesn't suck."

"Crap." Hope sat for a moment, then turned to her computer and locked it down. Grabbing the water bottle by her desk, she took a quick shot, recapped and stood. "Where's your little friend?"

Erik consulted his list. A failure to plan, he knew, was a plan to fail, and so far, this had been the case. The small bag of drawer pulls and handles clanked in his pocket as the leash stretched to its limits and he tugged it back until it was slack again in his hand.

"What is that doing in my store?"

Angry Chick Hope stood ten feet away, staring at Ruger.

"It's too hot to leave him in the car." Eric pulled out the schematic drawn up from his leather folder and looked at his options. If he had to replace every single piece of hardware in his bathroom, at least he was ready for it.

Hope was still talking. "This is a place of business. You can't bring this dog in here. There are health codes!"

He studied the ebony color of the knobs in the bin in front of him. "Do you serve food here?"

"No. Why?"

"Then health codes don't come into play. Relax. He's housebroken." He and Ruger looked at each other. "Mostly."

"Fine. But if it makes a mess or gets hurt--"

Erik focused on her and smiled, loving the way it turned her to ice. "You keep grinding your teeth like that and you're going to make some dentist very happy. And very rich."

She smiled back and he could almost see the freshly drawn battle lines. "Such a pleasure to see you back here. And so soon! How can I help you today?" She paused. "Erik."

One gauntlet, thrown. Check.

"Well, *Hope*," he paused, hating the fact that her emphasis on his name was so much more effective. "I need a new handle for a cabinet in my bathroom."

"Didn't you just get one the other day?"

He studied the antiqued bronze collection. "Yes. But I chose one that didn't work."

"Okay." She stood next to him and gazed at the seemingly endless array of knobs, handles, pulls and hinges. "What made it not work?"

He picked up another piece of metal, grimaced, and returned it to the bin. "It didn't work. It didn't fit."

"It was the wrong size?"

"No, it—Here." Erik pulled out the bag of hardware he'd removed from the bathroom and compared it to the brushed nickel display. "See? Like this. It doesn't work."

"Okay. So it wasn't the same design."

"That's what I said." This time, he kept the bag in hand and held up the bits of metal and wood to the shelves in front of him.

Hope leaned in and peered at his bag. "May I?"

He handed her the small parcel and returned to the shelves. "Gotta be one here. Where is it?"

He heard a sigh and turned. "What?"

"You can stop looking for this style."

The blonde kid who'd helped him before walked down the aisle. "Hey, did you get it worked out, boss?"

Hope held up the largest handle and Erik saw the kid's eyes widen. "Uh oh."

Hope nodded. "This is a design we carried, but it's not in stock anymore."

Erik gave a quiet groan. "All right. You have to special order it. Realistically, how long a wait should I expect?"

The denim and khaki twins exchanged looks. Hope spoke up. "This isn't something we carry because this wood," she tapped the handle, "is an endangered South American hardwood. It only grows in the rain forest."

"You're kidding."

"No. I'm not." She actually looked sympathetic.

"Okay, fine. You don't carry it, but someone does." Erik thought of his bathroom, with its missing handle. "One of your competitors."

Hope bristled, all sympathy gone. "If Home Again doesn't carry it, it's not worth carrying. But feel free to call around. We'll even write down the design style number for you."

"If you want to waste your time," the kid chimed in.

Erik felt the leash tug and reeled the puppy back in. "What do you mean?"

"I mean this is the Pacific Northwest. You'd have a better shot at getting a baby seal pelt here." He shook his head at Erik.

He blew out a breath and faced Hope again. "Okay. Fine. What do I do?"

She gazed at him for a moment and held out her hand. "Let me see your plans."

Erik pulled the paperwork out of the file and passed them over to Hope, jostling as Ruger tugged on his leash again. "Ruger, settle down — oh, man."

The three of them looked at the growing puddle underneath Erik's Ferragamos.

"Oh, jeeze," he sighed. "Bad dog."

It was a disaster waiting to happen. Resigned, Hope watched Erik roll the overflowing shopping cart through the exit doors and shook her head. Her assistant manager sidled up and sighed a little.

"That man gets hotter every time I see him," Caitlyn said. "He comes in here again, I may pass out."

"You've seen him twice. And you're married. You have a baby."

The younger woman giggled. "Doesn't make me blind. He's been in three times."

"Three?"

Caitlyn nodded, her eyes glued to Erik's admittedly stellar behind. "Mmm hmm. Wow. Look at him lifting all that stuff."

"You're staring," Hope snapped and turned away, then paused. "When was he in?"

"Um…oh, watch the puppy, Mr. Hottie Man!"

"Caitlyn. Focus." Hope waited until the other woman looked at her. "When was he in before this?"

"Well, the night he came in after hours, remember?"

"Yes, I remember." Hope prayed for patience.

"And then a couple days later, but it was really quick. He came in, exchanged the handle and practically ran out." Caitlyn contemplated that for a moment. "He might have been on lunch or something, and had to get back to work. He was in a suit." She grinned and made a growly sound.

"And why didn't you tell me he'd been back?"

Her assistant blinked. "Was I supposed to?"

Hope walked behind the customer service counter and pulled out the returns log and flipped through it. "No, of course not."

Caitlyn trailed after her. "He's not one of the owners, is he? Because you said--"

"He's not an owner," Hope made a note from the log and returned the heavy book to its shelf.

"Then why…" she trailed off and a huge grin split her freckled face. "Oh, my God! You're *dating* him!"

Hope stopped dead and stared at her. "Are you insane? Guys like that do not date me. Or anyone who looks like me."

Her assistant made a rude noise. "That's stupid; you're really pretty. You could totally date him."

"I'm not dating him."

"You *could* date him."

"I'm not dating him!"

"Then why did you ask about him? And you were helping him, and I know how much stuff you have to do." Caitlyn leaned her elbows on the countertop and rested her chin on her hands.

"I was helping him because he's a customer and Aaron asked me to help him." Hope printed the register reports and skimmed them.

"Hope." She grinned, unfazed by Hope's steely glare. "You have a crush."

"Ha! A crush. You are ridiculous." Hope stacked the papers from the day's sales and walked around the desk. "Don't forget to give the cashiers their breaks. I'll be in the office."

She strode away, ignoring the sound of Caitlyn's giggle.

"Shit! Shit!!!" Erik scrambled to turn off the water that led to the faucet in his bathroom sink, one hand fruitlessly covering the top of the spraying hose. Grabbing a towel from the rack, already soaked from the spray, he stuffed it down the open-ended pipe while cranking on the cold water handle. There was a snapping sound and more cold water sprayed him directly in the crotch.

He looked at the water flow valve in his hand, snapped cleanly off at the base.

The curses that flew from his mouth would have made Marty and his drill sergeant proud.

By the time he'd plugged the holes with towels, wash cloths and the bathmat, and called building maintenance to shut off the water to his condo, every inch of his bathroom dripped. Ruger danced through the puddles on the tiled floor and stopped to challenge a stray towel to a duel, barking happily at the limp, wet cloth. The instructions Hope had written down and his own drawings of the hardware replacement plan were still taped to the wall, but the ink had washed off the paper and ran in rivulets to the floor.

This was going to require a better plan.

Chapter Five

After the mayhem of the work day, the quiet of the nearly empty grocery store welcomed Hope in. It was a relief to be somewhere she didn't have to have all the answers. She could just go and shop and get ready for the family barbecue that weekend. At her house. For her birthday. No problem.

She just prayed it didn't rain. The last thing she needed was her whole family inside her house on a rainy day.

Grabbing a shopping cart, she dumped her purse into the child seat and fished out her list. She didn't like the new purse that Miriam had picked out and insisted she buy, but she had to admit, it was a better choice than the one Thor's dog had destroyed.

Thor. And his little dog, too.

It had been several days since Thor – *Erik* had visited the store, and she hadn't thought about him at all since then. At all. Or much.

Okay, she admitted to herself, she'd thought about him way too much.

Not that it mattered. She was done with men. If the past two weeks had accomplished nothing else, Hope thought she might have gotten that through her sister-in-law's head. Maybe. Miriam was a tough nut.

Rolling the cart down the nearest aisle, Hope stared blindly at the array of soft drinks and mixers. She might be done with men, but the sad fact was whether she was interested or not, Erik wouldn't look twice at a woman like her.

Grabbing two large bottles and resting them on top of her new bag, she continued down the aisle to the chips. She did a quick head count and filled half her cart with several varieties. The way her family ate, too much was always the safer way to go.

Too much. That was the man's problem, she thought viciously. He was too much everything. Too tall, too blonde, too handsome. He was every stupid girl's dream and he…he knew it.

And guys like that always got everything they wanted. Snatching bags of rolls for hamburgers and hot dogs, she tucked them into her cart. They had gorgeous women, women like Miriam. Although, she admitted, Miriam hadn't gotten suckered in by a smooth operator like Erik. She'd gone for quality materials, just like she'd advised Hope. She hadn't slipped up on a shiny surface.

But that was Miriam. Despite her beauty, there was a shrewd and sensible brain under all that hair. And with all the choices she'd had, she still made the wisest one.

Sorting through the packages of hamburger, Hope felt a kinship with the ground meat. Chewed up, squeezed out and slapped down on a disposable plate. All of her choices left her pureed and covered in plastic for everyone to see, and she was sick of it.

"And some people think because they're handsome, they can just push me around, well, they're wrong." She spun the cart around and slammed into an immovable object.

Both two-liter soda bottles tumbled off her purse and bounced at her feet.

"You're going to want to wait a little while before you open those."

She raised her eyes to see Erik, struggling not to grin.

"Are you kidding me?" Hope pressed her fists to her closed eyes and prayed that she was imagining things. She opened her eyes to find the man she didn't want to see, ever again, handing her back the shaken bottles.

"What are you doing here?" She ripped the bottles away from him and tossed them into the cart.

"Oh, hey, you squashed your buns."

"Leave my buns out of it!" Hope sputtered. "What are you *doing* here? Why are you freaking everywhere?"

"What are you talking about?" Erik drew back and the look on his face, that small, smug smile pushed Hope over the edge.

A low, inarticulate sound erupted from her. "You! I'm talking about you!! You're everywhere. Why are you here, now? Why aren't you somewhere with your stupid purse-eating dog?"

The smile was gone and now he looked at her as if she'd just slipped a gear. "Ruger's in the car," he began.

"I don't care!"

"But you just said--"

"Arg!" she shrieked. "What is the matter with you? Are you some kind of stalker? Do you have some sort of sick need to follow me around and make me look like an idiot?"

He'd stopped listening to her rant a couple minutes before her lips stopped moving, watching her coldly, pretending not to see the flush in her perfect skin or the way her luscious mouth looked as it opened and closed. He latched onto the last thing he heard before switching off the sound.

"A stalker? You're calling me a stalker?" Erik asked her, oddly pleased with the way she stammered unintelligibly in reply. "Are you kidding or just crazy?"

"What--I--you--"

He gave her another moment to see if she could form an actual sentence. When none appeared to be forthcoming, he continued, derision dripping from his words. "Sweetheart. Look at me."

She stared at him mutely as he spread his arms.

"I have been fighting off women since I was twelve years old. Do you think, even for a minute, that I need to stalk anyone? Especially you?"

He knew it was arrogant. But dammit, she was his friend's sister, and some things a decent man just didn't do. Stalker. Ha!

"In case you haven't been paying attention, stalking is a serious crime. It's one of the most common precursors to violence against women and most women who are murdered in this country have been stalked by their killers. And you're accusing me of that? What kind of sick--" he stopped himself. "What kind of man do you think I am?"

It occurred to him that she hadn't responded to his reassurance but simply stood there. She'd gone ghost-white, almost as bad as the first time he'd seen her, before she threw up.

She made a sound he couldn't define and spun her cart around.

"Hey!" he called after her, watching her nearly run through the aisles.

What the hell was wrong with that woman?

Why did he even *care*?

Hope sat in her workshop, a cup of coffee steaming on the bench beside her. She knew she shouldn't be drinking it this late in the evening, she knew she'd be wide awake later, but dammit, she needed something to chase away the chill.

Her new cell phone rang in her pocket. She sighed and pulled out the phone and peered at it. Miriam's pictures floated on the screen. Pressing the speaker option, she set the phone on her workbench and picked up her cup.

"Hi," she said, not bothering to sound happy.

A small silence spilled from the phone and Miriam demanded, "What's wrong?"

"Nothing."

"You are full of crap."

Despite herself, Hope felt her lips turn up. Only Miriam could say that and still sound charming. It had to be the accent.

"Hope. What happened?"

"Nothing, okay? I just...ran into that stupid Thor guy again." She wrapped both hands around the cup and breathed in the steam. She really needed to run heat to this work room, she thought. Something to add to the list.

"And? Why are you so upset? Was he mean to you?"

"Yes. No. He's just so full of himself and...I don't know." Hope stood and wandered over to the tool wall, idly examining the mishmash of equipment on the pegboard. Her bench was cluttered, too; she really should straighten it out one of these days.

"He's full of himself and this makes you sound as though you lost your best friend." Doubt poured out of the phone's tiny speaker.

"I don't sound like I've lost my best friend." Hope gathered a few of the scattered screwdrivers and replaced them in their drawer.

"Yes, you do. This is exactly how you would sound if I dumped you."

She snorted. "You can't dump me; you're my sister-in-law. You'd have to divorce Daniel."

"Or I'd have to take him with me as I left you in a cloud of friendless dust."

"Jeeze, Miriam, how much time have you spent thinking about this?" Hope sat back on her stool, shoulders slumped, coffee cooling and forgotten in her hand.

"I don't have to spend time thinking about things, I just think. It is the magnificence of my mind, darling."

Hope could all but see her, flipping her hair over her shoulder. She smiled ruefully. "Now, why is it you can be a conceited twit and it doesn't bug me at all?"

"Good question. Why does this guy bug you? Do you have feelings--"

"NO. Miriam, we've talked about this," Hope warned.

"I know we have. But, darling, if you do not have any feelings for this man, why are you so upset?"

"I don't know," she whispered.

"Hope? Are you there?"

She cleared her throat. "I'm here. Right here."

There was another beat of silence, and Miriam spoke again. "I'm coming over."

"No, don't. I'm fine." Despite herself, Hope smiled as Miriam made scoffing sounds. "I am. I just need to figure some stuff out."

"Like how you really feel about this man?"

"Jesus, Miriam. Can't you just give it up for once?" Hope reached for her phone and scowled at Miriam's picture on the small screen.

Another beat of silence. "Have you *met* me?"

Hope raised her cup in salute to the disembodied voice of her sister-in-law. "Good point."

Erik dangled from the chin-up bar as sweat poured off of him to puddle on the mat covering the hardwood floor. A twenty-five pound dumbbell hooked onto his ankles as he pulled himself straight up to the bar and eased back down.

Despite the sweat, despite the near trembling exhaustion that made his arms, chest and belly quiver, he kept at it, round after round. The hardcore trainer from the gym, Stephanie the Sadist, would be telling him his weight was insufficient if he could do this many reps, but he pressed on, waiting for the screaming of his muscles to drown out the memory in his head.

Stalker.

Was she kidding? What kind of man did she take him for? Stalkers were sick bastards who needed to be roasted over a slow fire, every last one of them. Catching the dumbbell as he released the bar, he eased the weights onto the padded floor mat.

Taking up the coiled jump rope, he started a series of double-unders, jumping high enough to whip the cord two revolutions before landing. He'd never been great at double-unders and doing them after weighted pull-ups took all his concentration. Across the room, on his cushion, Ruger chewed blissfully on a new bully stick, safely out of range of the whip-fast rope.

He'd managed to put Angry Chick and the bathroom disaster out of his mind for two whole minutes. And then…

His phone rang.

Muttering a curse as he missed a jump and stumbled, he dropped the jump rope and scooped up the phone. "Yoriksson."

"Erik. Daniel. What are you doing?"

"Home workout."

"Stephanie's?"

Erik grunted.

"She is *brutal*, dude."

"Tell me." Erik rubbed a towel over his face, trying to absorb more of the sweat running down his body like a river.

"Don't have to; you already know."

He laughed and felt some of the tension leave his body. "Yeah, guess so. What's up, Dan?"

"Barbecue. Saturday. Three-ish."

"This Saturday? Outside?"

"It rains, we eat inside. Meat, potato salad, decent beer. Burgers and dogs for the kids. My wife wants to meet you."

Taking a quick swig from his water bottle, Erik flipped through his calendar mentally. "Can't do it. Little sister's going to be in town and my parents want us all to get together at my place. Ever since she and her husband had the kid, it's all they can talk about."

"Bring 'em along!" Daniel plowed through his objections. "There's always enough for twice as many people at our barbecues. Besides, if you're there, I get out of clean up."

He considered the tentative plans he'd had for his family gathering and discarded them. This would be easier and he wouldn't have his mother and sister pawing through his stuff.

He also wouldn't have to explain the bathroom and why the door was locked shut.

"What do you want us to bring?" He reached for the dumbbell and stood beneath the pull up bar again.

"Anything you want. There's going to be killer brisket and the wife always has chicken to go on the grill, but if you want something else, like steak, bring it along."

"Text the address to me."

"Done."

"Three?"

"Ish," Daniel snorted. "Don't worry about being on time."

"Good enough. See you then," Erik pressed a button on his phone and tossed it onto the chair closest to him.

Bracing the weight between his legs, he stretched up to the bar and lost himself again in the workout.

Chapter Six

"Sweetheart, why did you get soda pop? You knew we were bringing it." Rebecca Lindstrom bustled around Hope's kitchen, wiping down already clean counters and stove top. "I hope you got enough chips and things."

Hope watched her mother's impression of a tornado from the relative safety of the breakfast bar with the comfort of long practice. "I think I did, Mom."

"Well." Her mother glanced around the spotless kitchen, taking in the granite counters and brushed nickel fixtures. "We can always run to the store if we have to."

"Okay."

Running her fingers over the faucet, Rebecca frowned. "This is…interesting. Why did you choose this one, sweetheart?"

Hope smiled into the coffee she'd been sipping while her mother re-cleaned her kitchen. "Well, you're touching the metal now, right, Mom?"

Rebecca pulled her hand back. "Am I not supposed to? Is it wired to electricity?"

Hope sighed. "No, of course not. But you just touched the faucet. Can you see any fingerprints?"

Her mother leaned in and examined it closely. "No. But my hands are clean."

"Uh huh. But this doesn't show dirt or smudges as much."

Rebecca sniffed. "Hmph. Well, I think it's still a little dirty, down around the base."

"Really?" Hope widened her eyes. "After *you* cleaned it?"

"Gamma!" a small voice shrieked from the hallway before the thunder of three small children rolled into Hope's small house. Rebecca lit up like Christmas and went to greet her grandchildren.

"Paul, stop yanking on your grandmother. Hello, beautiful one," Miriam swept into the kitchen on the heels of her children and dropped a kiss on Rebecca's still unlined cheek. The sleeves of the sheer white shirt fluttered and the open sides danced against the white lace inserts on the sides of extreme low-rise jeans. Miriam's perfect abs rose out of the low-slung denim to the sparkly white bra top. Hope glanced down at her loose jeans and nearly knee-length baseball jersey.

Oh, well. She was comfortable.

Turning to Hope, Miriam embraced her lightly. "Happy birthday!"

"Don't you look pretty!" Hope said clearly before muttering, "Where have you *been*?"

"Sorry. We got here as soon as I could pry your brother away from his computer. Has it been bad?"

Hope smiled brilliantly at her sister-in-law and said under breath. "She cleaned my kitchen. Again."

Miriam grimaced. "Hang on," she whispered.

Swooping down on the children, she laughed with her mother-in-law. "I swear, you are their catnip! Come, darlings. Gamma isn't to be mauled like this."

Rebecca preened. "Oh, they're fine."

Miriam tossed her hair back and Hope wondered, for the millionth time, how she didn't get neck strain. "Well, we don't want to take advantage of your sweet nature."

"Oh, Mirrie, I'll just take them outside. They can run around a little, wear themselves out a little bit."

"Are you sure?"

Hope turned away to top off her coffee and hide her grin. As tough as her mother was, she never seemed to see through Miriam's maneuvering. Or maybe, she just didn't mind it.

"Hope, sweetheart, don't drink too much coffee. You'll never get to sleep tonight."

Hope turned to see her mother herding the children out the back door. "Yes, ma'am."

They watched from the window for a moment and Miriam plucked at Hope sleeve. "Come on."

"Where are we going?"

"Your room." Miriam flashed a devilish smile over her shoulder. "I have a birthday present for you."

"We're opening presents later. Mom finds out I opened one early—wait up! How do you move so fast in those ridiculous shoes?" Hope lengthened her stride and still came in second in the race to her bedroom.

"They're not ridiculous, they're Christian Louboutin." Miriam turned out her heel and admired the white basket weave and four inch platform spike of her shoe.

She frowned. "Those shoes make no sense. The bottom of it is red. It doesn't match."

"Darling."

Hope waved her hands. "I know, I know. You've told me all about it before. It still doesn't make sense to me."

Though her room was a work in progress with its unfinished trim and unmatched furniture, she always felt a surge of pride when she walked through the doorway and laid eyes on her gorgeous bed. She'd made it herself, inspired by a museum exhibit of a Tudor bed chamber. Dark panels and sheer hangings made her bed a haven, a cocoon against rainy mornings and cold nights. She absolutely loved it, every ridiculous and romantic inch of it.

Miriam shook her head and set her purse on the bed to rummage through it, muttering in Norwegian. Hope bristled.

"I know some of what you're saying there, so watch it. I'll get your kids jacked up on sugar."

"You'll do that anyway. You or one of your parents. Ah ha!" Miriam pulled out a pink and black gift bag and rattled it. "Happy birthday!"

A little squeal escaped Hope as she snatched the bag away from her sister-in-law. "Thank you!" The black lace bow that held the top of the bag closed was quickly untied and unthreaded and Hope plunged her hand into it. Through the pink, glittery tissue paper, she found her quarry and pulled out…

A vibrator.

The deep purple device rested in the palm of her hand and Hope gaped at Miriam, who beamed at her.

"Isn't it pretty? It's a Rabbit!"

Sure enough, there was a small rabbit figure on the top of the sex toy. Hope felt her lips move but no words came out.

"See, I listen to you. I know you think I don't, but I do. And this is exactly what you need right now." A flick of golden hair punctuated Miriam's statement.

"What?" Hope finally managed.

"You told me you were done with men, yes?" Miriam waited for Hope's nod before continuing. "And we both know how cranky you are without…." She waved her hand and waggled her eyebrows.

"Oh, my God! Miriam!"

"You're going to argue?" Miriam shot her a meaningful look and draped herself across Hope's bed. "This way, you can be less cranky and no man to worry about. So there. I listened!"

Hope stuffed the vibrator back in the bag and looked around the room for a place to hide it. Giving up, she tucked under the bed and prayed none of the kids would use that as a hiding spot for hide-and-go-seek. That, she thought, was all she needed.

"And there's yummy lube in there, too. Strawberry. Oh, and honey dust," Miriam chirped. "I didn't know if you'd need it or not, but I thought…better safe than sorry!"

"Miriam." Hope closed her eyes and summoned patience. "You said you listened to me."

"I did." Even with her eyes closed, Hope could imagine the wounded look on Miriam's face.

"And that I was done with guys."

"Of course. Therefore…your present!" Bewilderment mixed with insult.

"Miriam." Hope opened her eyes and leaned in. "If you bought me something for…solo activities, why did you think I'd needed flavored lubricants and honey dust?"

"Oh." Miriam sat up and toyed with her necklace as she pondered the question, then shrugged. "Well, no one says you can't lick them off yourself."

"Oh, my God."

Hope turned and walked out of her work-in-progress bedroom. She didn't turn around but she could hear the clicking of Miriam's heels as she was followed by her sister-in-law; anything Miriam said was lost to the buzzing in her ears. Or maybe that wretched vibrator had turned on and was buzzing the whole house….

Escaping to the deck, she breathed in the scents of the unseasonably warm day and slow barbecuing meat. Her father's brisket was a thing of beauty and what she asked for every year on her birthday.

"Hey, birthday brat!"

Hope turned to her brother with relief. "Hey, yourself." They shared a quick, hard hug that ended with Daniel's traditional back thump. Hope coughed and tried not to stumble.

"Getting some guns, there."

Daniel had always been the classic nerd through high school, brilliant, quirky, skinny as a rail. It was only as an adult that he'd found a workout regime that gave him some muscle mass and allowed him to hold his own when facing down bullies. It also helped him land Miriam.

Daniel struck a dramatic weightlifter's pose. "Kid, you're going to need tickets to this gun show."

"There's my girl!"

She and Daniel turned to find their father coming up the steps of the deck with Lene on his shoulders. The little girl gripped Jonas Lindstrom's tonsure with both fists, pulling his eyes into a slant.

"And there's *my* girl," Hope answered. "Hi, peanut."

"Lene, don't pull out Farfar's hair. He has so little left." Daniel reached up for his daughter, who shrieked and clung to Jonas' balding head.

Jonas tipped his head back and smiled at the little blonde scrap. "See, you know it's best with Farfar, huh?"

"The meat smells really good, Dad." Hope walked over to the cooler on the deck and selected a can of cola. "Anybody want anything?"

"Beer." The men spoke in unison and each held out his right hand. Without looking closely, Hope pulled two bottles of beer from the nest of ice and tossed them to her father and brother. The bottles were caught mid-air and opened as swiftly.

"Daddy! Come play!"

Daniel saluted with his beer. "Duty calls." He winked at his daughter, who giggled, and loped out to the yard to wrestle with his boys.

Hope walked over the edge of the deck and studied the dining area set up there. Last year's wisteria vines were just starting to show green and framed the small mountain of food. "Wow, Mom outdid herself this year."

Jonas nodded. "Well, when Danny called, she knew we'd need a lot more of everything. I've got some extra chicken, too, in case they don't eat beef. Your mother's idea." He winked.

"Why did Daniel call?" A shriek interrupted them and they turned to the yard. Both boys ran full tilt at the gate on the side of the house. Ecstatic barking echoed between Hope's house and the detached garage that created the corridor between the buildings. "What the he--heck is going on?"

"Oh, that must be Daniel's friends." Her father headed down the steps of the deck, a shrieking Lene bouncing on his shoulders.

"Goggy! Goggy!"

"Yes, I hear the doggie, Lene." Hope trailed after them. "Daniel invited people to my birthday party? Who did he invite?"

"He invited me."

Hope stopped dead on the last step and stared right into Thor's ice blue eyes. "Oh, my God."

"But he didn't tell me it was your birthday." Ruger continued to bark madly at the squealing children as Angry Chick stared at him with all the dismay he felt. He saw her gaze shift to his parents and then his sister and her family and struggle into a nearly welcoming smile.

"Hello." Her smile evened out a little, he noticed, when she wasn't looking at him. "I'm Hope. Please, won't you all come in?"

"I'm Jonas Lindstrom." A man who could only be Hope and Daniel's father stepped forward and offered his hand. Erik found himself nearly eye-to-eye with the tiny blonde angel perched on the man's shoulders. "You must be Erik."

"I am, Mr. Lindstrom. A pleasure to meet you." Erik set Ruger down as he shook the older man's hand, but kept a tight hold on his long line leash. The two small boys crowded around the puppy, who alternated between smothering the boys with dog kisses and rolling onto his back for belly rubs.

"Oh, call me Jonas, boy. And who else do we have?" The older man's smile was as broad and bright as a sunbeam as he turned to the others.

"These are my parents, sir, Astrid and Bosse Yoriksson. And my sister Tilda, her husband William and the Squirt."

"Baby!" crowed the little girl on Jonas' shoulders. "Baby, hi! Hi, baby!"

Erik's sister smiled at the little girl. "This is Henrik. What's your name, little one?"

"I'm Lene. Hi, baby!" she chirped. "Down, Farfar. Down. See baby."

Jonas obliged and Henrik had the courtesy to wake up as new faces peered into the carrier William held. The little girl cooed and patted his blanket. "Pretty baby. Come! Show Mama! Show Gamma!"

Daniel appeared then, a neon green and blue Frisbee in his hands. "Hey, you made it! Dad, did you meet Erik?"

Erik glanced over as Daniel and his father chatted with the new arrivals; Angry Chick—no, *Hope* was busily pulling out chairs onto the generous cedar deck at the back of the house. She paused long enough to count them then turned to his family. "Please, everyone. Be comfortable."

Carrying a bottle of wine as well as their child, Tilda and William moved up the steps first, escorted by Lene's unintelligible babble as she held on to the other side of the baby's carrier. Hope dragged over a huge, low table to hold the carrier, then turned to his parents. "May I get you something to drink, Mrs. Yoriksson? Mr. Yoriksson?"

The music of Sweden still sang in his mother's voice. "Thank you...Hope, is it? And I did not bring a vase." She offered a swath of bright spring color in the bouquet.

"Thank you, ma'am. Oh, they're beautiful!" Hope dipped her head and he saw her close her eyes as she inhaled the scent before collecting herself. "We have white wine chilled and some red in the house, and several beers. If you'd like a soft drink or coffee or tea, we have that, too. What would you like?"

"White wine sounds very nice."

Hope nodded and turned to his father, who unbent enough to smile at her. "You have beer?"

Her own smile warmed several degrees. "With this crowd?" She nodded to her brother and father. "I'd be drawn and quartered otherwise. Would you like to look in the cooler?"

Still carrying the flowers, she escorted his father to a large ice chest and splayed open the lid. A large urn sat on the corner of the deck railing; she popped the bouquet into it and poured water from a pitcher on the nearby table. Erik caught the odd word about the variety of ales, lagers and stouts that peppered the white mounds, and without missing a beat, pulled out a cold bottle of wine and opened it with the skill of a seasoned bartender. Glasses waited on the table next to the cooler, and she filled one while his father made his selection. His bass rumble mingled with her voice as she handed him the bottle opener attached to the corkscrew she'd just used. Daniel joined them and accepted two more bottles, which he handed to Tilda and William.

"Oh, I can't," protested Tilda. "The baby...."

Hope interjected with a murmur, handed Bosse the glass of wine and disappeared into the house while Daniel moved over to the barbecue next to Jonas. The conversation between his sister and his friend continued over the gleaming silver beast of a grill, punctuated with laughter and comments from the older man and William. His own father returned to hand the glass to his wife and held out an extra bottle to Erik.

"Thanks, Dad." He accepted the bottle and glanced at the label.

"Yah. She has Carlsberg." Bosse drank from his own bottle and sighed his appreciation. "A good girl."

"Very nice," added his mother, though Erik wasn't really sure if she referred to Hope or the wine. He'd barely taken a drink of his beer when Hope came outside again, carrying a large glass, filled with something pale gold and bubbly.

"Here, try this. It's got ginger ale and some fruit juice, so it's safe," he heard her say as she set the drink in front of Tilda. "My sister-in-law swore by it while she was pregnant, because of the ginger. Helped her stomach and after the babies were born, she was hooked."

Tilda smiled and hummed in appreciation and Hope laughed. She leaned over the carrier and smoothed Henrik's blanket. Cooing at the baby, she chuckled as his fists flailed in the air and scooped up her niece to see the little boy.

Turning to the yard, he watched the two older children playing with the puppy. The long leash allowed for a little wiggle room for the small dog and his new friends, but not as much as they all would prefer. "Hey, Daniel?"

"Yo!"

"How secure is your fence?"

Daniel looked nonplussed for a moment. "No clue. Hope!"

"Busy here." Hope called back.

"We just need to know if your fence is secure."

Erik closed his eyes. *Her fence.*

Hope laughed. "Secure from what? Alien invasion?"

Daniel just pointed his tongs at Erik and Ruger, still playing with the boys. As he watched, Erik saw the tight set return to her mouth. But she nodded. "As long as the gate is latched, it should be fine." Without waiting for a reply, she turned and walked back into the house.

Her house. Crap.

Erik walked over to the deliriously happy puppy and crouched down as he unhooked the long line. "Okay, guys. You've already met, but this is Ruger. Who are you?"

"I'm Paul and this is Sebastian." The older boy spoke, his eyes never leaving Ruger.

"I'm Erik. Good to meet you men." The children giggled and he continued. "Can you play with the puppy and keep him busy, but also keep an eye on him?"

A chorus of assent filled the backyard.

"He's just a baby, so sometimes, he doesn't do the right thing. If it gets to be too hard, you come get me. Okay?" He stood and coiled the leash as he walked back to the deck, pausing when he realized there was a woman standing on the steps, watching him.

It wasn't Hope.

This was the kind of woman everyone expected him to date; blindingly beautiful, a hotter-than-lava body, enough confidence to pull off the outfit she was almost wearing. He hoped to God Daniel wasn't trying to set him up.

"Well," she said, tossing nearly waist-length golden hair over her shoulder. "You have a brand new fan club."

He let the rhythm of her speech roll over him. "Norwegian?"

She smiled. "Snakker du Norsk?"

"Do I speak Norwegian?" he waited for her nod. "No, not really. I understand a few phrases, most of which have to do with beer."

The beautiful woman laughed. "Then you speak Norwegian, my friend. I'm Miriam."

He took the hand offered and shook. "Miriam. Daniel's Miriam?"

His relief at her nod must have shown because she raised her eyebrows and studied him. "And you are?"

"I'm Erik. Erik Yoriksson. I'm a friend of Daniel's from the gym."

A small frown danced across her face. "I see."

He leaned forward a bit and lowered his voice. "It's a little awkward being here because it's Hope's birthday."

Now she folded her arms. "How did you know it was Hope's birthday?"

"She said so, when we came in."

"And 'we' would be…?" Miriam turned toward the deck and checked out the crowd.

"My parents, my sister and her family and Ruger. The puppy," he added. "Daniel said we should all come. I didn't know it was her birthday, and I really didn't know it was her house."

"Daniel said." Her frown deepened. "And do you know Hope, too? Are you friends of the family?"

"No, I--"

Her eyes widened suddenly. "Oh, my dear God. You're Thor!"

"What? How did--?" he sputtered. "No, my name is Erik. I hate it when she calls me—how did you know she called me that?"

Miriam giggled. Actually *giggled*.

He glared at her and she struggled to control her mirth. "Oh, this is excellent. And I have front-row tickets. Boys!"

At first Erik thought she was making reference to him and all his kind, but he saw the children scramble up, the larger one clutching the puppy.

"Mama! Did you see? He's Ruger." The smaller of the boys jumped up and down. "Can we keep him?"

"Oh, darling, no. No. The dog belongs to Mr. Yoriksson here."

"He's not actually my dog, I'm just watching him for-- Yes." Erik threw accuracy to the wind as Daniel's gorgeous wife shot him a killing glare. "Yes. The dog belongs to me." He nodded at the boys for good measure.

"He would be sad without his dog. Wouldn't you?" She leveled another speaking glance at him.

"Yes. Yes." Erik did his best to look sad despite a strong desire to find Hope and throttle her. "I would miss him a lot."

"There, you see? You cannot take the man's dog from him, darlings. Now come and wash, it's time to eat. And then, Auntie Hope's birthday cake."

"And presents," piped the smaller boy.

"Yes, the presents." The golden goddess of a woman led her sons into the house, leaving Erik to stew.

He walked around the garden, studying the fence with its painted concrete block base and sturdy wood planks. A wide band of lattice topped the fence; between it and the greenery in the yard and the surrounding area, the city garden was surprisingly private.

"Erik, c'mon." He turned and saw Daniel. "Food's ready."

"No, really, Daniel. I've got it," Hope muttered under her breath as she dragged the large folding table from her storage shed. The table banged against her shins and she muffled the curse that leapt to her lips. A quick glance confirmed the area clear of tiny ears.

Thank God. Miriam had been very unhappy when Daniel accidentally taught Paul how to say "shit."

Easing the table up the side steps, she wrestled gravity to keep it from banging into the expensive railing. Even at cost, she'd nearly had to sell a kidney to buy the cedar decking.

"Here." One large hand reached over her shoulder and lifted the awkward table with no apparent effort. Thor in action, she thought sourly.

Bastard.

He carried the clumsy piece of furniture to the space she'd cleared and with a few swift movements, had it unfolded and set in place. He hadn't even had the courtesy to struggle with the stubborn hinges that always needed a little more oil than she gave them. With deliberate effort, she unclenched her jaw. "Thank you."

"Least I can do." He spotted the tablecloth and dishware on the buffet she'd found at a garage sale. "These for here?"

"Yes. I can—or you go ahead. I'll just stand here."

"You do that."

The nip in his voice surprised rather than hurt her. She caught the end of the tablecloth as he snapped it across the length of the folding table and smoothed down over the edge. "I know why I'm angry at you. Why are you pissed off at me?"

"I'm not pissed off."

Hope watched him setting the table for a moment. "You're doing that wrong."

He braced his hand against the table and breathed in through his nose. "Of course, I am."

She bristled. "I'm not saying that to be snotty, it's--"

Erik laughed and went back to placing cutlery next to plates precisely, to her eye, one-half inch from plate and table edge. "Really."

"Look, Thor, this isn't about you," she snapped. He raised his head slowly and before she could stop herself, she shrank back a bit.

"Do you think," he said quietly, so quietly she nearly had to strain to hear him, "that you could be bothered to remember my name? Let me help you with it. My name is *Erik*. And I would appreciate your using it."

She locked eyes with him and reminded herself that this was her house. Her deck. Her freaking squeaky folding table! Lifting her chin and straightening her shoulders, she
—

"Sweetheart! Why are you setting the table like that?"

--turned to face her mother.

Erik watched Hope deflate like a balloon with a tiny hole, then summon a pretty smile. Or it would have been pretty if he hadn't seen the frazzled edges.

"Hi, Mom. Have you met…" she paused a moment, her smile turning to a blade, "Erik?"

He bared his teeth back at her before facing the blonde dumpling of woman beside her. "Hello, Mrs. Lindstrom."

"Hello, dear. Oh, and you call me Rebecca. My! You are a tall one, aren't you?" She beamed at him. "And so good-natured; I see Hope's been putting a guest to work."

"No, ma'am, I just wanted to help--" he began. He caught a glimpse of Hope sighing and shaking her head slightly.

"Well, you just go on and relax. I'll fix this."

To her credit, Hope didn't quail under the steely look her mother gave her, and he wondered if he'd have been able to do the same. Instead, she merely gave her mother an innocent look as the older woman rearranged the cutlery Erik had just laid out.

"Mom, would you like a cocktail?"

Rebecca's head popped up like a gopher from a hole. "Oh! One of the pretty ones?"

Hope nodded. "In a nice glass."

"Well…" Rebecca fussed with the cloth and tugged the table over what was obviously a critical two inches. "If you're making one anyway."

She dropped a kiss on her mother's cheek and the sweetness of it made him blink. He'd caught the criticism fired at her and despite being Angry Chick with him, she obviously didn't let her mother's treatment affect her. He watched as she strolled inside, pausing to speak to his mother on the way. It appeared the same offer was made and accepted, and then more casually to Miriam as she exited the house with the two boys. Laughter rang out between the women as Hope disappeared back into the house.

As he watched, Miriam strolled over to the grill and leaned into her husband's side. Daniel bent his head to her and even from the distance, Erik could see him wince and his shoulders hunch. Someone was getting a trip to the woodshed.

Good.

Despite the discomfort of his family's invasion, everyone appeared to be having a good time. His notoriously stiff father laughed—okay, chuckled at something Jonas said. Miriam had walked away from her sheepish husband and lounged on the arm of the chair while her children dipped newly clean fingers into hors d'oeuvres arranged on small tables.

And Hope walked back onto the deck with a large tray.

Sweat beaded on his back.

Maybe he was just hungry, maybe it was the unseasonably warm weather. None of those things explained the way the peach colored froth in the fancy glass pitcher caught the sunlight and reflected the velvet of her skin.

Whoa.

Erik shook his head. Coming up behind him, Rebecca patted him on the back. "You must be hungry, dear. Hope should have gotten you a plate."

He smiled at the diminutive tyrant. "Actually, she did take care of all of us. Look, my mother has one of the drinks Hope made for you ladies. We better get you a glass before she gets it all." He offered his arm in an exaggerated courtly manner.

Well, at least he could make Hope's *mother* giggle and blush.

They joined the group and Erik held the chair for the older woman at his side. Wordlessly, Hope handed him a tall crystal beaker of a glass, lightly frosted and decorated with a sheer slice of peach, and nodded to her mother. "What do you think, Mrs. Yoriksson?"

"It's very nice." Erik's mother sipped at her own glass. "It is all fruit juices?"

"Well…" Hope smiled a little. "There's some alcohol in it, just for a little sparkle. You aren't driving tonight, are you?"

"Oh, no. Bosse likes to drive." Erik watched his mother sample the drink again, a light pink tingeing her cheeks. "Mmm. I do like this."

Daniel reached over Hope's shoulder for the remaining glass and Erik choked back a laugh as she held it out of his reach. "Oh, no. You can't have this. This is for your wife."

Daniel sputtered. "But…I always…."

"You have to be the designated driver." Sugar all but dripped off of her as she smiled at her brother. "Here, Miriam."

"Thank you, darling." Miriam accepted the glass and slid an arm around Hope, pressing her cheek to her sister-in-law's. The two women beamed identical wicked grins at Daniel. "I love your drinks. And it is Daniel's turn to be the driver."

"I agree. In fact," Hope nipped the beer bottle out of Daniel's hand. "We'll make the switch now."

"Hey!" Daniel tried to grab back his beer but Erik plucked it out of Hope's hand before he could reach her.

"The boss say you're driving, buddy."

Daniel looked mournful. "Whose side are you on?"

Before Erik could answer, Jonas lugged a huge platter of grilled meat to the table. "Why isn't anyone at the table? Danny, I told you to round 'em up."

Evidently, Daniel's trip to the woodshed was far from over.

The two families clustered around the table and settled into the serious business of eating the small mountain range of food. Warm potato salad and roasted asparagus vied for space with smoky barbecued chicken and tender, marinated beef brisket. Hope carried over the remainder of the appetizers and topped off the ladies' cocktails before handing her brother a soda.

"Thanks," he muttered sourly.

In the warm, nearly hot sunshine of mid-afternoon, laughter and chatter almost drowned out the clink of cutlery and glasses. Jonas stood and raised his glass. "Happy birthday, little girl."

"Thanks, dad." Hope stood to receive kisses and hugs from her family. Even Daniel kissed her cheek before ruffling her hair, earning a reciprocal smack upside the head.

Erik passed platters and trays around the table, rising to grab another drink for his sister. The sound of his mother's voice stopped him in his tracks.

"We did not know it was your birthday, Hope. Birthdays are such nice family occasions, yes? And here we are." Her musical voice, so rarely heard, had blurred a little around the edges. "And not even a gift. I am sorry."

"Oh no, Mrs. Yoriksson, please don't be." Hope smiled at her and rose again to bring another serving bowl to the table. "And it's great to have you here."

"Erik said his friend's wife had insisted we come, otherwise we would not have intruded." Astrid Yoriksson contemplated her nearly empty glass and frowned. "It is gone again."

Erik glanced at his sister and saw the same expression of disbelief on her face. He walked around the table and stood behind Hope as she refilled his mother's glass. "Just how much 'sparkle' is in that stuff?" he whispered.

"I'll thin it out, next pitcher," she murmured back then spoke in a normal tone. "Mom? A drop more?"

Astrid hiccupped. "Leffe, this is a very nice drink. Did you try this drink?" His mother sipped again and Erik smiled at her.

"Is it? Should we get the recipe?"

Hope passed another platter of food in front of him, raising her brows at the chicken and indicating his mother with a tip of her head. "Would your mom like a little protein?"

"Thanks."

Answering her mother's call, Hope returned to the house with an empty bowl and pitcher. "I'll write down that cocktail mix for you, Mrs. Yoriksson."

Erik forked a piece of barbecued chicken onto his mother's plate and listened as conversation eddied around him when he heard Ruger's happy bark.

"Look, Mama! Ruger got a toy!"

Erik dropped the platter with a thump and dashed around the table, visions of priceless antique somethings, chewed to shreds and dangling from the puppy's mouth.

The small dog had dropped his prize, already gnawed on the end, and stood over it, slightly crouched with his tail high and waving madly. Astrid's tipsy voice floated over.

"It is a play bow, you see, children? He asks you to play with him and his new toy...." She trailed off as everyone stared at the purple pipe-shaped object between the puppy's paws.

Miriam drew in her breath and covered her mouth.

"What is it, Mama?" One of the boys tugged his mother's hand and Tilda muffled a giggle.

Daniel chortled. "It's a sign that Auntie Hope's been— OW!" Several hands smacked him at once.

Erik dove at the small dog and stifled a curse as Ruger scooped up his contraband chew toy and hopped backwards. Locking eyes with the dog, he stepped forward and made a low growling sound as the dog took another bounce back.

Astrid tutted. "Leffe, you are letting the dog control the circumstance. He will not recognize you as the alpha."

Hope's mother leaned toward her. "The alpha? What is that?" Rebecca asked.

"In a dog pack, the alpha is the leader. If a dog does not know who is the leader of his pack, he is uncomfortable. He wants to know who is in charge."

Erik caught Rebecca's frown as she watched his antics. "But, Astrid, there's only one dog."

"And Erik is his pack." Astrid nodded. "We had a small business in dog training, and Erik knows better than this."

Biting back a curse as he rapped his shin on a deck chair, Erik swiped an arm at the little dog, who responded by racing around the seating area. The purple object in the pup's mouth bumped the table leg as he zipped by and the sudden buzzing startled him enough that he dropped it on the floor. Gleefully barking and pouncing, Ruger chased the vibrating tube that wiggled under the furniture on its own.

The little dog's distraction gave Erik the break he'd been looking for. He nabbed the puppy, scooping him up with one arm. Ruger snapped up the stolen toy and set his white, sharp teeth in the pliable exterior. "Ruger." Erik stared down the small dog. "Drop it."

Button black eyes met his and the dog gave a sigh of disgust and defeat. Erik sighed, too, and glanced at the chewed object in his hand. "Great. Now we have to replace Hope's...." he trailed off. At the sound of the gasp in the doorway, he looked up to see Hope holding a fresh pitcher of cocktails. In the background, Rebecca and Astrid continued to discuss dog training while Miriam and Tilda muffled laughter. Wordlessly, he held out the gnawed vibrator.

Hope closed her eyes. Erik cleared his throat.

"We'll replace it. I promise."

Chapter Seven

"Mom! How could you???" Hope leaned her forehead against the cool metal of her stainless steel refrigerator.

Her mother sipped at her cup of tea. "You'll smudge the front of that fridge, Hope. Stand up straight."

She pushed herself off the fridge and stood at the sink, leaning her arms against the sink. "I can't do it. Please, Mom. Call Mrs. Yoriksson and tell her you made a mistake."

"Hope Oda Lindstrom!"

"Well, it *was* a mistake to tell her that I would watch that horrible little dog." Hope could feel her face scrunching up, much the way her nephews' faces did now when stubbornness set in. "Besides, I'm allergic to dogs."

"What?" Rebecca laughed. "Who told you that?"

Hope held her arms out to the side and stared, dumbfounded, at her mother. "You did!"

"I did not."

"Mom. All through our childhood, you told Daniel and Edvard and me that we were allergic to dogs and cats. This is why Daniel's kids can't have a dog now. Remember?" She peered at her mother's growing look of comprehension. "How much did you drink tonight?"

Rebecca's cheeks flushed a deeper rosy hue than half a pitcher of Hope's magic cocktails normally made them. "Oh, that. Of course I remember. It's just...."

Hope watched her mother fuss with the cup and saucer in front of her, smooth the napkin, reach over and take a cookie. "Mom?"

"You're not actually allergic."

"What?"

Rebecca rolled her eyes and bit into the cookie. Knowing the delaying tactic for what it was, Hope waited for her to chew and swallow, and sip her tea again.

"You have to understand, Hopie, three children are a lot to deal with." Rebecca smiled gamely. "And I knew if we got a dog or a cat, I'd be the one who ended up taking care of it."

"I don't believe this." Hope walked to the drying rack and stacked the clean dishes there.

"Oh, you didn't suffer a deprived childhood." Recovering, her mother nibbled the sugar cookie again. "Look at this way; now you can play with the puppy all you want. And you don't have to worry about sneezing. Or hives!"

"I'm not doing it." Scooping up the serving dishes, Hope walked to the built-in cabinet of the dining room. Refinishing it had taken her every evening for a month, but the satin smooth finish on the old wood, the clean lines of the craftsman styling soothed her now. She placed platters and bowls into their spots, checking the padded shelf liner as she did so. Satisfied, she turned to leave the dining room and shrieked as her mother appeared behind her.

"Mom! God!! I hate it when you do that!!" Hope pressed her hand to chest, mostly to keep her heart from escaping in terror. "Stop with the ninja moves already."

Rebecca folded her arms. "You're just being silly."

"I am not. That stealth-parent maneuver is going to kill me one of these days." Walking through the living room, she paused by the couch and dropped a kiss on her snoring father's forehead before continuing on to the deck. Miriam and Daniel had done most of the outdoor clean-up, leaving her to hide in the kitchen after the humiliation of dinner was over.

"No, you're being silly about the dog." Her mother huffed out her breath as she followed Hope around the deck. "No one will remember about the...toy he chewed."

"Mom. Please. I beg of you, *never* mention that again." She pulled the deck furniture back into place and shut off the strand of lights that illuminated the deck for parties and returned to the house, Rebecca trailing after her.

"And Astrid explained it to me. It has to do with the relationship, training a dog." Rebecca pronounced. The Voice of Authority had governed Hope's childhood and it hadn't been until college that she realized the effectiveness of it. You didn't really have to know anything, you just had to sound like you knew something.

"So you have the dog for a few days while that nice Erik is out of town on business, you show it who's in charge, and Astrid and Bosse have time with their grandson." Authority turned to reproach. "You can't keep a little, tiny dog for a few days? Just so some very nice people can spend time with their new grandchild? A grandchild they *never* get to see?"

Hope tasted defeat. "You are the most horrible woman I know."

"That's the spirit, sweetheart. Here's Erik's address; pick the dog up tomorrow."

He wiped the worst of the sweat off his face and opened the door to his condo to find her standing there. Resignation draped over her like a banner.

"I'm here to get the dog."

"Yeah, hey, thanks for doing this. I know my mom talked you into it." Erik led the way into the living room. "Want a beer?"

"No. Thank you. I just--" She paused at the lift bar suspended in the doorway and studied it, brow wrinkled.

"I've got half a bottle of chardonnay; Mom was here." He scooped up the dumbbells and rolled the exercise mat into a thick cylinder and pushed open the closet next to the marble tiled gas fireplace. Swiftly, without much thought, he replaced the weights and mat into their correct places and turned to find her peering into the storage area.

"No, thank you. What is all that stuff?"

"This? It's just some workout equipment. Weights. Stuff I can do at home when I can't get to the gym. Excuse me." He walked back the doorway and dismantled the pressure-mounted bar and returned it to its holder in the closet as well.

When he turned back to her, she was studying the room. He glanced around, checking that there wasn't anything embarrassing left lying around. "Nice place," she said finally.

"Thanks."

"So." She fiddled with the strap of her purse. "The dog?"

"Oh. Yeah, hang on."

Smooth, Yoriksson, he thought as he opened the office. Shredded newspaper greeted him, but he didn't see any other major casualties. Ruger looked up from the sports section he'd been methodically tearing into strips. "Nice work, buddy, but I think you're being a little hard on the Mariners."

The puppy yipped and hopped to his feet.

"Come see the lady. You're going to stay with her." Erik held open the office door. "Come on."

Ruger went from zero to blur in nothing flat, racing to the living room. Excited barks punctuated the yell that drifted down the hall to Erik.

"Arg!! Stop it! Stop it!!"

When he entered the room, Hope was backing away from the small dog, faster and faster. Delighted, Ruger leaped and licked. "Ruger! Off!"

The pup dropped down to all fours again and wiggled toward Hope again.

Erik's voice dropped. "Ruger...."

With a sigh, he laid down, looking up at Hope with adoration and longing.

"Why did he do that?" she asked, bewildered.

"He was playing."

She raised her eyebrows at him and he laughed. "You should see your face. When you get agitated, dogs sense that. When you act like other dogs do when they play, they get excited and go into play mode."

Her mouth dropped open. "You're saying I'm acting like a dog?"

"Only in the best way." Swallowing another chuckle, he grabbed the large red duffle bag he'd readied. "All right. Here's his food, his toys, a crapload of bully sticks--"

"Gah."

"I get that it skeeves you out, but they will save your life. His bed is in here and I've included a bunch of newspaper." He pulled out the bundle he'd wrapped in plastic.

"Oh, God." Horror spun across her face. "He pees on that?"

"No, no way." Erik shook his head then muttered under his breath. "Or he shouldn't."

"What?"

He hurried on. "The newspaper is for him to tear up, to keep him busy when you want to do something else. It lets him burn off a little of the crazy."

"Okay." She took the duffle, weighing in her hands. "How long are you going to be gone?"

"You going to miss me?" At her level look, he relented. "Two or three days. I'm aiming for two, but it's not unusual for these to go an extra day."

"All right. What do I do if..." She flapped a hand.

"Hang on. I had this all set up."

The folder he'd assembled was on the shelves next to the kitchen and he flipped through it, then whistled softly for Ruger and hooked his leash to his collar. "Okay, I have his vet information, microchip numbers and here's an emergency credit card. If you need anything extra at the pet store, I've included the type of food he eats."

When he looked up, she was standing at the photo collage on the wall, the duffle at her feet. "What's this?" She pointed to one of the frames.

He handed her the leash and looked. The picture she indicated showed a much younger Erik in camouflage fatigues, crouched in front of a tank, arm slung around...

Magnus.

"I was in the Army."

Studying the picture more closely, she asked, "And they let you have pets?"

"He wasn't a pet."

She turned to him, obviously surprised at the edge in his voice. "What was he, then?"

"He was a military police dog."

"What was his name?" Her voice was quiet enough he could have pretended not to hear her, if she hadn't been looking him right in the eye.

"Magnus. Okay?" He drew in a breath and blew it out, changing his tactics. "Hey, after I get back, you'll have to let me take you to dinner to thank you. I really appreciate this." He held out the leather folder and clasped her hand as she reached to take it. He smiled at her as she looked up at him.

And her face changed again.

"You know what?" she asked.

Uh-oh, he thought.

"You don't have to talk about this dog is you don't want to. You don't have to talk about it ever. But I would really appreciate it if you wouldn't try to manipulate me into dropping the subject."

"Hey!" More than a little insulted, he drew himself up and looked down at her. "It's called being nice. Maybe you've heard of it."

"Oh, that?" She circled a finger around. "That was just being nice? I don't think so."

"Maybe you just didn't recognize it."

She laughed. "Oh, I recognized it. You didn't want to talk about the dog and instead of saying I don't want to talk about it or please, let's not talk about this, or even, hey Lindstrom, back off, you got all smarmy."

"Smarmy?" Was his head still attached?

She nodded and kept talking. "And when I said something about it, you stood over me. Like you were trying to intimidate me. Which, actually, I don't mind as much as the other charming crap, especially since I don't even know if we play on the same team."

"*What?*" It wasn't his head popping off his neck, it was an alternate universe. What the hell...?

"It's one thing to use your looks and stuff to get your way with women, but if you're doing that and you're gay--"

"What the f—what are you talking about? Where the hell do you get that?"

She spread her hands and shrugged. "The working out. The apartment. The hair."

He couldn't form words and in the growing silence, he could see the uncertainty on her face give way to a deep, dark peach flush.

She shrugged and tucked the folder into the duffle, leash looped around her wrist. "I guess not. My mistake."

Duffle and dog in hand, she darted out the door before he could say a word.

"You asked him *what?*" Miriam's screech rocked her eardrums and made the new earpiece tremble.

"I know, I know! It's none of my business and I shouldn't have said it. Dog, stop it!" Ruger barked out the window of Hope's truck, darting back and forth across the back seat. Streaks of dog snot now decorated the passenger windows.

"Forget the dog for one second! You honestly thought that man was gay?!"

"Miriam, you didn't see his apartment."

Her sister-in-law snorted. "What, did he have 'art' photos of naked men on the walls?"

"No, everything was just—ARG!" Ruger leapt into the front seat and scrambled into her lap, sticking his nose out the crack of open window. Shrieking as her arms were filled with small, wiggling dog, she swerved and righted the truck just before side-swiping an SUV in the neighboring lane.

Miriam's panicked voice filled her ear. "Hope! Hope! What happened? Are you okay?"

"Oh, my God...oh, my God." She managed to dislodge the puppy into the passenger seat and gripped the steering wheel with shaky hands. He yipped happily and rested his paws on the handle of the door, standing on the power button for the window.

He'd made it halfway out the nearly opened window when Hope grabbed him by the tail and dragged him back.

"Are you all right? Hope, say something." Miriam sounded seriously worried now.

"I'm fine, I'm fine. The stupid dog is just making me crazy and...oh, no."

Blue and red lights flashed in her rearview mirror.

Chapter Eight

"Erik Yoriksson."

"Oh, thank GOD. Why the hell haven't you been answering your phone?"

It was a woman's voice, of that, Erik was certain. She was agitated. That was pretty clear, too. Beyond that...it was anybody's guess.

Erik hooked his briefcase handle with a finger and used his other hand to unlock the door to the temporary office given to him for his stay in Southern California. Unlike the nearly unrelenting gray and rain of the Seattle area, the skies here were blue, the sunshine warm and the beaches inviting.

Not that he had seen any of this.

The past day had been a barrage of endless meetings and phone conferences, market analysis and production projections. Erik tried not think about the amount of work he had to wade through to make it home in two days, the two days he told Hope this trip would take.

The woman's voice crackled in his ear. "I can't get the dog to settle down. How do you get him to settle down?"

Speak of the devil.

"Hope?" he asked incredulously. She'd never sounded so panicked, even after slamming her head on the underside of her car.

"Yes, it's Hope."

"I think we have a bad connection, you sound--"

"It's not the connection!! The dog chewed on my earpiece!!"

"Uh oh." Erik winced as he set his briefcase on the ugly desk in the tiny room. "What kind of earpiece was it?"

The aggravation in her voice doubled. "The stupid expensive one! And he keeps stealing my underwear!"

He took a moment to sort out this non sequitur and sighed. "Dirty underwear?"

"Yes! It's disgusting."

"Yeah, it is. I thought I warned you about that in the folder." Pulling out his sleek laptop from his case, he booted up the small machine.

"Oh, you mean the Gutenberg bible of dog information? Sorry, I'm still on chapter six."

Erik laughed. Pissed off or not, she was still pretty funny.

"Did you know he jumps all over the car? And he can lower the window on his own!!!"

"You aren't using the carrier?" He closed his eyes.

"What carrier?"

"The hard plastic one. Next to all of his stuff."

There was a small silence on the other end of the line. "You have a carrier for him."

"Yes. He's supposed to be in it every time he's in the car."

"Oh. That would have been really good to have, before getting in the car."

"Did something happen when you were driving?" he asked warily, pulling up the presentation he was supposed to make in under an hour. He'd worked it over last night until he was sure it was right, but in the light of day....

It took him a moment to realize she hadn't answered him and he felt his chest tighten. "Hope? Did something happen while you were driving?"

"Nobody got hurt."

"Oh God."

"And I didn't actually hit the other car."

Erik stood and started to pace. "You hit another car?"

"No, I *didn't* hit the car. It was just...closer than it should have been. The police officer said--well, never mind."

"Police officer." He scrubbed his hand over his face. "Are you in the car now?"

"No, we got home a little while ago. I had to take him to work, something my mother conveniently forgot when she voluntold me to babysit him for you."

He winced again. "Yeah, I'm really sorry about--"

"And he chewed a special order of crown molding medallions in my office! In like five freaking minutes! Do you have any idea how long it will take to replace those for the customer who special ordered them for his remodel?"

Erik thought about it. "No idea. How long?"

Another beat of silence. "Well, the factory happened to have extra on hand, but that's not the point!"

"Uh huh." He held the mouthpiece of his cell phone out as he muffled his laugh. "So where is Ruger now?"

"I don't know."

"You don't know?"

"No, I don't...Oh, my God. I don't know where the dog is."

Even with the crappy reception on her abused earpiece, he could hear her rapid-fire footsteps over the floor.

"Dog? Dog! Booger!"

"It's Ruger. Like the small handgun."

"That's what I said."

"No, you said--never mind. Did you find him?"

"Not yet, but he couldn't have gotten out." She was starting to sound panicked again.

"Yell that you have a cookie," he advised, taking his seat again, resting his head on his desk. By his calculations, Ruger had been unattended for at least four minutes. It was a small miracle the house was still standing.

"Cookie! I have a cookie!"

Erik heard the faint yip in the background and Hope's shriek in response. "No no no!! No toilet paper! You're dragging it all over the house!! Drop it! Drop--"

The phone went dead. Erik took a moment to pray Ruger wouldn't meet the same fate.

The automatic glass doors slid smoothly shut over Ruger's leash and did nothing to slow his forward momentum into the pet store. Hope tripped over the curb and, losing her balance, was dragged forward to smash, nose first, into the glass panel. She was still bent forward and holding her nose when the doors slid open again. Ruger barked impatiently at her.

"Are you all right?"

"Oh, sure." She stood upright and opened watery eyes to see a shock of reddish hair flopping over a freckled forehead. "Opie?"

He grimaced and rubbed his hand through his hair.

"Sorry. Dr. Evans, right?" Hope felt a flush heat her face. What was it with her foot-in-mouth disease lately? The dog yanked on the end of the leash again and she nearly toppled over again.

"Yeah." He grinned. "Auntie Hope?"

"Cute."

"That's what I'm told." He gave her a shrug and a modest smile. Hope realized there was a large dog seated next to him, so still it might have been a statue. Its long, feathery fur looked remarkably similar to Miriam's hair.

"Really, Dr. Evans? Is that what you're told?" Hope tore her eyes away from the placid beauty of the dog and grinned back at him. It felt as comfortable as ribbing Edvard, her younger brother.

He laughed, a deeper sound than she expected. "Please, call me Rory."

"Rory. Seriously?"

Now his cheeks reddened. "It's short for Gregory, okay? I grew up being called that."

She pressed her lips together and swallowed the laugh. "And who is this?"

"This is my best girl, Serena."

The tension on the leash in her hand eased as Ruger spotted the other dog and rushed forward. Yipping and jumping, the puppy all but turned himself inside out despite Hope's hissed commands to stop. The bigger dog eyed him calmly, only dipping her head a few inches to sniff him in return.

"And who's this guy?" Rory held out his hand to the puppy, who attacked it with a frenzy of love and licking. The man laughed and scooped up the small dog, chuckling as Ruger corkscrewed his body. "Easy, fella. You're okay. What's your name, huh?"

"This is Boog—I mean, Ruger. His name is Ruger." She exchanged a look with the large dog, still seated calmly by her master's side. She couldn't be sure, but she got the feeling that Serena didn't think much of Ruger's antics, either. "He's a fox wire--no, that's not right. A terrier--"

"Wire hair fox terrier?" Rory grinned.

She pointed at him. "Yes. That. Yes."

"Nice little dog. How old is he?" He rubbed the triangular flaps of the puppy's ears, who sighed and pressed his head into Rory's hand.

"I have no idea."

Russet brows rose. "You don't know how old your dog is?"

"He's not my dog," she explained. "I got voluntold to dogsit. For three days."

"Voluntold?"

"By my mother."

"Ah." He looked down at Ruger, laughing and sputtering as the puppy nailed him with a lightning strike of doggy kisses. "Looks like you have your hands full."

She laughed, too, and heard the faint edge of hysteria. "Yes. Hands full." She pressed her fingertips to her temples and rubbed.

Opening her eyes, she found Rory looking at her with sympathy and good humor. "You know, Serena was a hellion as a pup. Weren't you, girl?"

The blonde goddess of a dog gazed up at her master and shook her head, as if denying the accusation.

Hope looked back at him. "I think she disagrees."

Rory ruffled the dog's fur and set Ruger down. The puppy immediately ran to Serena and started mauling the older dog. "Well, we better get going. Kibble waits for no man."

"Yeah, okay." She opened her mouth, then shut it again. "Well, have a good day."

Rory waved and took a few steps, then turned and walked back to her. "Are you okay?"

She looked around the brightly lit store and scanned the colorful displays. "You know, I work in retail."

"You do?"

"She nodded. "I manage Home Again."

"Nice. Cool place."

She was momentarily diverted. "You've been there?"

"Yeah, my brother lives near here and was redoing their basement. Got some great stuff there." He tilted his head at her, waiting, looking remarkably like his dog.

"The thing is, I know retail. I know how to ask for help and I usually can find stuff in a well laid out store. But..." She fiddled with the handle on the leash and jerked in surprise as Ruger dove at a passing standard poodle. Both the poodle and its human gave the puppy a frosty look and streamed by, snouts elevated.

"What are you looking for?" Rory asked after she'd wrestled the small dog back.

Panting slightly, she hauled back on the leash. "Cut it *out*. He's supposed to have a carrier, or something, for the car. He has one, but I left it at his owner's house."

Nodding, Rory added, "It's a safety factor. And is he kennel trained at night?"

"What's that?"

The way his jaw dropped and eyes widened made Hope squirm. There were other things she hated more than feeling stupid, but not many.

"Oh, man. Have you been dealing with him loose, at night?" The sympathy in his voice made her blink rapidly and look upwards to the left to stop the tears. She nodded.

"Have you slept at all?" He reached out and touched her arm.

"Not very much."

"Come on," he said, slinging his arm around her shoulder and knuckling her head. "Let's get you set up."

The call switched straight to voicemail again, and Hope's even tones invited him to leave a message. Frowning, Erik ended the call. Where was she? Was there another incident while driving? Did she get into his condo and retrieve the carrier? Had Ruger survived the night?

The alarm on his phone chirped at him. With a curse muttered under his breath, he stood and closed the briefcase on the desk and walked out to his next meeting.

Chapter Nine

The small mountain of dog paraphernalia wobbled as Hope wheeled the cart to the checkout counter. "You really think this will help?"

"Absolutely." For a guy who looked like an overgrown twelve-year-old, Rory Evans sounded pretty darn sure of himself. "That carrier can be secured in the car and the kennel will give him a place to sleep tonight. And these things saved my life when Serena was a pup."

She pulled out the oddly shaped rubber dog toy Rory indicated and turned it over in her hand. It looked like someone had taken three rubber balls of graduating size and smashed them on top of each other, to resemble a slightly squashed snowman, then hollowed out the toy. "And what do I do with this thing?"

"You can throw it for the dog," Rory explained, "like a ball. It bounces in all different directions because of the shape."

"Okay."

"But the best part is, you can stuff the cavity with treats or even kibble, then top it with peanut butter or cream cheese." She made a face and he grinned at her.

"And then what? Just...give it to the dog?" She looked doubtfully at Ruger, whose leash was tied to the handle of the shopping cart. As he lunged at another customer, yapping at the top of his lungs, the cart shuddered and the pile of carriers and toys and training fence sections wobbled, threatening to crash to the floor. She yanked on the leash. "Stop it. You're embarrassing us."

"It'll take him forever to get every bit of treat out of the middle. By the time he's done, he'll be ready to fall asleep." Rory put a medium-sized sack of kibble on the desk of the other checkout counter and before he could grab one of Hope's items to help unload from her cart, a loud tone rang. Pulling out his mobile phone, he scowled at the screen and punched a reply out on the glowing screen. "Crap."

She paused, holding the car carrier. "Everything okay?"

"No, not really. I've got to go into work. Dammit, I was supposed to be off the entire weekend." He shoved the phone back into its holder, clipped to his belt. "My brother is going to be bent."

"You have to go right now?"

He nodded as he signed the credit card slip and took the receipt from the clerk. "Thanks. No, no bag. Listen, Hope," he turned to her. "I feel really bad about this. I was going to suggest a walk in the park to help your little guy blow off some steam."

She smiled. Rory Evans really was a very nice guy. "Maybe another time."

"Yeah. That'd be good. Here." He pulled out his wallet again and extracted a business card. "Call or text when you have free time and we'll set it up. My schedule's a little packed, but..."

"Can't even imagine. But yeah, I'll do that." She took the card and studied it. "Well, go on. You have work to do. Slacker."

He leaned forward and pressed a friendly kiss to her cheek and clucked his tongue at his dog. A wave and a smile, and he disappeared.

"Okay, ma'am, that'll be $542.31. Do you have your Pet Central Furry Friends card today?" The clerk behind the counter looked up from bagging half of the store's inventory.

"How much did you say it was?" Hope sputtered.

"$542.31, but if you have a preferred customer card, you'd get discounts on a lot of this."

Hope tapped her debit card against the counter. The new flooring she'd ordered for her bedroom had nearly drained her checking account until payday and while she could swing this, it would leave her a little tighter than she liked. Reaching into her bag, she pulled out the Dog Tome, as she called the thick leather folder Erik had left for her. In the back, in a zippered plastic envelope attached to the binding, marked "Emergency; Dog," was a gleaming gold card. She removed it slowly.

Ruger huffed his breath out and sat as she looked at him, wagging his tail a little. His eyes and nose gleamed like new buttons on a fluffy winter white coat and for a moment, she could have sworn he winked at her. She sighed.

"What do I have to do for the discount?"

Erik saved the document he was opening and clicked over to his personal email. He was right, he *had* heard the beep that signaled a new email. With a grin, he opened the message from Jasper Martin.

Hey, buddy--

Yeah, I'm still alive. I don't know if I would be if I was standing there, but I'm safer here than wherever you are right now. I can't take Ruger back as soon as I thought I would.

I got stop-lossed. Or I will be, once my time is up. I know I said it would only be while I was deployed and I get that you don't want this dog, so if this isn't going to work, let me know and I'll find another way.

Got an email from Amanda. She said she'd consider taking me back but the dog was a deal breaker. Guess what I said? The bitch had it coming.

It sucks that I'm doing this, I know that. Sorry, man. I owe you muchas cervezas.

Marty

Erik stared at the message. It hadn't occurred to him that he'd have to hand over Ruger to anyone but Marty. Ruger wasn't his, so it wouldn't be a problem.

"This is going to be a problem."

Erik contemplated the email on his computer screen a while longer then reached for the desk phone. Even as he considered calling his parents for input on the rescue societies Marty had listed, he found himself dialing Hope's number. After several rings, crackles exploded in his ear?

"H...o? Hello?"

"Hope?" Erik strained to hear her response.

"Yeah, this...k?"

Barely able to make out her voice, he pressed the volume button on his own handset to max. "Can you switch off the earpiece?"

"...in the car." Her voice, suddenly clear, burst through the speaker. He winced and held the phone away, tapping down on the volume again.

"Okay. Did you get the carrier for the dog?"

"I had to...carrier. And I got...in..." The crackling began again in earnest, but he was almost certain she'd gotten the small kennel from his condominium. His mother had probably given her the key.

The crackling disappeared again and he spoke quickly, unsure how long this break would be.

"Good. I got an email from Ruger's owner and—well, it doesn't matter. I'll just have to deal with it when I get back. Speaking of..." He took a deep breath, like a diver headed toward the deep end. "Listen, I know I said I'd be back tomorrow, but it's looking like I'll have to stay a few more days."

Absolute silence.

"I realize it's inconvenient, and if you can't watch Ruger any longer, I can ask my mother to pick him up."

Still, she said nothing.

"Oh, come on, Hope. The silent treatment? You can't seriously--" A shrill beeping chimed in his ear and Erik realized that he'd been talking to a dead line for several minutes. "Yoriksson," he said out loud, "you are losing it."

Hope ripped the earpiece out and threw it into her purse. The pup in the carrier yipped from the backseat and she scowled into the rearview mirror. "Don't bark at me. You're the one who chewed the earpiece. All I heard was something about your stupid carrier."

Ruger grumbled.

"No, I'm not going back to the phone store. Your human will have to take care of that. I'm not going through that crap again...

"Oh, my lord. I'm talking to a dog." She pulled into her driveway and sat for a moment, gripping the steering wheel. "I am losing it."

After grabbing her bag, she opened the back door of the car and peered into the carrier. Gleaming eyes and the thwack of a tail against hard plastic greeted her. "Don't tell anyone, okay?"

The carrier wasn't heavy, even with Ruger in it, but Hope struggled to balance it and her bag as the small dog's scrabbling and wriggling made it rock like a fishing boat. The puppy had taken to riding in the carrier in the car well enough, but how would he react to the larger wire crate in the house?

As she struggled with the door lock, Miriam's mammoth SUV pulled up behind her car. "Hi!" she called out.

Miriam stood on the running board of the huge vehicle. "No, you stay in the car until I've spoken to Auntie Hope. Because I said so. What did you—excuse me, Hope." She popped back into the vehicle for a short, intense discussion with one of the kids. Hope had money on it being Paul.

Miriam reemerged. She walked around to the passenger side of the car and opened the heavy door with ease, and lifted Lene out of her car seat. "You both will sit right there until I say so. Not another word, young man."

Hope left the carrier and her purse on the porch and joined them on the front walkway. "Hello, my princess. How's Lene? How's the prettiest girl?"

Lene launched herself into Hope's arms, babbling a mile a minute. Miriam smiled at her daughter and shook her head. "Darling, I know she's going to be a nightmare when she's fifteen, but you must remind me of days like this when I complain. Paul and Sebastian have been at each other for a week."

"Uh oh." Hope smiled at her niece and pressed her forehead to the little girl's. "Mama is not happy, is she?"

Lene giggled and shook her head.

"Where have you been? I tried to call you to come with me to the Mother's Lunch."

This explained Miriam's outfit. In a decidedly conservative move, Miriam had put together a silver ruched skirt the size of a bandage and relatively modest lavender halter top. Deep purple platform stilettos winked back at Hope as she studied their silver and crystals flowers. "I'm sorry I missed it. How are the mothers today?"

"They're very well. They like me better now that I've started dressing down." Miriam flipped her hair over her shoulder and planted her hands on her hips. "And guess who's in charge of the Cookie Committee?"

"No! Really?"

Miriam preened a little more. "Which means I'll need your help."

"Of course you will." Hope rolled her eyes. "As long as it's not this weekend."

"No, it's not. What do you have going on this weekend?"

Ruger barked and rattled his carrier and Miriam and Lene made identical cooing sounds after spotting him on the porch. "Oh, you still have the funny little dog!"

"Yes, I do. In fact, we just back from the dog park." Hope laughed as her little niece shrieked. "Yes, ma'am. The doggie park. Doggies, all over. And we played with a doggie named Serena."

"Thank you very much, Auntie Hope. Now we shall hear of nothing but the doggie park." Miriam shot her an exasperated look.

"She's two, Miriam. She won't remember."

She pursed her lips. "True."

"Anyway, I got some suggestions from Serena's owner about how to deal with the devil's spawn over there." She bounced Lene to hear her giggle again. "If it works, I'll owe him a huge favor."

Miriam hummed. "Anyone I know?"

"No, no one you—no, actually, you have met him. The doctor from the emergency room, remember him?" Swaying to a modified waltz beat, Hope watched Lene yawn. Soon the little girl drooped like melted candle wax and rested her head on her aunt's shoulder.

"I do remember him. You had a date with *him*? He's twelve years old, darling." Miriam frowned and shook her head. "That is just not right."

"I know! He's actually twenty-eight, but I feel like I should be checking his homework." She shifted her now sleeping niece a bit higher. "Oof, she's getting heavy."

"Here, let me take her."

"No, no. No, I've got her." Hope hugged the sleeping toddler a bit closer. "You get to snuggle her like this all the time. My turn."

"Fine. Oh, darling! If you marry the child doctor, you could have your own babies!" Miriam grinned and folded her arms.

Hope rolled her eyes. "Mirrie, it was like hanging out with Edvard. Well, pre-marriage Edvard, when he was still fun. Or Daniel. Post-marriage Daniel, now that he has someone to keep him in line and he's not so annoying."

Several staccato barks in increasing pitch ripped through Miriam's response and Lene twitched and shifted in Hope's arms. "Uh oh."

Miriam zipped to the SUV and opened the door. "Quick, car seat. If she wakes up now, I'll never get her down for a nap."

She hustled over with the now-restive little girl and tucked her into her safety harness. Two sulky little faces pouted at her from the backseat, so she winked at Paul and Sebastian. "If you're good for Mama, we'll have a play day here. How's that sound?"

Sebastian's face brightened and he nodded but Paul remained mutinous. "Mama yelled at me and now I'm mad at her."

She nodded soberly. "How come she yelled, Paulie?"

"'Cause Sebastian was bad an' I was just standing there."

"Really?" Playing the fascinated auntie card, she turned to the younger boy, whose eyes were starting to swim. "Are you a troublemaker, Sebbo? Are you?"

A watery giggle answered her.

"You know what this means when you come over next?" She wiggled her eyebrows and pressed her finger over her lips. "Tickle torture!" she whispered.

Both boys giggled this time and Miriam started the vehicle with a muted roar. Since Lene didn't move, she assumed it was safe to give the boys one last wink and back out of the SUV. Waving, she watched her family barrel down the small road and turned back to the house. The carrier had gone silent again. "All right, let's give this a try."

Before getting Rory's call, she'd set up the larger wire crate for Ruger and lined it with blankets. She'd literally had the treats in her hand with Ruger dancing around her feet when the phone rang.

"It was worth it, wasn't it, furface?" Happy scrabbling answered her. "You ran your little guts out and slept in the car. Must be how Miriam feels," she mused.

Hope set the carrier on the floor of the living room and opened the door, prepared to see Ruger saunter over to the fireplace rug that was his new favorite spot and flop there a while before investigating his new kennel. What she didn't expect was Ruger...

...being Ruger.

He did his traditional bullet-out-of-a-gun exit and proceeded to rip around the living room and dining room in figure eights, running full tilt. She'd watched him do this in the backyard, but this was the first time he'd pulled the maneuver indoors. "My God. It's the Terrier 500."

In a final, show-stopping move, Ruger leapt over the ottoman and spun into a crouch on his belly, front legs splayed and a huge doggy grin on his fuzzy face. He barked happily.

"So much for you being worn out." She took the treats she left on the buffet and sat on the floor next to him and the kennel. "Let's see if this will work."

Pulling out one of the smelly liver treats Rory swore would drive Ruger into a frenzy of obedience, she held the disgusting thing inside the wire box. "Ruger, kennel up."

Sniffing at the treat, Ruger walked into the kennel and nibbled at the morsel she held. Setting it down on the blanket, she closed the door to the box. "Good kennel."

Ruger chomped down his snack. She waited a few minutes and opened the door again, letting the little dog bounce out again. "Well, that wasn't so hard, was it?"

The pup yipped and spun in a circle.

"I know. But we have to do it again. Rory said so." Getting another treat, she held it inside the kennel again. "Ruger. Kennel up."

Fifteen minutes later she left the dog cookies on the buffet and stood across the room. "Ruger. Kennel up."

With no fanfare, the little dog got up from his spot on the area rug and trotted into the kennel. She walked over to the kennel and shut the door. Ruger blinked up at her and then laid down. She pulled the cookie out of her pocket and sat down, too, right next to the kennel.

"Holy crap. It actually worked."

Chapter Ten

"Hey, buddy, how're you doing?" Erik squatted down to thump Ruger lightly on the ribs. The little dog wriggled with delight and rolled over to show his belly. "Good boy. Were you a good boy?"

Hope closed the door behind them and he looked up at her. "Was he a good boy?"

Hope opened her mouth and paused. He waited for the avalanche of crap that Ruger had pulled to descend on his head, braced and ready. For what seemed like a year, she was silent. Finally, she spoke.

"He was fine."

Erik didn't move. "All right," he said slowly. "Who are you and what have you done with Hope?"

She folded her arms and raised her eyebrows at him.

"Kidding."

"Uh huh." She walked over to the red duffle he'd packed for Ruger. "There are a few other things in here. I had to get a few things."

He looked into the bag. "Wow. You aren't kidding."

Ruger yapped and danced around her feet. Erik realized that she had a small bag of treats in her hand. "A friend of mine helped me with something and I don't know if you want to continue with it."

"A friend?" he repeated.

"Yes. I don't know if you've started kennel training him, but Rory says it helps a lot, especially with active dogs."

"Rory?"

She nodded. "He's got a golden retriever and she used to be really hyper."

"Who's Rory? Or what's a Rory?"

"Huh?" She paused in her dissertation and blinked. "It's Gregory, actually. Evans. He was the doctor in the ER who took care of me after I hit my head."

"I see." Frowning, he clucked his tongue at the dog and rubbed Ruger's ears as the little dog put his paws on Erik's leg. "He's a doctor and a dog expert?"

"Well, I don't know if he's an expert, but he was very helpful. Look." She walked to a good sized dog crate made of thick wire and opened its door. "Ruger?"

The dog's head swiveled around and he dropped down from Erik's lap. Wagging slightly, his focus on Hope was as intense as the smell emitted from whatever was in the bag she still held.

"Kennel up!"

With a joyous bark, Ruger raced to the enclosure, spun around and stuck his nose out of the door. Erik watched in disbelief as Hope handed the dog a treat and latched the door. She sat down in the armchair and picked up the newspaper, sending a speaking glance at Erik. He closed his mouth.

Following the order given by a jerk of her head, he stood, walked to the couch and sat, ignoring the puppy in the kennel.

"How was your business trip?" she asked casually.

"It went well, thank you," he replied, eyes fixed on her face. He could still see the dog, standing at the wire doorway, but avoiding looking at him. "Longer than I expected."

A few minutes of nothing conversation later, Ruger laid down on the blanket in the kennel and rested his fuzzy chin on his paws. Hope folded her paper and rose from the chair. "Are you thirsty? Would you like something to drink?"

Erik mirrored the nod she gave him. "Yes. Yes, I would."

In the kitchen, he had a brief impression of dark wood and gleaming granite before she turned to him and grabbed his hands. She bounced up and down a couple of times before whispering, "Did you *see* that?"

Her gray eyes sparkled and he grinned back, enjoying her obvious glee. "Yeah, I can't believe it."

"I know!" She bounced again and gripped his hands tighter. "I couldn't believe it, either, the first time he went in. It doesn't happen every time, but it happens."

He was pretty sure she had no idea she was holding his hands. They were surprisingly tough, for all their smallness, and he could feel small calluses on her palms. Running his thumbs over the backs of her hands, he was distracted enough by the contrasting softness to miss what she was saying, until the name snapped him back.

"...And Rory's been showing me how to walk him without letting him think he's in charge, because they get really unbearable."

He let go of her hands and took a small step back. "So you've been spending a lot of time with this guy? With Ruger?"

She pursed her lips and appeared to ponder that. "Not a lot, because you know, the doctor thing. He works some crazy hours. But we've met at the park a couple of times."

"I see."

She leaned back and studied him in a way that made him want to leave the room. "Is that a problem?"

"No, it's just..." he shrugged. "I don't even know this guy and he's spending a lot of time with...the dog."

Splaying her hands, she laughed. "You don't really know me, either, and you left your dog with me for almost a week."

"You're exaggerating. Four days."

Now she threw up her hands and turned to some sleek, stainless steel machine. "Whatever, Thor."

He closed his eyes and breathed in through his nose. "You know I hate it when you call me that."

She sent one of her knife smiles over her shoulder. "Yes. I do."

"What are you, nine?"

"Pardon me?" She turned fully to face him, the bag of coffee beans forgotten in her hand, disbelief etched on her face. "You're questioning *my* maturity level?"

He stuffed his hands into his pockets and pulled them out again. Opened his mouth and shut it again. "Thank you for watching the dog."

"You're welcome." Turning back, she fussed with the coffee maker.

"And for getting all that stuff for him."

She shrugged. "Don't thank me; you paid for it."

His jerked back as if he'd been slapped. "Well, please, allow me to pay you for your time."

"Don't bother." Her tone matched his in temperature, if not courtesy, and that slight fraying of temper pleased him. He couldn't say why, but it did.

Taking out his wallet, he laid a small stack of bills on the shiny stone surface of the kitchen island. "Enjoy your coffee. I'll find my own way out."

Striding from the kitchen, he collected the dog, still in his kennel, and the red duffel bag and walked out, shutting the door gently behind him.

She didn't follow him.

It wasn't until he was in the car, dog secured in the original car carrier the back, wire kennel folded and stowed in the trunk, that he paused. What the hell just happened?

"What the hell just happened?" Hope asked the empty room.

She realized that she had no idea. It'd been nice, actually nice, for once, talking to Erik. And then he'd gotten all...

What?

Ignoring the insult of cash left on the counter, she took the cup of freshly brewed coffee with her into the living room. He'd cleared out Ruger's stuff without any effort and barely any sound while she stayed in the kitchen, trying to collect herself. Now everything was back to normal. No rotten little dog to chew her newspaper or bark when she tried to sleep. No cranky Viking god to act all pissy for no damn reason at all. She wouldn't have to assign staff to take the dog out to potty during the work day.

There she had to pause. The staff at Home Again hadn't minded walking Ruger. In fact, in the past couple of days, it had turned into a competition. Whoever finished their section work and cleaned the best and fastest, got to walk the dog. The store had never looked so good.

Of course, that didn't discount the chewed merchandise and equipment and the occasional puddle or pile Ruger left behind. She sighed and sat on the couch, studying the empty space where the dog's kennel used to be.

Shifting, Hope tried to find a comfortable position. She usually sat in her armchair; had her couch always been this uncomfortable? After a moment's thought, she dismissed the idea. Her family surely would have said something.

Loudly. And repeatedly.

Shifting again, she stuck her hand behind the couch cushion to adjust it and pulled out a small stuffed pig. Ruger's small stuffed pig. She squeezed it and it oinked and wriggled in her hand and she laughed out loud. Leaning back on the couch, she studied the toy.

Until something else poked at her back.

Five minutes later, she'd pulled every cushion off of every piece of furniture in her living room and amassed a small mountain of toys. She couldn't really blame the dog for it, her nephews had obviously been storing toys in her furniture for months. Ruger had just been copying the bigger kids. After dividing up the toys, she looked over the puppy pile and groaned. The Kong, the treat toy, was on top of the pile.

It wasn't her responsibility, she reminded herself. He wasn't her dog. And *Thor* could just suck it up and deal with it.

Ruger's fuzzy face flashed before her. His excitement when he saw the bright red toy, stuffed with a cookie and topped with a smear of peanut butter. His contented gnawing on the toy and the blissful silence as he fell asleep mid-chew. The way her employees had laughed like loons when he'd chase after the toy, which never bounced the way she thought it would. How would Erik keep him calm?

Erik.

"Dammit."

"Hi, I brought--"

Erik watched her eyes widen and cheek flush as she looked away from him. He glanced down and realized that during the last explosion of water from the sink, he'd stripped off his shirt and hadn't put on another. "Come in, I'll just grab...something." Leaving her at the door, he walked to his bedroom and threw on the damp t-shirt he'd draped over the laundry hamper.

Excited barking echoed through the hallway as Ruger discovered Hope's presence. "Off! Off!" he heard her shout. "We've talked about this!"

"Ruger." With one stern look, the puppy dropped to the floor and danced in place. Hope stood by the door, a canvas bag in her hands. "I didn't expect to see you."

She laughed, discomfort tingeing the edges. "I bet. I didn't expect to be seen." She held out the bag to him.

"What's this?" He opened the bag and peered inside, then looked at Ruger. "How much crap do you have, dog?"

Pulling out a stuffed pig, he squeezed it and watched for the puppy's reaction. Ruger leapt into the air, barking and twisting, then spun in a tight circle before tearing around the condo at top speed.

"The Terrier 500," Hope murmured.

He chuckled. "No kidding. Is this thing legal?"

Ruger zipped by them, nearly careening into the wall.

"It was in the stuff you sent with him, so you'd know better than I. He buried it in my couch," Hope said absently, eyes on the dog. "Along with the rope, three tennis balls and the Kong."

"The Kong?" He wrinkled his forehead. *When did she learn about dog toys?*

She pointed to a small, red, rubber toy in the bag. "Rory told me to fill it with a treat and some peanut butter. Keeps him busy when you put him in the kennel. He doesn't cry that way."

He realized they were still standing by the door. "Come on in. Can I get you something?"

"No, I--"

"You like coffee, right?" He led the way into the kitchen without checking to see if she'd follow. Sure enough, by the time he was setting the cups under the spout of his much less impressive machine, she was there, standing by the breakfast bar at the edge of his streamlined kitchen.

"You didn't have to make me coffee. Plus, it's a little late for it." She sounded uncomfortable.

"Least I could do." He pulled open the drawer under the coffee station for spoons. "You brought Ruger's stuff back."

Erik opened the fridge and checked the date on the carton of half-and-half. A small sugar bowl was already near the coffee maker and he slid both to Hope across the counter while motioning her to a bar stool. "Besides, it's decaf."

She lifted the mug he handed her to inhale the steam. "Yes, I did bring the toys over. And after you were a jerk to me." She narrowed her eyes over the rim of her cup.

"You were a jerk to me first."

She pursed her lips, something he'd noticed she did when she was thinking. "True enough. But I had good reason."

So did I, he thought.

She studied him for a moment, sipping her coffee. "Nice place. Good coffee. I didn't know those machines made good coffee."

He braced himself, waiting for the other shoe to smack him upside the head or assault his masculinity, but nothing happened. "Thank you."

"Do you cook a lot?" She nodded to the gourmet kitchen his ex had designed. He laughed and pointed to the laminated list of delivery numbers on the refrigerator.

"You are enjoying the sum total of my culinary expertise." He sat down and saluted her with his own coffee cup.

"But...." She looked around the kitchen again, with its stark white counters, convection range and mosaic backsplash.

"I know. But the lady who did the whole place said it would increase the value. Now if I could just get the bathroom fixed."

Hope perked up. "You're redoing your bathroom? What kind of fixtures?"

The idea of fixtures stymied him for a moment, but he shook his head. "I'm not redoing, I'm just trying to rescue it. After Ruger chewed the handle, everything's gone from bad to worse."

"The drawer pull, that's right." She set her cup down and leaned forward. "And then you came in after for a new faucet?"

Grimacing, he got up to make another cup of coffee. "Another?" She shook her head and he sat back down. "Yes, I got a new faucet. And you helped me with instructions."

She studied him. "You do not sound happy about this."

He shook his head.

"Uh oh. But you haven't been back in." She tapped her fingers together. "It's been weeks. It's not done?"

Before he could answer, she stood and carried her cup to the sink. "Come on. Let's take a look."

Erik looked like a scolded child faced with two weeks without a favorite toy and she bit her lip not to laugh at him. Reluctantly, he rose from the bar stool. "You don't have to do this. I'll figure it out."

Her best reassuring smile in place, she nodded. "I know, I'm just curious."

He led her through his gorgeous—really, there was no other word for it—condo and through his bedroom to the master bath. Maybe it was the mountain of perfection in the rest of the place that made the bathroom such a shock, but she actually tripped as she entered the spacious room.

It wasn't torn up, she realized. It was simply swathed in plastic sheeting to protect the beautiful dark wood. She could see the new tools he'd purchased laid out in descending order of size and type, on a folding table covered in butcher paper. It was weird, looking at such an organized mess. It was unsettling.

It was...sweet.

In an odd mix of embarrassment and pride, he showed her the faucet set he'd purchased, which worked really well with the new drawer pulls and cabinet handles that replaced all the endangered wood ones. He'd managed not to scratch the ebony wood in all of his demolition and when Ruger joined them, with all of his curious nosing about, he was sent to a padded dog bed with the ubiquitous bully stick. Which was probably why he came into the room in the first place.

Hope had a feeling the dog knew how to work his owner.

It didn't take long before she was under the sink, checking his work and subtly fixing a few of his rookie errors. The fact that her butt was sticking out of the cabinet didn't even register until she heard Ruger yip and felt him dart past her.

"Ruger, no. Bad dog! Drop it!"

The shock of a large, warm, male hand on her rear end shot through her and she dropped the shiny new wrench she was holding and jerked, slamming her head on the underside of the sink. "OW!"

"Oh, sweet Jesus, not again!" Erik pulled her out from under the sink, more gently than he had from under the car, and ran his hands over her head. Despite the sharp crack of skull against metal, she hadn't hit it that hard. That had to be the reason his hands felt so good now.

"I'm okay."

"Are you sure? A second concussion could be really dangerous. Maybe--"

"Erik." Cradled in his arms, she looked up into his beautiful eyes and smiled. "Your sink is fixed."

He nearly dropped her and she yipped, almost the way Ruger did. At the sound, the puppy clambered over to her, checking her health in the age-old method of smothering her with doggy kisses. Hope and Erik spoke in unison.

"Off!"

Ruger sat on the floor of the bathroom and laid his ears back, beseeching their forgiveness.

She pressed her hand to her forehead. "I hate it when he does that. I feel like the meanest woman on earth."

"I know. Here, stand up." Before she could act on his suggestion, he lifted her to her feet and brushed her off. "You're sure you're okay?"

"Yes. Thank you. I'm fine."

"And you're sure..." he paused. "Not that I'm doubting you, but you're sure the sink works?"

She grinned and before he could shout a warning, twisted on the faucet handle, sending a rush of water into the sink. A matching grin spread across his face and he crouched down to look under the sink. "It's not leaking."

"I know."

"And the water didn't spray me in the face when it went on ." He sat back on his heels and Ruger trotted over for an ear rub. "Not bad."

She shrugged, feeling her cheek heat under his appreciation. "You would have gotten there eventually. I just finished it up for you."

He paused in the process of putting all the shiny new tools away in a gleaming red toolbox roughly the size of a Volkswagen. "Really?"

Meeting his amused gaze and crooked smile, she opened her mouth to utter the nice lie. "No. You really suck at this."

Hope turned away from his shout of laughter and started washing her hands, the flush in her cheeks turning to a wash of fire. "I wasn't going to say that. I was going to be nice and...it just...."

"Don't worry about it." The tools neatly stowed, he turned his attention to the plastic sheeting that covered most of the bathroom. In swift, economical movement, he pulled and folded the lightweight tarps before she finished getting the pipe grease off her hands. "You hungry?"

"Oh, I'm fine, I should just get home and--"

"I was thinking Thai food. You like Thai?" He tucked the sheeting bundle under his arm and hefted the mammoth tool box with no apparent effort. A whistle had Ruger skittering after him and she trailed after him, too, feeling like the puppy. Well, minus the fur. And the disgusting chew toy.

A large cabinet by the kitchen was open by the time she got there and he paused and pointed to an accordion file on the counter. "The menu's in there." All of the stuff he'd just pulled from the bathroom fit neatly into the cabinet and instead of looking at the takeout menu, she peered over his shoulder.

"Wow. It's all labeled and everything."

"How else do you find stuff?" He stood and she stepped back, his fluid movement startling her. "What?"

"Nothing, you're just tall." She fiddled with the file. "I don't expect you to move that fast. You alphabetize your takeout menus?"

"I'm not that tall."

She snorted.

"You're just short."

"I am not short!"

"Oh yeah, a petite flower of a girl." He smirked at her and she bristled. "So delicate, I bet you can't even eat a whole entree by yourself."

She folded her arms. "I think I'll start with summer rolls."

"Angel wings are better."

"Then you order them. And the coconut soup, with lemongrass? I want that, too."

"That sounds good."

She spoke over his next comment. "And phad thai with prawns and Swimming Rama." She angled her chin up at him.

"Perfect. Not that you'll eat of that."

"Ha!" She leaned on her elbows on the counter as he picked up the phone. "Watch me."

With the order placed, the teasing died for a moment and Hope shifted a little. It was fine when there was a project, but really, what was she doing there? She studied the ripple of muscle as Erik rummaged through the refrigerator.

"There it is!" He pulled out an enormous bottle of champagne and held it out to her.

"Wow, that is one big-ass bottle of champagne."

He nodded and read the label. "Yup, that's the official name of this size. Big-ass bottle. Oh, come on," he coaxed when she shook her head. "To celebrate. Victory over the sink demon."

She felt herself wavering. "I really shouldn't. I don't drink a lot and I have to drive."

He was already unwrapping the foil from the neck of the bottle. "Then I'll drive you home."

"No, you can't do that."

"Actually, I can, but we'll let that go. I could call a cab for you." A discreet pop made her jump a little and she cursed herself. She wasn't a giddy schoolgirl and this man was just a man. She could handle it.

She hoped.

Erik opened the cupboard by the sink. "I don't have the flute things for champagne, but I do have these." Triumphant, he held out a tall, narrow glass with a footed base.

"What is it?" Hope took the glass from him and he tipped the bottle, filling it halfway then pausing to let the bubbles recede, then tipping the bottle again.

"It's a pilsner glass. For beer. It's pretty close to a flute, right? Skaal." Filling his own glass, he tapped it to hers.

"Cheers. Sure. Other than the size, it's practically the same thing." She sipped and sighed. "Oh, that's good. That's really good."

"It's not bad. It's not a good beer, but it'll do." He set his glass on the counter when a buzzer sounded. Walking to a small speaker on the wall, he pressed a button. "Yes?"

She tuned out the muffled voice on the speaker and sipped from the glass again. As a rule, she didn't drink much and when she did, it was usually a mixed drink. All the champagne she'd tried in the past was sour and left a bitter aftertaste in her mouth, but this...this was heaven in a glass. She hiccupped.

Lost in the delight of the champagne, she didn't realize Erik had returned until the wave of aroma hit her. She looked up from her glass to see him laying out carton after carton of food. "Wow. That was fast."

He checked his watch. "Fifteen minutes. About right."

She choked on the next sip. "In what universe?"

He shook his head and held a set of chopsticks. "They're right across the street. And..." his grin flashed. "I tip very, very well."

Picking up the champagne bottle, he topped off her glass which had magically half-emptied.

"Let's eat."

Angry Chick had transformed.

He wasn't sure when it had happened, but somewhere along the way, Hope had lightened up. She'd gotten nice. She smiled. She laughed at his jokes. She'd pulled the stick out of her butt.

He really hoped it wasn't just the champagne.

"This looks...wow. All sorts of yummy goodness." She pressed her lips together and inhaled.

"Yummy goodness?" He handed her a plate and started loading up his own. The way she piled on the food made him bite back a smile as well as one of the chicken wing appetizers; there was no way she'd be able to finish what she put on her plate. Well, more for him.

It was less than a half-hour later that he looked up, prepared to take Hope's leftovers. What he saw was an empty plate and a pretty blonde finishing her glass of champagne. "Holy crap. You ate all of that?"

"Yes. I. Did." A slightly sloppy smile illuminated her face and she held out her glass. "And I wanna try those chicken thingies now."

He pushed the carton closer to her and took her glass. "You sure you want another one of these?"

"I'll tell you something." She leaned forward and wagged a chicken wing at him. "I don't usually drink a lot."

Nodding, he pulled out a bottle of water from the refrigerator. "I guessed that."

"And I eat way too much when I do drink."

"You eat just the right amount. See?" He tapped the empty dish between them. "You're a member of the Clean Plate Club."

She looked sadly at the plate. "I shouldn't have eaten that. I should be dieting. I mean, have you seen Miriam?"

"I've seen Miriam," he said cautiously.

"Maybe if I were thinner, I could be sexy like that." She chewed the last bite of chicken wing appetizer and made a happy sound as she spotted the smear of sauce on her fingers.

The sight of Hope licking her fingers made him shift a bit on his bar stool. "You're sexy. Don't diet."

She paused mid-lick. "Really? You're not just saying that?"

He looked her over. Dark honey hair, cool, though slightly blurry gray eyes, dimpled creamy skin and peach-luscious lips gave way to a body he'd never seen revealed, only hinted at. "Believe me. Not just saying anything. Very, very sexy." He gulped back some of the champagne in his glass.

She smiled, droopy eyes and sultry promises and reached across the breakfast bar to grip a handful of his t-shirt. With no real resistance from him, she pulled him over the bar to her. Her mouth was a breath from his when she paused long enough for him to open his mouth, to say something, anything and then...

He kissed her.

As sweet as he imagined, her lips parted beneath his and he deepened the kiss, tasting spicy Thai and tart wine on her. It was the taste of her, the spicier, sweeter, hotter taste of woman that drew him in and made him reach across the counter for her. He shoved a path through the food containers and hooked his hands under her arms, pulling her up and over the bar to his lap. Without breaking the kiss, she straddled him, wrapping her legs around his waist and arms around his neck. He felt her shudder as he moved to her cheek and jaw, felt her heart pound against him as trailed his mouth down the side of her neck. She clutched at him tighter, pressing her crotch to his and in the roar of blood that followed, he lifted her up and onto the cleared space of counter in front of him.

Raised up on the countertop, Hope was almost level with him as he stood between her legs. Her eyes stayed closed and she gasped a little as he pressed closer. "Hope," he whispered.

"Kiss me some more," she whispered back.

"Hope." This time his voice was louder. "Open your eyes."

She did, dazed and so beautiful he couldn't think for a moment. But she looked at him and smiled again and slid her legs up and down the outside of his thighs. Even through the layers of clothing, he could feel her softness and strength. She pulled up his t-shirt and in self-defense, he grabbed her hands and held them behind her back. "What?" she asked.

The hungry, frustrated tone to her voice almost made him throw all caution and sense out the window. "How drunk are you?" he asked, between gritted teeth.

She arched against him and his cock screamed at him to shut up, shut up and do this woman now! "I'm not."

"Yeah, right."

"No, really." She pulled back and gazed him with the earnestness of the deeply tipsy. "I couldn't drive right now to save my life. Or operate a backhoe."

"I'm being serious here."

"So am I!" Some of the tipsy faded into indignant. "You think a backhoe is easy to operate? They're not. And you really have to be on the right ground for them--"

"Hope. Focus." He threaded his fingers through her hair to grip her head. Wide-eyed, she stared back at him. "We can't do this if you're hammered."

"Do what?"

With a muffled groan, he let go of her and stepped back.

"Oh. Oh! Oh, wait," she scrambled off the counter and smiled in a way he was sure she meant to be reassuring. "I understand. I'm not totally sober."

"No kidding." He forced himself to think of anything other than her mouth. Taxes. He could think of taxes. And swimming with elderly members of the family, who still thought Speedos were the only bathing suits worth wearing.

Yeah. That killed it.

But Hope wasn't finished. "But I know that. I know I can't drive. I know I shouldn't have anything more to drink because then I'll get a headache. But I'm okay. I'm okay for...you know. For that."

He stuffed his hands into his pockets. "Absolutely. You're fine. But we're just going to hold—oh, my God."

Hope had pulled off her sweatshirt.

Under the folds of fleece and jersey knit, her skin was the same delicate peachy hue of her face. Smooth shoulders sloped into delicious breasts, cupped lovingly by a bra only a few shades darker than her skin and sheer enough to show the darker circles of her nipples through the fabric. Language deserted him as she kicked off her sneakers and socks and pushed her jeans down smooth thighs. Her matching panties hid nothing from him.

She stepped out of the wreckage of her clothes and moved toward him. Sliding her hands under his shirt, she lifted up the cloth over his ribs until he caught the hem and yanked the shirt off. With almost a purr, she ran her hands over his belly and chest, pressing into his flesh. He saw her knuckles go white and her fascinated gaze.

"So hard. How did you get this way?" Mischief danced across her smile. "Are you this hard all over?"

He caught her hands and pressed a kiss to her palm. "Swear to me you're sober enough."

"I swear I'm sober enou--" She shrieked as he swung her up in his arms and fused his mouth to hers.

"That was all I needed to hear," he whispered, walking back to the breakfast bar.

He lifted her like she weighed nothing, she thought dimly, trying to stay focused, trying to concentrate on everything that was happening, trying not to be distracted by the hot press of flesh as he slid his hand over her butt, under her panties. The shock of cold granite against flesh made her shriek again, but laughing as she did. And the laughter turned into a moan as he spread her legs and stepped between them. Somewhere in there, her underwear had disappeared, and now she was naked, except for her bra.

Sitting on the granite slab of the kitchen counter. Legs spread. The most beautiful man she'd ever seen kissing her neck, sliding her bra straps down her arms.

He was really good at this. Hope found herself arched back, breasts lifted to the worship of his mouth and tongue and teeth, shuddering.

"Erik...oh my God, yes, please, Erik!" Who was that rabid woman, babbling?

He worked his way back up her neck and murmured in her ear, "Thanks for getting my name right."

The dark velvet rumble over his voice and press of the not-quite-smooth skin of his belly against the wet center of her made her whimper. "Please."

He murmured again and she didn't catch what he said, because his fingers were on her now, stroking her clitoris, teasing the entrance of her vagina. She pressed closer to him, stretching her legs farther apart to pull him in. In desperation, she scrabbled for the buttons on his jeans and they gave way with the soft popping sound of old cotton and she filled her hand with him.

His shudder and swallowed curse delighted her and she squeezed him lightly, stroking the bulbous head. He dropped his head on her shoulder and groaned, then thrust a finger inside of her. She cried out again.

"Oh, GOD, Erik, now now now now NOW!"

"Wait. Wait." He sounded like he'd run a marathon. "We have to stretch you a little."

"No, we do NOT. In me, now. Now!" She let go of his cock, making him groan in disappointment and caught his face in her hands. The ice blue of his eyes had almost disappeared behind the dilated black of the centers. "Please," she begged. "Please. Now."

He eased the finger he'd pressed into her out and adjusted her thighs. She could feel her own moisture on his hand as he touched her. "Nice and easy," he whispered.

The shock of pleasure as he eased the tip of his cock into her made her tremble and he froze. "Do you want me to stop?" He sounded like his skin was being peeled off of him but he didn't move. She couldn't even feel him breathe.

"Erik," she panted. "Now, come to me. Do it now, please, now."

He cursed again, at least she thought it was a curse, because he pushed past the tightness in her and all she could hear was the roaring in her ears as he started to move. The perfect rhythm of it loosened her bones until she felt like she was melting and then he sped up. She choked out his name and clutched his shoulders.

"--won't last. Hope, you've got to come now."

She screamed.

Everything fell away as wave after wave of pleasure shook her and his breathing in her ear as he pumped faster and harder only lifted her higher. His own muffled shout vibrated against the skin of her neck and he clutched her to him as he came after her.

Chapter Eleven

Her bed was incredibly warm.

One of the feathers from her pillow must have worked its way out and she brushed away the tickle at the end of her chin and nestled deeper in the bed for another few minutes of sleep. She was just about to slip down under the covers when a tiny cold tap against her nose roused her again. She moved her head away, eyes determinedly shut.

Five more minutes.

Tap. Tap. Tap.

She opened one eye, squinted, really, since bright morning sun streamed through the window, and saw Ruger's face, an inch from hers. His black eyes gleaming in a frenzy of puppy love, he attacked her with kisses.

"Arg!" She jerked her head back and heard the crack as well as felt the back of her head smash against something hard. A muffled shout had her jerking around in surprise.

This wasn't her bed, she realized. Nor was it her bedroom and despite his insistence on cuddling with her at night, this was not her dog.

She was in Erik's bed.

"Oh, God! Sorry! Sorry!! Are you okay? I'm sorry."

She clutched the crisp white sheet to her, barely noticing its smooth, nearly silken texture, but suddenly aware of her nakedness as his broad, equally naked form rose from the covers.

His broad, golden tan, seriously freaking built form. He bent forward and clutched his face. Or, more precisely, his nose. Which was bleeding. A lot.

"Oh, jeeze." He looked at his hand tried to swipe at the blood trickling across his face. "What happened?"

"I'm sorry. I was just here and the dog came and he licked me--" Hope sat up and tucked her feet under her, tugging up the sheet to wrap under her arms. She got enough slack in the fabric to feel safely covered but Erik was now completely uncovered.

Well, hello, Mr. Goodbar.

"Here," she said briskly, not looking anywhere at all. "Pinch your nose. No, like this."

The bleeding slowed and she reached for the box of tissues on the bed table. With a few dabs and wipes, he was cleaner but still a little scary looking. He muttered clogged thanks and rose from the bed and walked into his bathroom.

Oh, dear God in Heaven.

Hope had an overwhelming flood of pity course through her. Pity for the sculptors of ancient Greece. Pity for the male models who struggled to convince the world of their beauty. Pity for every woman, ever born, who would never seen T. Erik Yoriksson in the buff.

It almost made up for the fact that she'd thrown herself at him and practically ravished him. And that she was here, now, naked and undoubtedly hideous-looking, with coordinating fetid breath and body odor. In his bed. Naked.

Did she mention that she was naked?

He came back into the room, still naked—naked!!--and drying his face with a fluffy white towel. "Oh, man, it's nice to have my bathroom back. Every time, I was having to go into the hall bath and...hey. Good morning."

Hope ducked her head and missed committing a felony with her breath, feeling his lips brush her forehead. "Yeah. Hi. Good morning."

He pulled back and she was miserably aware of the unmistakable aroma of last night's activities drifting up from her and the bed. He was probably completely repulsed by her.

"What's your schedule today?"

"Today?" She glanced at the sleek little clock on his night table and stood. "Oh my God! I have to work, I have to—oh, my God!!"

Erik paused with a pair of boxers dangling from his fingers as he watched Hope leap out of bed as if her extremely fine ass were on fire. "I guess breakfast is out, then."

He supposed he should have been a little freaked out to be seeing Angry Chick—or The Woman Formerly Known As Angry Chick naked. Especially since he was still naked himself. But this morning, he just couldn't get too worked up about it. Even the headbutt didn't faze him, despite the fact that his whole face felt swollen and hinted at the soreness that would be arriving soon.

It was probably an accident.

"Where are my clothes? I know I had clothes." Stumbling over the tail of sheet she wrapped around her, she looked so panicked, he didn't have the heart to tease her.

"Hope. Stop. Go take a shower, I'll get your stuff." With a gentle shove, he pushed her toward the bathroom, catching her as she stumbled again.

"I'm going to be late!" she wailed from the bathroom.

He looked at the clock. "It's 6:17. Where do you have to be at 6:17?"

"At the store. It's springtime and everyone does stuff in springtime. And if I don't get there in time, I'm not ready for the day--" A rush of water as she turned on the shower cut off her words and he left her to find her clothes.

It wasn't hard to find the things she wore the previous night. They weren't exactly in a tidy pile and he winced as he looked at the congealed mess of leftovers still on the counter.

First things first, Yoriksson.

Gathering up her things, he took a moment to appreciate the peach colored confection of her panties and bra. He'd been more than a little shocked when she peeled of the dull, baggy clothes she seemed to live in to reveal these. Delighted, but shocked.

What wasn't really shocking was finding Ruger chewing on the remains of one of Hope's socks. Sighing, he threw the tattered remains of white cotton into the trash, ignoring the puppy's plaintive dismay. On the way to the bathroom, he stopped at his dresser and searched for the smallest pair of socks he could find.

He walked back to the master bath and left the small pile, socks and everything, on the towel stand. After pulling out a new toothbrush and leaving it by the sink, he returned to the kitchen to start coffee and clean up.

He was just wiping down the breakfast bar when she rushed into the room. "Okay, thanks for finding my stuff. I think I can still make it in close to on time, if I don't hit every single red light." She patted her pockets and looked around.

He held up a small ring of keys. "These what you're looking for?"

"Yes. Thank you." She reached out for them and he lifted them out of reach.

"Say good morning to me."

"What?"

He stared her down.

She rolled her eyes and sighed. "Good morning."

He lifted his eyebrows and she frowned, pressing her lips together.

"Good morning, Erik."

He smiled and tossed her the keys.

She caught them between her hands, like she was clapping, and studied them a moment. "Why does this seem familiar?"

He laughed and walked to her, grabbing up the travel mug of coffee and a protein bar. "Here."

"Thanks. What—coffee." She popped the seal on the lid and sipped. "Ohhhh, beloved nectar of heaven."

He left her to enjoy her morning caffeine while he checked Ruger's potty pad. Sure enough, the little dog had done as he was supposed to and relieved himself on the absorbent material. Swiftly, Erik bagged the soiled pad and slipped a fresh one in the holder. After adding the small bag to the garbage he'd take out later, he washed his hands and tossed Ruger a small treat for his reward.

He turned to find Hope looking at the protein bar and coffee in her hands. "You gave me a cookie."

"No, it's a protein bar. Hey, I thought you had to go." He cupped her elbow and walked her to the door. "The traffic should be fine. It's Sunday. Practically still dawn."

"You gave me a good-girl cookie." She waggled the travel mug at him. "That's what this is!"

He'd eased her into the hall and pressed a quick kiss on her lips, then stepped back into his condo. "Have a good day, dear."

"You're *training* me, aren't you?" she called as he closed the door quietly.

The barely audible yowl of frustration through the door made him chuckle. He looked down at Ruger, who sat expectantly in front of him. "That went well, don't you think? Come on. I'll get dressed and we'll check out the dog park." Erik tested his nose. "Ow. That woman has a hard head, Ruger."

The dog barked and grinned.

The clear weather hadn't lasted through the morning. Erik sipped his own cup of coffee and tugged back on Ruger's leash, which the small dog completely ignored. Stretched almost flat, he pulled and yanked at Erik's hand. The fact that he was outmatched on every level never seemed to occur to the dog.

Erik had to respect that.

They passed through the double-gated fencing and, once safe inside the enclosure, Erik unleashed the terrier. Most dogs took a moment to shake off the feeling of the leash, he saw, but Ruger...Ruger just flew.

Racing circles around other dogs, he barked happily at a huge black dog, who lowered his massive, square head to sniff the pup, then returned to what Erik could only assume was guard duty. Undeterred, the puppy raced off in a different direction, romping and cavorting with as many dogs as he could smell.

The other dogs were tolerant of Ruger, he was relieved to see. The park seemed to be open territory for all the canines and surprisingly enough, everyone seemed to coexist peacefully.

He winced at the cacophony of barking, baying and outright dog screams as a small pack of beagles entered the park. Maybe "peacefully" was the wrong word.

Ruger didn't seem particularly put out by the beagles; he'd spotted one of the most beautiful golden retrievers Erik had ever seen and raced toward it, adding his own barking to the noise. The two dogs halted in front of one another, sniffed luxuriously and proceeded to race in circles. In the midst of the race, the larger dog paused and trotted back to a red-haired man, followed closely by Ruger.

As Erik watched, the young man seemed as pleased as his dog to see Ruger. He didn't even flinch when the puppy jumped up with muddy paws.

And placed them squarely on the man's khakis.

"Oh, jeeze. Ruger!" He strode across the muddy ground to the man, who was brushing ineffectually at his pants. "Hey, sorry about that."

"No problem. Ruger and I go way back."

Erik paused. "You do?"

The red-headed man straightened. "Yeah, I'm friends with the lady who watched him last week. You must be his owner. Rory Evans." He held out his right hand.

Erik shook his hand, resisting the urge to crush the smaller man into a whimpering pile of snot. "No, I'm just watching him for a friend. Erik Yoriksson. So you're the doctor/dog expert, right?"

Rory laughed. "I don't know about that, but I think I was able to help Hope a little. Is she here today?"

Keeping a bland smile fixed on his face, Erik shook his head. "No, not today. She had to go into work. All freaked out because she got up later than the crack of dawn." He sipped his coffee and watched Ruger chase the golden retriever.

"Oh." The infant doctor blushed and stuck his hands in his pockets. "Well, I'll just give her a call later."

"I'd be happy to pass on a message."

"That's okay. Thanks, though."

They stood side-by-side, watching the dogs play until the rain started in earnest. Rory pulled up the collar on his jacket and shivered a little and Erik smiled into his coffee cup.

"Okay, we're outta here." Rory whistled for his dog, who raced to his side and sat as he hooked her leash to a metal loop hidden by a pile of yellow fur.

Struggling not to smirk, Erik nodded. "You didn't grow up in the Pacific Northwest, huh?"

"No, I did."

The men locked gazes for a moment. "Oh." Erik sipped his coffee again.

Rory smiled and held out his hand to shake again. "Good to meet you, Erik. Great dog. Hope's worked with him here, so you shouldn't have any trouble getting him when you're ready to leave. Come on, girl."

Erik released the younger man's hand and looked over at Ruger, who danced over when the retriever obeyed her master's command. Meeting Erik's eyes, the puppy dropped his head and chest to the ground, butt in the air, tail wagging madly. As Erik moved to stretch out his hand to the dog, Ruger spun around and raced off.

"Well...shit."

Chapter Twelve

"Hey, boss."

Hope's head popped out of the crate she was unpacking. "Kyle, just the guy I wanted to see. Look at this vanity."

Obligingly, the lanky young man pulled aside the packing material. "Yeah. Okay."

"It has to go back. All of them have to go back."

"What?" He paused in his examination of the wooden cabinet. "Why? Didn't these just get ordered?"

She nodded. "Look closer."

Kyle studied the vanity, walking around the crate and folded his arms across his chest. "It's total crap, Hope."

"How do you know?"

He pointed at a hairline crack running through the wood grain. "There, and there. And I think—yeah, it's all broken at the base, too. Aren't these things, like, stupid expensive?"

"Yes, they are."

His face scrunched up. "Did you order these? Like, on purpose?"

Chuckling, she moved to the desk and gathered the paperwork there. "The samples were a completely different quality. Now, they all have to be returned."

"And you want me to take care of the shipping stuff while you make the disappointed, but not taking any crap phone call," Kyle guessed.

"No."

"Huh?"

She held out a small stack of papers. "I want you to make the disappointed, but not taking any crap phone call."

"No WAY!" A huge grin broke across his face and he accepted the paperwork.

"And also take care of the shipping stuff." She picked up the travel mug that had been handed to her that morning and sipped. She'd already refilled the cup twice and examined the base for a clue where Erik had gotten it.

Erik.

She quickly derailed that freight train of thought before it left the station and focused on her excited employee. "You'll need to be tough when you talk to the company, but professional, Kyle. They need to refund Home Again one hundred percent, no restocking fees, no shipping and handling charges. And if you feel like it's slipping away from you, page me or Caitlyn to take the call."

"What call?"

Both she and Kyle turned to find Caitlyn standing in the doorway, a quizzical look on her face. "Kyle's going to call the manufacturer for the new vanities and handle the return."

"Ooo, Kyle!" Caitlyn grinned and held out her fist, bumping knuckles with him. "Big stuff. Big move."

"I know, right?" The young man giggled, actually giggled and Hope hid her smile behind her cup.

"Try not to do that on the phone, Kyle. Go be a manly man."

He saluted and grabbed the loading dolly. "Crap cabinet and I are on it, boss."

Caitlyn stepped back to allow him room through the doorway and at Hope's signal, followed her to the office. She dropped in the soft chair in front of the desk with a sigh. "Well, well, well. Extra responsibility for Kyle."

"Yes, indeed."

The younger woman nodded. "He'll do a good job."

Hope pointed at her with her coffee cup. "He's got big shoes to fill."

Laughing, Caitlyn held out a small work boot. "You better be talking about yours. I've got Cinderella feet."

Hope propped her own foot on the desk and hiked up her pant leg to compare. "Mine are definitely bigger shoes."

"Whoa..." Caitlyn leaned forward. "And definitely bigger socks! What the hell are you wearing?"

The thick wad of sock bunched up around Hope's ankle, stubbornly refusing to let her yank the hem of her khakis back down. "Nothing. Socks. Hey, cut it out."

Caitlyn had grabbed her shoelaces and now held her foot hostage. "Let me see. Oh, my God. Those are *men's* socks."

"So? Let go of my shoe."

She complied but didn't even bother to hide her delighted smile at her boss. "And that's your just in case shirt, that you keep here."

Hope made a dismissive sound. "How would you know?"

"Because the cuff is all old and thready. You wouldn't wear that unless you had to. And you had to, huh? Huh?"

"Caitlyn. We need to get your meds adjusted."

"You got some last night!" the assistant manager crowed.

"Shhh!" Hope checked the open door of her office for humiliation potential. No employees. No store owners. No random camera crews. "These could be my brother's socks."

Caitlyn giggled. "Whatever! Who? Who was it? Do I know him? Can I thank him?"

"What? Why would you thank him?" Hope managed the tuck the offending sock back under her pant leg.

"Ah HA!!! See? I knew it! You got lucky! It's not the ex, is it? Because we hate him. Or...." She trailed off, her eyes rounded. "Oh, my God."

"What?" Hope said crossly.

"Oh, my *God*!"

"What is wrong with you?" She peered at Caitlyn. "You're pale, all of a sudden. Are you sick?"

"It was *him*, wasn't it?" Caitlyn pressed her hands to her heart. "You did the naughty with...Thor."

Words deserted Hope for a moment and she pressed her lips together.

"Hope? Did you? Did you do Thor?"

She shook her head. "His name's Erik."

There were worse things than waiting for her employee's gleeful laughter to stop, she supposed, marking off her morning checklist. War. That was bad. And famine. Nobody likes famine. Pestilence. The name alone was unpleasant. Yes, far worse things than being the butt of the joke existed in the world.

She just needed to remember that.

Finally, Caitlyn subsided, wiped her eyes and plucked the walkie-talkie off her belt. "Nick, Aaron."

Hope looked up from the paperwork on the desk. "What are you doing?"

Her assistant held up a staying hand and spoke into the handheld speaker as the other employees answered. "Twenty bucks, losers!"

Chuckling still, she dialed down the volume on the walkie, quieting the jeers and complaints.

"You bet on me?" Hope felt her face heat. "You bet on whether I would sleep with him or not?"

"Oh, please, Hope. What do you take us for?" Caitlyn pulled her own checklist off her clipboard and passed it over the desk. "We didn't bet on whether or not you would sleep with him. We bet on when you would sleep with him."

"Oh. GOD!" Unable to face the horror of her life, she covered her face with her hands.

Caitlyn tsked. "The guys were all, 'no, she's not a slut,' but come on, Thor? Are you kidding me? Plus, you know how you are during a dry spell."

Hope dropped her head onto the desk. "Please, please shoot me. Shoot me now."

Papers rustled as Caitlyn pulled out one of the forms under her arm. "Believe me, it's been discussed."

Hope lifted her head and passed the till report to the other woman. "Here."

"How do you always know what I'm looking for?"

"Because I trained you. And remember what I've told you about murdering your boss."

Caitlyn stopped marking her clipboard for a moment, wrinkling her brows. "Establish your alibi first and use a high-quality tarp?"

"No. Okay, yes, good to remember in any murder situation, but no. Killing the boss always reduces your bonus." She took the report back and turned to the computer. "And why are you guys plotting my demise this time?"

"Because you're horrible when you're not doing the horizontal mambo." Caitlyn sat back in the chair again. "And now that you're dating Thor, things will be better."

Hope could only shake her head. "No. No, no, no."

"Yes, it will. You're so much nicer and—oh, hey, Hope! I didn't mean anything bad." She leaned forward and clutched her hands together. "You're the best boss, really.

The murder threats hardly ever happen. We really love working here."

"No, I didn't mean that. I know, Cait. Don't get upset—oh, shit." Hope spun her chair and grabbed the box of tissues off the file cabinet. Pulling a couple from the pop-up dispenser, she walked around the desk to press them into Caitlyn's hand.

Sniffling, the younger woman mopped at her face. "I just know that no one would ever trade you for anybody. You always take care of us, and--"

"Caitlyn, stop. It's okay. I know."

"But you must've thought--" She shook her head. "I'm such an idiot."

"You are not. All I was saying was I'm not dating Erik."

"But...you were with him." Caitlyn forgot her own misery to process this. "You don't do that unless you're dating the guy."

"Usually. But I'm not dating him." Patting Caitlyn's shoulder, Hope returned to her place behind her desk.

Erik dropped the barbell onto the padded mat and stepped back, breathing deeply. Stephanie, the Sadistic Trainer, was in full force today. A series of thrusters, a front squat followed by a military press, and then a matching number of pull-ups, added up to the most hated workout in the gym. Sweat and exhaustion pounded his body like a prize fighter.

He loved it.

"Wow, Erik, nice time there." Sarah sidled up to him and ran a finger down his arm. "You've got really great form. Maybe you could help me with mine. I think my thrusters need a little work, you know?"

"Uh, well, I don't--" he began, only to be interrupted by another voice.

"Sarah, I can help you with that." Stephanie's voice was sweet, but her smile reminded him of Hope when she was in work mode. The brunette trainer was the opposite of Sarah in almost every way; she was slim but hard-muscled in a way that only countless hours of work would create. She was serious as a surgeon in the gym and was respected and feared by nearly every other person in the room.

"Oh, I'm okay, really, thanks, Steph," Sarah stammered.

"No, no. That's what I'm here for, to help." Stephanie rested her arm across Sarah's shoulders and led her away. "Erik, elbows up on those thrusters."

"I hate you," he called after her.

He chuckled as she winked and flipped him off and kept walking a protesting Sarah to the other side of the gym. Steph was one of his favorite people at the gym; she was happily married to the facility's co-owner and helped keep the focus of the gym on the workout. *Blood, Sweat & Tears* wasn't a pick-up joint.

"Oh, she is going to be sorry." He didn't realize he's spoken out loud until he heard an answer behind him.

"Who is?"

Erik turned to find Daniel at his side, watching Stephanie put the screws to a loudly protesting Sarah. "Watch the master at work," he advised.

"Or mistress, as the case may be." Daniel got semi-dreamy expression on his face. "She just needs some black leather."

"And a whip. Not the Indiana Jones kind, but one of those little ones." Erik nodded, trying not to grin, admiring the strength of movement as well as the near-perfection of Steph's rear end. It wasn't as beautiful as Hope's, but it was a thing of beauty and wonder.

Hope's butt. He sighed. Oh, yes. Beauty, wonder, perfection. And he'd held all of that in his hands.

Remembering it was Hope's brother beside him, he cleared his throat and steered his mind firmly away.

"Oh yeah. You know, I think I'll ask the wife to wear those black boots tonight--"

Stephanie's voice broke through their happy musings. "If you two are just going to stand around gossiping and staring at my ass, move out of the lift zone, please. People who are here to work out need the room."

"I wasn't staring, it was Erik." Daniel stepped away from him and even pointed.

"*Dude.*"

"Sorry, man. Survival of the least in trouble."

"Asswipe."

They moved out of the central area to the benches on the side of the gym, dodging the trio of college boys throwing medicine balls at each other with lethal speed. Tossing one of water bottles to him, Daniel opened his own and took a swig. "So I hear you and Hope got together."

Erik choked on his water, coughing as Daniel pounded him helpfully on the back. "What?" he managed. "Who said--"

"You're worse than my kids!" Daniel laughed. "You okay?"

"Yeah, I'm fine, I just--" Erik shook his head and coughed again. "What did you say?"

"Huh?"

He drew a deep breath in through his nose. "About...your sister?"

"What, that you two got togeth—oh, man!" Daniel barked a laugh. "You and Hope? My sister? Yeah, that'll happen. I'll hold my breath for it."

"Okay..." Erik studied Daniel, waiting for signs of complete insanity. "What are you saying, Dan?"

"Please, all the hot women crawling all over you and you're going for my geek sister?" The laugh turned to a guffaw. "Yeah, sure. Alternate universe, but sure."

"Your sister's not a geek," he protested. "You're the geek."

"I know it, but it got me Miriam." Another smug smile. "No, dork. I was talking about the dog thing. My mom said it went well."

"Yeah. Yeah. It did. Hope was really nice about it." He cleared his throat again and weighed the odds of her mentioning him to family members. "She even dropped off some of Ruger's stuff that got left behind and ended up helping me with my bathroom sink."

Daniel gave him a congratulatory shoulder punch. "You suckered her into helping. Nice! You may be a pretty boy but you're making it work for you."

"Shut up," he laughed.

"Helps to work on the plain girls, though." Daniel hefted his bag and Erik paused in pulled out his towel.

"Huh?"

"Plain ones. Like Hope." Daniel pointed at him with his water bottle. "She probably still doesn't even know what hit her."

"Hey!"

"Not that you'd be an asshole about it, I'm not saying that," Daniel walked next to him toward the door of the gym, lifting a hand in farewell to a couple of the men still working out. "If I thought that, I'd have to kick your ass. You know, on principle."

"You have no principles," he snorted, pointing his remote at his car. The lights flashed, reflecting off the freshly washed surface and he frowned.

"What's the matter? Something wrong with your car?" Daniel turned to frown at it, too. "There've been kids around lately and they could have keyed it."

Startled, he looked back at Daniel. "No! Or they better not have. No, I was just trying to remember when my next scheduled maintenance was."

"Yeah. Gotta keep this baby running sweet, huh? She's a beauty, though." Hitting his own remote, he unlocked a burgundy luxury sedan a few spaces over and sighed. "Want to trade?"

"No. Thanks." Erik grinned. "Your car screams married. Mine tells the world hey, I like women."

Daniel snorted. "Just for that, I'm kicking your ass at racquetball on Thursday."

"Uh huh. Sure, you will."

Daniel walked backwards to the car. "I've held back until now. You're toast, man."

"Better bring backup," Erik called.

Daniel started his car with a roar that made Erik laugh as he watched the older man drive out of the parking lot. Despite his covetous looks, he knew Daniel wouldn't trade anything in his life, not his car or his kids or, especially, the woman. He had a good head on his shoulders, Erik mused.

But what the hell was Daniel thinking, calling Hope plain?

Hope knocked briefly at Miriam and Daniel's front door before coming inside. "Hello?"

"Why do you knock? You know I'll hear and think I have to come open the door myself?" Miriam's aggrieved tones floated from the kitchen. "Now get back here and help me!"

The kitchen had been designed by Hope herself and laid out with the same care she'd shown to her own space. The work triangle of fridge, stove and sink was the exact length and width that matched Miriam's long-legged stride without making it unusable to potential future buyers, should they decide to put the house on the market. Only the best materials were used, not only for appearance but also for longevity. The kitchen was beautiful and functional and inviting.

Just not right now.

She estimated that not every single cooking implement had been pulled from the drawers, cupboards and walk-in pantry, only about ninety percent of them. Of that ninety percent, seventy-five percent mounded the counters and balanced in the sink, held together with something indefinably sticky. Hope looked around the room, her vision blurred by the destructive capabilities of not a band of marauding Vikings, but of one woman.

"Miriam."

"What? Hand me the big spoon, fast." Miriam faced the stove, stirring frantically.

"What the hell have you done here?"

"Hope, darling. The spoon, now. Before I burn this and am forced to kill you." The stirring motions grew more frantic.

With a sigh, she switched off the heat on the cooktop and pulled the pan across the smooth surface to a cooler area. Taking the smaller spoon from her sister-in-law, she stirred the pale yellow liquid as she tilted the pan around to check for scorching at the base. "I don't think it burned."

A sighed barrage of Norwegian escaped Miriam, something Hope could interpret as *oh, thank God.* She studied the cooling mass and leaned down to sniff. Nice. Vanilla-y.

"What is this supposed to be?"

"It's not supposed to be anything, it's crème brulee. I have to bake it now." She peered at the spattered paper taped the wall beside the stove. A wall that had been treated with Venetian plaster and glazed to protect its finish.

Hope sighed.

"It's going to be delicious. You will see." Eight ramekins stood ready as Miriam hefted the pan and started to pour the hot liquid.

"Wait! Miriam, good God. You're a menace." Pulling a large ladle from the depleted utensil holder, she portioned the fluid into the white ceramic bowls. "Do you have the water bath ready?"

Miriam looked at her blankly. "I don't need a bath."

"No, for baking these. Where...let me see your recipe." Hope scanned the smudged paper. "There. See? Bake in a hot water bath for thirty minutes and cool for one hour, or overnight."

"Overnight?" the other woman shrieked.

"No, for one hour OR overnight. Miriam." Hope sighed. "Get the big roasting pan out."

"It is out." She pointed at one of the double ovens.

"Okay. Hmm. How about a baking pan? Like for brownies?"

Within a few short moments, she had the dessert in the oven, the dishwasher crammed full and running and had started on the dirty dishes. Miriam had started on a glass of wine. "Okay, Miriam. Out with it. What's with the big dinner?"

Before Miriam could answer, a shout come from the front of the house. "I'm home!"

"In the kitchen," Miriam answered.

Daniel breezed in, a cloud of sweat and stink, and dropped a kiss on his wife's perfectly painted mouth. "What's all this?"

"This is your sister, saving your smelly ass from all the dishes." Hope scrubbed at a particularly stubborn saucepan. "No, no. No need to thank me."

"Really?" Daniel and Miriam exchanged a look. "You don't want to be thanked?"

"No. What I do want--"

"Ah ha!" Daniel grinned. "I knew it."

"What I do want," Hope continued, ignoring the snickers, "is for you to take a shower and wash that stink off."

"Awww..." Daniel extended his arms as if to hug her and in warning she pointed the sprayer at him.

"Freeze."

"You watch too many cop shows," he complained as his wife laughed at them both. "Besides, you think I sweat bad, you should come to the gym and see the guys there. Like Erik!"

Hope hunched over the bowl she was scrubbing and grunted in response. "Just go clean up, would you? Your wife made you a lovely meal." Rinsing the bowl and placing it on the drying rack, she caught the speculation in Miriam's eyes and sighed a little. Busted. Don't say anything, Miriam, she thought. Not now. Not in front of Daniel.

Daniel rummaged around in the fridge. "I'm going, I'm going. Babe, where's the beer?"

"Move the milk, darling."

"Got it." Brandishing the bottle in a mock toast, he kissed his wife once more and headed upstairs, then popped his head back in the kitchen. "I didn't miss anything, did I?"

Before Hope could stutter out an answer, Miriam laughed. "Because I cooked? No, darling. You're not in trouble."

"Whew! Last time you did a big meal like this was before Lene was born!" He clomped up the stairs with the grace of a lame elephant, whistling.

Hope and Miriam looked at each other, Miriam's expression mirroring the one Hope felt. "Miriam...."

"Don't say it." She placed a hand on her belly, just above the button on her low-rise jeans.

Hope bit back a smile. "Are you pregnant?"

"No. I can't be." She rolled her eyes at Hope's snort. "Okay, yes, I could be, but it's too soon to know for sure. And I know what you're doing."

Hope looked up from her examination of a wheel-shaped implement. "Huh?"

"You're trying to avoid talking about Erik. I saw that!" she crowed when Hope flinched.

"Shut up. I am not. Shut up." She ignored her sister-in-law's chortle and held up the oddly-shaped kitchen tool. At least, she hoped it was a kitchen tool. "What the hell is this?"

"It's a spaetzle maker."

"What's it for?"

"Making spaetzle."

Now Hope rolled her eyes.

"You know, the little dumpling things." Miriam pushed the nearly full wine glass to her. "Here. Pour that down the sink. Just in case."

Hope took the glass and rinsed it, setting it aside. "Why do you have a spaetzle maker out and covered with...what is this? Glue?"

"It's not glue! It's spaetzle...oh, what is the word?"

"Batter?"

"Yes. Batter." Miriam walked to the fridge and pulled out a container of orange juice, accepting the tumbler Hope handed her without a word.

"Fine. You made spaetzle. Where is it?"

Miriam focused on pouring her juice with the intensity of a brain surgeon. "It didn't turn out."

Hope paused in her scrubbing. "What was wrong with it?"

"Too gluey."

She gave up and laughed. "Oh, Miriam."

"What?" Miriam glided back over to her seat. "Stop laughing at me, you bad girl."

Hope laughed harder.

"You are still doing it! I know what you're doing." Miriam sipped her juice and waggled her finger. "You are trying not to talk about Erik."

She snorted. "You're crazy."

Miriam raised her eyebrows and smiled.

"There's nothing to talk about."

Miriam rested her chin on her hand and stared her down.

"There isn't."

Miriam hummed a little.

"Fine." She tossed the scrubbing pad into the sink and walked over to the built-in coffee machine. "What do you want to know?"

"Did you sleep with him?"

"Miriam!" Hope's jaw dropped. "Jeeze!"

Her sister-in-law smiled into her orange juice. "I'll take that as a yes. Yes?"

She gave up even the pretense of battle. "Yes."

"I knew it!"

"How did you know? What, am I wearing a sign or something?" She made a small sound of disgust. "And really, what did you know? That I slept with some guy I'd never even kissed beforehand? We're not even dating."

Miriam hummed again. "So we won't tell your mother."

"No kidding." She filled a mug with the freshly brewed coffee and plunked down at the table. Miriam reached out and covered her hand, squeezing it lightly.

"Was it...not good?"

She paused with the cup halfway to her mouth. "Huh?"

Sorrow and sympathy all but oozed from her sister-in-law. "The sex, darling. Was it bad? You seem so upset. He did not hurt you, did he?"

"No, no. He didn't hurt me."

The former model's golden head bobbed. "Because I would kill him for you. Or hire it done. You know this, yes?"

"Yes. But you don't have to. It was..." Hope searched for the right words to describe the previous night.

"What?" Miriam leaned forward.

She folded her arms on the table and rested her head on them, like a kindergartener at quiet time. "It was amazing." She ignored Miriam's crow of delight and sat up again. "No, seriously. It was like...."

"Oh my God, tell me!" Miriam all but bounced in her seat.

"It was like the world stopped. Just stopped. I don't know. Maybe held its breath for a minute." She turned her coffee cup in slow circles, remembering.

Miriam smiled dreamily. "I remember the first time your brother did that for me."

"Ew! Miriam!!"

"Oh, stop being such a child." A light swat punctuated her words. "You were saying? The earth stopped, angels wept, for a moment, all nations were at peace. Go on."

Hope giggled. "It was that...whew. But then this morning, oh Miriam."

Her sister-in-law made a happy humming noise. "Morning sex is the best, isn't it? Who needs coffee?"

"I do," she snorted. "And there wasn't any morning sex."

"Aw."

Lips twitching, she shook her head. "No, he was going to the bathroom to clean up. Oh, shoot. I'd forgotten this part. I think I broke his nose."

"Hope!" Miriam wailed. "How many times do I have to tell you? A man stops the world for you, you *do not break his nose.*"

"It wasn't on purpose. And you're missing the point."

"What's the point?"

"I watched him walk away, Miriam."

"Ahhhh." Miriam looked dreamy again. "And the angels wept once more, did they?"

"Sweet lord, but he is a beautiful man."

"Tcha!"

They sat in silence, each sipping her drink until Miriam got up from the table and started gathering plates and utensils. "Well, I thought you two were right for each other. This is what I meant when I told you to look for a quality man. I think he'll be good for you. And his family likes you already."

"What are you talking about?"

"About you and Erik."

"There is no me and Erik. Haven't you been listening to me?" Hope accepted the stack of plates and began setting the table.

"I hate it when you ask me that."

"I hate it when I have to repeat myself." Hope didn't exactly slam the forks and knives into place, but she set them down with emphasis. "He's beautiful, Miriam."

"I know."

"He's what Michelangelo was trying to create, and failed."

"Lucky girl. You are a lucky, lucky girl."

"No, I'm not! That's what I'm saying. Yeah, I got lucky with him. Once. But it's not going to be more than that."

Miriam paused, fridge door open, a bag of salad mix in her hand. "Why not?"

"Because he's too good-looking for me! We don't match. That's the way it works." She felt her shoulders sag and deliberately straightened them.

Setting the bowl of salad greens on the table, Miriam studied her. She could feel it, the careful examination, and braced for Miriam's comment. "I think I speak English fairly well, you know."

Before she could respond to that non sequitur, the timer for the oven buzzed. Hotpads in hand, she eased the crème brulee out of the oven and set the dish on the stovetop, then looked at her sister-in-law. "Of course you speak English well. Better than I will ever speak Norwegian."

"Mmm, yes. But this isn't saying much, darling." Miriam waved a hand sparkling with diamonds as if erasing what she'd just said. "I am always frustrated, you see, when I do not understand a word that has been said, even though I know it is English, and I know my English is very good."

"Miriam...."

It was as she hadn't said anything. "Because I do not understand why his good looks should stop you from dating him."

"First, we're not dating. It was a random act of sex. And champagne. But that doesn't mean we're dating." Hope passed over the hot pads and watched Miriam extract the pork tenderloin from the second oven. Miraculously, nothing spilled and not a drop splashed onto the sheer red silk of her shirt. "Second, when it comes to dating, pretty people stick together."

"You're being ridiculous. Would you refuse to date him if he were unattractive?"

"No. Well, depends. I don't know if I could date the Elephant Man or anything."

They both paused, thinking about that. "Fair enough. But unattractive in the normal fashion? Would you say, 'no, I am sorry, you are too ugly and I am too beautiful?'"

"Of course not!"

"Then why are you being such a snob about Erik?"

"I'm not! It's just that people who are really good-looking know it, and if you're not as good-looking, then pretty soon, they're looking around. And other people start saying, 'Oh, what is he doing with her? He could do so much better.' And then suddenly, he's too busy to call or hang out, and then it's just over."

Miriam didn't even blink. "And perhaps, darling, if he is a good man, who sees you and how beautiful you are, he's happy with you for the rest of your lives. Look at your brother and me."

Hope snorted. Loudly. "You're gorgeous and he knows how lucky he is. He's never going to be named Sexiest Man in the World, you know."

Her sister-in-law smiled. "Yes, I know and he would, if I ruled the world. Should I say to your brother, no, I cannot be with you because you are not beautiful enough for me?"

"It's different." Hope shook her head.

Miriam muttered under her breath in Norwegian.

"I heard that! I know that word!" She folded her arms and glared at her sister-in-law, who mirrored her pose.

"Which word? The one for stubborn? Or for stupid?"

The front door crashed open and three small pairs of feet clattered into the house. Hope heard her mother's laughing rebuke to the children.

"This conversation," Miriam said ominously, "is not over."

Hope sighed. "I didn't think it was."

Chapter Thirteen

"What do you think of this? For Ruger?"

Hope froze. She'd been easing up behind Erik, determined to catch him by surprise, as he kept doing to her. Now that she thought of it, he probably wasn't trying to surprise her. If Caitlyn hadn't told her "the super hottie" had returned, she wouldn't have even know he was in the building.

Maybe he didn't even want her to know he was here.

Suppressing a sigh, Hope looked at the some-assembly-required end table that Erik was considering. While it looked like a clean-lined, simple piece of furniture, it doubled as a dog crate and storage device. There was even a place for deodorizing material, kept far enough away from the dog for safety purposes. "That's a good choice," she told him. "Some people have had a little trouble with the assembly, but all in all, it's a good product."

"What do you mean, problems with the assembly?" He turned to her with a frown and she saw that he had Ruger under his arm. Oddly, the small dog seemed to have fallen asleep. She decided not to wake him.

"I mean some people have had a little trouble putting it together." She turned the box on the shelf and skimmed over the print on the side of it. "But that's usually only people who have trouble with most home repair projects."

"Ah."

They stood in silence for a moment, looking at the table. "How did you know I was behind you?" she asked.

"I can smell you."

Once again, the floor refused to open up and swallow her.

"Oh. Okay. Good to know." She took a step away from him. "It's been a busy morning. I guess I got a little sweaty."

Erik gave her a sideways glance and smirked. "You've been sweatier."

She swatted his arm. "Thanks. Now I feel better."

"You dope. I didn't say you smelled *bad*, I just said I could smell you." He picked up the box he'd been studying, shifting the dog as he lifted the large box with one hand.

She swallowed.

"Where are you going to put it? The table?" she asked after clearing her throat.

"In the spot by the couch in the living room."

She frowned, trying to picture his condominium's layout. "Right by the wall? Where that little divot is?" She made a square shape with her hands, but dropped them when his shoulders started shaking.

"No, that was great. I think that's the international sign for 'space by couch next to wall.'" He grinned down at her.

"Shut up." She ignored his chuckle and suppressing her own smile, peered at the box again. "I don't think this is going to fit."

"No, it'll fit. I can make it fit."

Pointing to the box, she shook her head. "Look at the dimensions, Erik."

"Well, that could still...no. It's not going to fit." He tipped the box back. "Ruger would have liked it, too."

At the sound of his name, the puppy woke and blinking, spotted Hope. Corkscrewing his body, he yipped with joy. Hope watched in disbelief. "But how would you be able to tell?" she murmured.

"What?"

"Nothing," she said quickly. "I was just—hey, maybe you can cut these pieces down. Make it fit in the space."

Erik turned the box again, studying the picture of the table, where she'd pointed. "I could just cut that piece and it'd fit?"

"It *might* fit," she corrected him. "You just need to measure it right, and with a little luck and a jigsaw...."

He nodded, listening closely. When she paused, he asked, "The jigsaw. Is that the round one?"

Hope stared at the beautiful man who stood in front of her, one hand holding his silly dog, the other, the corrugated box containing the end table. Obviously, neither task took a lot out of him; the muscles in his arms barely bulged holding the heavy box and the puppy wriggled happily, restrained but not harmed. So beautiful. And such a klutz with tools.

"I can fix it for you."

Who said that?

"You can?" He smiled at her, not the I'm-so-gorgeous-that-you'll-do-anything-for-me smile she hated, but an honest, happy, hopeful smile. She sighed.

"I'll give it a shot. But if I don't think it'll work, I won't try to alter anything," she warned him.

"That's great. Thanks, Hope." He leaned in, still balancing dog and box, and kissed her lightly on the lips.

She tingled.

Pressing her lips together, she turned and fussed with the remaining stock on the shelf. "I have to do a few things here. We can meet at my place in about an hour."

"Your place?"

"Unless you have a jigsaw. And the round one is the circular saw. The one that looks like a stick is the jigsaw."

"I knew that."

Hope walked Erik to the checkout register. "Of course you did. Did you get a measuring tape when you were here last?"

"Yes." He slid the box onto the counter and shifted the dog. Terra, the newest of the cashiers, cooed at the puppy. Ruger writhed in delight.

"Good, because I need you to measure the area--"

Caitlyn walked up next to them with her clipboard and shoved more forms to sign into Hope's hands.. "Hey, Erik!"

"Hi. How are you?" He smiled down at her and she all but dissolved, Hope thought sourly.

"I'm good, thanks. You remember the guys, right?" The assistant manager waved over Nick, Kyle and Aaron, who'd been skulking around the customer service desk.

After a round of reintroduction, Aaron spoke up. ""How'd the bathroom repair work out?"

Erik pulled out his credit card for the cashier. "There were a few problems, but Hope came over and helped me with them."

All five employees looked from Erik to Hope. "Ohhhhhhhh." Knowing grins were passed around like canapés.

"Shut up," Hope said under her breath.

"And now we're going to work on this table." Erik turned to her, his grin just a little bit wicked. "I'll see you at your place. Right...honey?"

Kyle giggled and was elbowed sharply by a snickering Nick. Hope turned to face them all. "Gosh, restocking is done already? And the mess in the garden center is cleaned up?"

Caitlyn moved over to help another customer and the cashier straightened her counter, deliberately not making eye contact. Delight dropped off the faces of her three stooges, as she thought of them in her more charitable moments, and they turned away. Crossing behind the registers, their voices carried back to Hope and Erik.

"Do you think he's really going over to her house for a project?"

"And is that what she's wearing?"

"What are you, a girl? He's seen her naked. You think he cares what she's wearing? Get real."

Erik stood at the exit doors, surprise and speculation mixed with laughter in his eyes. "You told your employees?"

"No, I didn't! Caitlyn was guessing and she guessed right and oh, my God." Hope pressed the heels of her hands into the forehead. "Some people are just a waste of a perfectly good tarp."

Erik's laughter followed her as she walked away.

She answered the door before his knuckles made contact.

"Come in. Yes, hello to you, too," she spoke to Ruger as he bounced on the end of his leash. With a quick tug, Erik eased both of them into the house.

"Ruger. Chill." Turning to Hope, he lifted the box he held a little higher. "I have the dimensions on the top there."

She pulled off the notes he'd taped to the top of the box and flipped through them. "You...drew sketches."

"Yeah, and I have pictures on my phone, too. I don't draw that well, so I thought it would be better to have an accurate idea of the location."

She pressed her lips together and studied the pages he's hastily assembled and he began to feel foolish. But then she smiled at him. "This is great. It's really going to help. Let's hit the shop."

The shop was attached to the garage in the back yard, large and well lit. Erik perked up as they walked toward it. "Thanks for doing this."

"I haven't done anything yet." She paused, key in hand, outside the building. "I may not be able to make this work, Erik. And even if it works, it might not look the way you want it to."

He studied her for a moment, reining in Ruger as he would have started digging in the small flower bed next to the doorway. "Thank you for doing this."

She flushed and turned back to the door. "You're welcome."

"You know, my dad isn't a handy guy, so I'm looking forward to this," he said as he dragged the puppy into the building. He set the box where she pointed and blinked as she flipped on the overhead lights. "Whoa."

It was a large room with decent windows. He could see equipment lining the back wall, big and a little intimidating, cords twisting back to a wall-mounted power strip. A mammoth red tool chest hulked in the corner, drawers half open. And everywhere was the clutter of tools.

"Yeah. I know. I keep meaning to organize it, but I get in here and I start working on something else." Shrugging, she pulled out a utility knife and cut through the tape on the box carefully. "Let's keep the box intact, in case you have to return it. And one day, when I have time, it'll all be clean and straight. Tools will be hung up on pegboard with the little chalk outlines."

With equal caution, she unwrapped every piece, setting aside the plastic and laying out the precut pieces of lumber in order. He thought about making conversation, but seeing the absorbed look on her face, decided to look around instead.

"So this is a shop," he muttered.

"What?"

"Nothing, just looking around." He poked at a large machine in the corner. "What's this?"

"It's a lathe."

A sharp, dangerous looking blade winked at him from behind a plastic guard. "What's it do?"

"It shapes spindles and other turned wood pieces."

He thought about it for a moment, then gave up. "I have no idea what you just said."

He looked over at her as she laughed. She'd spread out his notes and was measuring one of the wood pieces, examining the edges. Without looking up, she said, "If your dog chews anything I will kill him. Then you."

He looked down at Ruger, who had a screwdriver's wooden handle in his mouth. With as much stealth as he could manage, he removed it and inspected the wood for marks.

"What did he get?"

"Nothing."

She put down the tool she was using and held out her hand. He gave her the screwdriver and examined the handle silently. "He didn't chew it. He was just holding it."

"Holding it."

"Uh huh."

"In his mouth."

"How else would he--" Erik stopped, and waited for the net of the trap he'd just stepped in to close around him. He didn't have long to wait.

"In his mouth, where his teeth are?" Hope tapped the handle of the screwdriver against her palm.

"Okay, he chewed it a little, but you can barely tell." A spurt of irritation flashed through him and he turned away, took a breath. "If it's such a big deal, I'll replace it."

"What if it's irreplaceable?"

Erik faced her again, ready to blast her into next week, when he caught the humor and challenge in her eyes, belying the stern expression on her face.

"What if this is the screwdriver that got me into woodworking and construction, which led to my job?"

Two easy steps separated them, and crossing the floor, he leaned into her. "I'd have to say, if it's that important to you, you probably shouldn't have left it lying on the ground like garbage."

The grin that broke across her face was brighter that the shop's fluorescent lighting. "I had you going, though."

"Yeah, you did." He gave a wisp of her hair a little tug. "Is this going to work?"

Her eyes widened and her delicious mouth dropped open. "Wh.... is what going to work?"

"The table." Erik watched with interest as she flushed and turned back to the work bench, rattling the tools she had laid out.

"Oh. Yeah, it is. I'm just going to cut these--" A shrill beeping cut her off and she pulled out her phone and glanced at it. "Oh, no."

"Problem?" he asked.

"It's a text message from Caitlyn. 9-1-1. Please don't let it be a fire," she muttered as she dialed. "Hey, it's me. What---okay. Okay. And the police are there? On my way." She pressed the end button on the phone and sighed. Erik put his hand on the back of her neck and massaged lightly.

"Is anyone hurt?" he asked.

"No. Not until I get my hands on them, anyway. I have to go back to the store. Now."

"Yeah, I figured. I'll get the dog and take off."

"No, don't do that. It shouldn't take too long and I'll be right back." She glanced up at him and smiled a little. "There's food in the fridge and a bully stick in the freezer, if you two want a snack. I forgot to give it back to you when you picked up the dog."

"You froze the bully stick?"

"It doesn't smell as bad that way. And it lasts longer." She shook her head and walked to the door. "I'll be right back and we'll get this finished."

He watched her leave, lifting a hand to wave goodbye. Left alone with the tools and the mess, he toyed with an idea for a moment before considering the dog. "Will you behave so I can organize some of this mess?"

Ruger wiggled a bit and wagged. A small yap punctuated his joy.

"Yeah, I didn't think so. Let's get you that bully stick."

Well. That was two hours of life she'd never get back.

Hope walked into the kitchen through the back door and closed it. The lights in the shop were out, but Erik's car was still parked in front of the house, but she didn't see any signs of the large man or the small dog.

But coffee was made.

He'd left an insulated mug on the counter with a note underneath it, denoting the time. She wasn't exactly sure what to make of this type of efficiency, but after opening the sealed lid of the cup and taking a sip, found that she didn't actually care. Half the cup was gone before she remember why she'd come back into the house. She wandered out of the kitchen.

The low sound of the television murmured from the living room and she stopped in the hallway. Erik was stretched out on the couch with Ruger draped across his chest and both of them were sound asleep. She tiptoed back down the hallway.

Taking the shop key and her phone, in case any other disasters happened at the store, she crossed the back yard. The slight drizzle that had started barely registered with her, other than the automatic gutter check she did when she was outside in the rain. When she'd moved into the house, roof and gutters for the shop had been one of her first projects.

She tried the door, pleased that Erik had locked up before he left, and fished out the key. Humming a little, she unlocked the door and flipped on the light.

And stopped dead.

What the hell had happened in here?

She stood, frozen, trying to take in the state of the shop when she heard him calling her name. The door opened and shut behind her and she turned her head to find him beside her, dog in hand, raindrops glistening on his hair like silver over gold.

"Hey, you're back." He set the dog on the floor and dropped a quick kiss on her cheek. "It's getting late. Want to get something to eat? We can finish this up another day."

"What have you done?" She leaned away from him and waved her arms around at the shop.

"Oh, just straightened up a little." Pride underlined his words. "Put a few things away."

"You...you...." Was he insane? "There's nothing on the workbench!"

"I know." He smiled at her, the smile she hated. "No need to thank me. I was happy to do it."

"I'm not going to thank you!" she shrieked.

He drew back as if he'd been slapped.

"You put everything away and I don't know where anything is now! You rearranged my power tools! A woman's power tools are sacred, Erik! And...and...look!"

She pointed to the pegboard. He turned to it. "What?"

"You put lines around the tools, like little corpses. This isn't a shop, it's a crime scene!"

His shoulders stiffened and he turned back to her. The ice blue of his eyes had turned glacial and when he spoke, she half-expected frost to develop on the walls. "It's not a crime scene. You're the one who said you wanted the outlines around your tools on the pegboard!"

"That's because I didn't know it would make them look like they've been murdered."

"Now you're being emotional and overly dramatic."

She sputtered.

"This place was a disaster area," he continued coldly. "Worse, it was dangerous. All I did was make it functional and a little less dangerous."

She pressed her palms to her eyes and prayed for patience, since she certainly wouldn't be able to move his body, if she killed him. As he so richly deserved. "Erik, how would you feel if I walked into your place and organized your stuff?"

A low, unpleasant laugh escaped him. "My place is organized. Unlike yours."

Teeth gritted, she tried once more to explain. "If I walked into your apartment and I took apart everything that you had done--"

"I didn't take apart anything. It was just mixed up in here. In piles."

"Hypothetically speaking!" she yelled.

He paused, then nodded. "Okay, hypothetically. You break into my condo, manage not to get arrested, and rip the place up?"

"Yes, and then, I put things away, but not how you had them. I make a completely different organizational system. Instead of..." She looked around for something to prove her point and picked up a jar. "Instead of labeling everything, I put it in alphabetical order. No matter what it is." She studied the label. "Where'd you get the label maker?"

"My car."

"You keep a label maker in your car?"

He shrugged. "Not a really good one. And the whole alphabetical thing doesn't make any sense. It only works if you're organizing the same kind of things or the same size."

"I'm just saying." She spread her hands. "So if I snuck into your place and took everything apart and put it back together according to my idea of what's right and accessible, how would you react?"

"It's not the same situation. You're comparing apples and oranges."

"And you're being deliberately stupid about this!"

"I'm not being stupid about anything, except maybe being here. But that can be rectified."

"Oh no, you don't." She pointed at him. "You're not going anywhere. I'm going to fix this table and you're going to take it home. Tonight."

"You think I'm just going to stand here while you play with your toys?"

She made a sound that had Ruger whining and hiding beneath the workbench. "No, you're going to go into the house and watch TV or play on whatever minicomputer you probably also have in your car or act like Mister Important Business Guy on your phone while I finish this and try not to go crazy looking for every damn thing in this shop."

"Too late." She stared at him as he smiled blandly. "You're crazy already."

"You ass!"

"You hysterical twit."

"Get out!"

Erik snapped his fingers at the cowering dog and left without another word. Ruger raced past him out the door.

Hope stomped around the blessed solitude of her shop and kicked the base of her big saw. Yelping, she hobbled back to the workbench. "Who the hell does he think he is?"

The small clamps she'd always had to root around for appeared like magic in the tool chest, in the drawer marked "clamps." Arranged according to size, she scanned them and selected the right size. "Comes into my home, my shop, and messes with my stuff."

Stomping back over to the tool chest, she yanked open another drawer and selected the correct Allen wrench from array there. "And then he gets snooty with me? Oh, I do not think so!"

Standing back from the table, she noticed an extra bit of wood glue escaping from the new seams. An array of clear plastic bins lined the shelving unit behind her and she spotted the rags immediately. A few swift dabs with a clean cloth and the table was done. "Oh, Mister I Know Better Than You Do! It's not like he works in this space! It's not like he has to find stuff in here!"

Still grumbling, she tossed the soiled rag into the garbage can near the door and picked up her tools to put away...then froze. The table gleamed in the florescent lighting as if laughing at her.

"Oh....shit."

Erik muted the television when Hope walked into the room. The Mariners had come back from a two-run deficit, but not even the potential win for his favorite baseball team held his interest. "All finished?"

"Yes." She took her keys from the small basket on the table near the hallway and faced him. "I could use a hand carrying it to my truck. I've got a tarp ready to go."

"I can take the table myself."

She must have heard the same childish response that he did because she looked at him in disbelief. "In your car?"

"I'm not walking home."

"It won't fit in your car." She picked up Ruger' leash and held it out to him. "Let's just get it loaded into mine and get it over to your place."

"No. I can handle it." Erik took the leash from her hand and caught the bouncing dog. Ruger knew the leash meant good things.

"Erik, come on."

He hooked leash to collar, no mean feat, and pulled his keys out, not bothering to look at her. "Don't worry about it."

She folded her arms. "Are you really going to sacrifice your car's interior just to show me how pissed off you are at me?"

He paused, hating that she was right. His car interior was as pristine as he could keep it, dog hair notwithstanding. "Fine. Let's get it done."

It didn't take long. Erik lifted the assembled table into the bed of Hope's truck and found her securing Ruger in his car carrier. They faced each other for a few moments, and she opened her mouth, undoubtedly to give him another piece of her mind.

He spoke first. "When you get to the condo, just pull up to valet parking. I'll get the table from there."

"Okay."

They brushed by one another and the feel of her arm, bumping into his, sent a shock of lust through him. What the hell was the matter with him? She was snotty and rude and he didn't like her. Why the hell....

Erik shut his car door with more force than necessary and drove away without checking to see if she was following.

For about thirty seconds.

The headlights of her undersized truck stayed about a block behind him as he headed for downtown and when he was sure she was on the right road, he sped up.

He estimated his arrival at the condo would give him just enough time to park and get to the front of the building before the doorman lost his mind over Hope being in the loading zone. Opening the carrier, he hooked the leash to the dog's collar. "Come on. Let's get this over with."

From the interior stair entrance to the lobby, he spotted Hope waiting by her truck, tailgate folded down and protective blanket pulled off the table. In the bright lights of the entrance to the condo, he could see how well it had turned out, and remembered that he hadn't said thank you.

No way in hell would he say thank you. Not now.

She'd eased the table to the edge of the truck bed and after a word to the doorman, Erik handed him the dog's leash and walked through the glass doors. "Okay, got it from here."

"Do you need--"

"No, I got it. Thank you."

Shit. He'd thanked her. Damn his parents' insistence on good manners.

"Erik, wait." Her hand on his arm stopped him, not the force of it, the surprise that she'd touched him.

He waited. She opened her mouth again, closed it and shuffled her feet. He could have eased her discomfort, he knew he could have.

But he didn't.

He checked his watch and caught her wince from the corner of his eye.

"The shop is perfect. Okay?" She slammed the tailgate shut and pulled her keys out of her pocket.

"It was not perfect!" he burst out. "You had crap everywhere and stuff on the floor--"

"No, not before! Now. Now it's perfect. I could find everything I needed and it makes sense and it's...I don't know. Tidy."

"Uh huh." The fact that she was still shuffling her feet pleased him. He knew it was small of him, but it was true.

"And I'm sorry I freaked out, but you have to see my point of view, too, you know."

"And what point of view might that be?"

She made a low growling sound and balled her fists. He raised his eyebrows and waited.

"The point of view that you rearranged my stuff without asking me. Yes, it's nice."

"Nice?"

She barreled on. "And it works, which is really the important part."

"Oh, that's the important part."

"But you did it without asking me!" she burst out, clearly determined to finish explaining her stupid point of view.

"Trust me, Hope," he said coolly. "It'll never happen again."

"I'm not the only one to blame here! And you're not even trying to see my side!" She folded her arms across her chest.

He wanted to agree with her. He could have said it. But he'd started to think about what she'd said.

The truth was, if she—or anyone—had gone into his home without his permission and changed things, he would have been...angry.

Okay, homicidal.

And now, it was time to come clean.

"You may have a point."

Her jaw dropped. "Pardon me?"

He stared over her head. "While I don't think your reaction was necessary or appropriate, I can understand that it wasn't altogether...unexpected."

He caught a slow smile from his peripheral vision. Dammit, this was not the time to notice how her face lit up when she smiled.

"So, you're saying you were wrong."

"No, I'm not. I wasn't wrong." He gave her a quick glare as she giggled. "I just wasn't entirely right."

"This is as much as I can expect from you, isn't it?"

It was the giggle that did him in. What *was* it about this woman? A slow smile spread across his face as he met her eyes. "Yeah, pretty much."

She nodded. "I'll take it."

They studied each other for a moment. "We're good?" he asked.

"We're good."

"Good." With his free hand, he hooked the back of her neck and pulled her to him in a steamy, ravenous kiss that made her gasp into his mouth and clutch at his shoulders.

"Dammit." She rested her head on his chest and trembled a little, he noted with something like glee. "How do you do that?"

He chuckled. "We could've been doing that—and more —this entire evening."

"I know. If only you hadn't been such a jerk." She peeked up at him from her resting place on his chest.

"You were a jerk first."

She laughed.

"All right." He gave her a one armed hug and released her, stepping back. "I better get Ruger before he drives my doorman nuts."

"Okay."

He kissed her again. "Bye."

"Mmmphf. Bye."

He walked away, barely resisting the urge to whistle.

Chapter Fourteen

"I don't know when I'm going to see him again, Miriam." Cradling the phone against her shoulder, Hope plucked some hand-washables hanging on the drying rack. "He didn't even say if he wanted to see me again."

Her sister-in-law sighed heavily. "And you didn't...guide him?"

"What am I, a Seeing Eye dog?" Hope demanded. "If he wanted to see me again, he'd have said so."

A small silence grew on the other side of the phone line as Hope carried her dry lingerie to her bedroom. Her sad, work-in-progress bedroom. The next day off, she promised herself, she would finish the trim around the windows.

Instead of chasing after some guy's stupid puppy.

Opening the top drawer of her dresser – another work-in-progress discovered at a flea market – she realized Miriam still hadn't spoken. "Mir? You still there?"

"I'm still here," came the slow reply. "I am trying to understand where I have gone wrong with you."

"What do you mean, gone wrong?"

"Do you really think the man even knows what he wants?" As usual, Miriam's accent thickened when she got upset. "That he can finds his ways in dark with no help?"

"Find his way. And in the dark." Hope tossed the mixed pile of panties, camisoles and bras she still held onto her bed. "This guy doesn't need my 'help.' He's been around the block. Hell, he probably built some of the block."

"This means nothing!"

"Like hell, it means nothing!" Giving up the pretense of tidiness, she dropped the pile of lingerie on the dresser and walked into the kitchen. Her to-do list was already as long as her arm and sat there, mocking her, next to an empty coffee cup. She scanned through the items, trying to decide what she could get done on a Monday evening. Caitlyn was opening the next morning, which gave her a little more time for some of the more involved projects, but it wasn't like she was going to be able to do anything really big. The patter of rain reminded her it certainly wasn't going to be the arbor she wanted to construct for the front yard.

Or the demolition of the upstairs bath. She'd have to leave the windows open in order to toss the garbage produced into an open dumpster. No demo in the rain. Dammit.

She really loved demo.

"Look, Miriam, this guy is hot and handsome and every girl's dream. That alone should be a clue."

"A clue for what?"

The doorbell chimed. "Hang on."

"Why do I always have to hang on?" Miriam asked plaintively. "You never have to hang on."

"Are you kidding?" She walked to the front of the house, scooping up a scatter of clothing on her way, reminding herself that she had a laundry hamper for a reason. "How many times have I had to wait because someone brought a frog into the house?"

"Twice."

"Twice?" She opened the door and froze.

"All right, three times, but really, you only have yourself..."

Her sister-in-law's voice faded in her ear as Hope faced Erik as he stood inside her screen door, collar raised. "What are you doing here?"

Wind picked up the thin rain and threw it at the open door. She shivered and grabbed his coat. "Get in here! Miriam, I have to go."

"What? Wait! I--"

Whatever her sister-in-law was about to say was lost to the kiss he pressed to her mouth. Without lifting his head away from her, he pressed the end button on the phone and placed it on the small table just inside the doorway. "That's what I'm doing here."

"I see." She glanced down at the carrier in his hand. "Is Ruger in there?"

"Uh huh." He leaned again and trailed a line of kisses up the side of her neck, ending it with a nip on her earlobe.

She gasped. "He's...he's being very quiet."

"Bully stick."

"Right." Stepping back from his dangerous mouth, she tried to rally her thoughts into coherent order. They resisted. "What are you really doing here?"

"Brought you a present." His grin was a slash of brilliant white across his wind-reddened face. He dangled a small pink gift bag from his forefinger.

"A present? What for?" Ridiculously pleased, she accepted the bag. Strangely, the black lacy bow that held the bag closed looked familiar. "What is it?"

"Well, it's not really a present."

She looked doubtfully at the festive wrapping. "It looks like a present."

He nudged her back into the living room and set Ruger's carrier on the floor. "Yeah, but that was for my own benefit. I had to tell the lady at the shop it was a present, so she wouldn't give me the fish eye."

The little pink bag looked less appealing now. "Why would she give you the fish eye? And what is the fish eye?"

"You know..." He turned his head to the side and gave her an exaggerated – and comical – look of suspicion, stretching his mouth and bulging his eyes for effect.

"This is not a good look for you."

He laughed as he stripped off his coat and slung the green Gore-Tex over the coat tree. "It's not a good look for anyone."

She shrugged and grinned. "Yeah, but you look almost unattractive. That's actually kind of great."

He stopped laughing. "It's great that I'm unattractive?

"Almost unattractive. There's a difference." With a wave, she indicated the couch and sat opposite in her wing chair, gift bag in hand.

"How is it different?" he asked, now scowling and looking like a displeased Nordic deity.

"Well, duh. Unattractive has no attractiveness at all. Almost unattractive is still attractive, just a little hint that unattractiveness might be possible." She toyed with the bow, wondering if she could open her present yet.

"And this is great?"

"It's totally great. So can I open this now?"

He snapped his fingers and gave her a triumphant look. "This is one of those Mars-Venus things, isn't it?"

She held up the bag, bemused. "No, it's a present. Remember? You gave it to me?"

"No, I mean...you know what, never mind."

"Okay," she said, ready to move onto important things. "So, present time?"

"It's not really a present. It's a replacement."

This man, she thought, couldn't confuse her more if he tried. Maybe she should explain that. "Huh?"

"It's a replacement for something Ruger chewed up."

"Oh! Okay, great." Smiling widely, she pulled at the black lacy bow tied in the ribbon that threaded the top of the bag and held it shut, running through the possibilities. It could be a hammer or the set of wooden barbecue skewers she stored in one of the lower drawers of the kitchen or--

Out of the opened gift bag, a purple vibrator fell into her hand. "Oh. My. God."

And looked up to find Erik smiling at her. "I think it's the same kind," he said.

"Oh, my God."

"And I know – Daniel told me – that he chewed some of the other stuff you had with it. I didn't know what you had, exactly, so...." He pulled another bag out of his pocket and dumped the contents onto the coffee table.

"Oh, my God!"

"Yeah, I got a little bit of everything." He studied the variety of lotions and lubes in bright packaging with a small frown. "But if I missed something special, you just tell me. This stuff looks great." He held up a small jar of honey dust.

"OH MY GOD!!"

The horror racing through her body and warred with the humiliation that danced across her burning face finally seemed to sink in for him. "What? What? It's the wrong kind? I thought it looked pretty similar." He took the cucumber shaped sex toy away from her and turned it over, examining it.

"No, it's exactly what I remember." She covered her face with her hands, tucking her chin into her chest.

"I know it took a while to get it back to you, but with the business trip and bathroom repairs, I forgot about it completely." He paused. "Hope? You okay?"

"No. Not really."

"What's wrong?"

She uncovered her face to stare at him in complete disbelief. "Other than I want to die of humiliation? Oh, gosh. Nothing much."

"I don't get it."

"Erik, I would never use one of these...things!" She flapped her hand at the vibrator and covered her face again. "And now you think I'm some kind of sicko who would."

"Okay. I don't know if you picked up on this yet, but I'm a guy."

She uncovered her face again and looked at him blankly before spreading her hands wide. "I know you're a guy. What does that have to do with anything?"

He'd picked up one of the bottles of flavored lotion and was taste-testing it. "I think this is mango. Not bad."

"Erik!"

"What? Oh, yeah. The guy thing."

"Yes."

He shrugged and tried another lotion. "Guys don't look at a woman with a vibrator and think 'sicko.' They think, 'wow, I hope I get to watch.'" He made a face and recapped the lotion. "Okay, this one is disgusting."

"Well, I would never use one of those."

"Then why did you have it?"

"Miriam had just given it to me for a birthday present. I wouldn't even know how to use it."

"Really?" A slow and wicked grin crossed his face. "I can help with that." He stood and scooped the vibrator and all the new accessories back into the pink bag, then held his hand out to her. "Let's go."

"Go where?"

The deep pink flush suffusing her face delighted him and he found himself grinning at her as she stared suspiciously at his outstretched hand.

"Your bedroom."

"What?!"

"Shhh," he cautioned, snagging her flailing hand and tugging her to her feet. "You'll wake the puppy."

They turned in unison to peer into Ruger's carrier. Sure enough, he'd passed out with his chin resting on top of the remains of his bully stick. "Do you think that's comfortable?"

"Probably not." Erik moved behind her and slid his arms around her waist. "But nobody's going to get that thing away from him without waking him up," he murmured into her ear, felt her shiver.

"I don't think...."

"Good." He nipped her earlobe. "Don't think."

"I have to," she said crossly.

"Really? Okay." He shifted to the other earlobe and nibbled, working his way down her neck. "Think of it as a learning experience."

She giggled and he turned her a bit. She was still flushed but humor had started to replace mortification on her face. Struggling to look sincere, he fought an answering smile. "And we all know how important continuing education is."

She laughed outright.

"Here." He stuffed the vibrator and a few of the bottles of lotion into her hands, ignoring her involuntary protest. "Hang on to these."

Without any further warning, he scooped her up and over his shoulder and headed down the hallway. He ignored her shrieks and laughter as he opened first one door then another, searching for her bedroom.

He had a vague impression of caramel colored walls and unfinished edges, of a closet without its doors, of stacks of thin pieces of wood against the wall.

And one enormous bed.

It was the kind of bed he'd seen in museums, heavy, dark wood, with actual bed curtains. It probably weighed a million pounds and was older than the hills. It looked like something out of the pages of history.

He felt his grin spreading wider. They were going to make history in that bed tonight.

He dropped Hope in the center of the mattress and climbed over to her. Her shrieks had stopped but she was still protesting. At least, he thought what she was doing was protesting; she was mostly incoherent with giggles. He noticed she was still clutching the pink gift bag like a life preserver.

After taking the bag and tossing it aside, he braced his hands on either side of her and studied. Cheeks, bright pink from embarrassment and humor, eyes growing darker with passion, lips flushed and full. She looked, he thought, like dessert. Framed by the fluffy white folds of her comforter, like dessert on a plate of whipped cream.

And he was hungry.

"Hope."

"What?"

Grinning again, he shook his head. "Nothing." His eyes locked onto hers and he lowered his head to kiss her beautiful mouth, waiting for her eyes to close, keeping his open when they didn't. It wasn't a deep kiss or a passionate one, or the kind that made a man wonder where he left off and she began, but for some reason, he felt the same way he'd felt in his condo when she opened herself to him. The same crazy, hard as a rock, no blood left above the shoulders feeling. And this time, she was even sober.

Bonus.

He deepened the kiss, easing his tongue past her lips and her eyes finally closed as she moaned and tipped her head back into the bed, shivering as he worked his way down to the collar of her t-shirt. She hadn't tucked it into her jeans, so slipping his hands under the soft cloth and onto her waist was as easy as pulling the shirt over her head. Her bra, a deep autumn gold satin with paler lace edging, cupped her breasts like hands. He pulled back.

"What?" Hope blinked as if waking up. "What's wrong?"

He chuckled and with some effort, tore his gaze away from the soft cream of her skin wrapped in gold, like fancy candy. "Absolutely nothing. In fact...."

She shrieked again as he reared up and stripped off her jeans in one smooth movement, yanking off the thick socks next. Her matching gold panties shimmered in the soft light of the dying day, coming in her bedroom window. Tracing the lace edging to the satin that tucked between her thighs, he growled, low in his throat. "Do you always wear matching underwear?"

She gasped and nodded as he rubbed the backs of his fingers over the silky, damp fabric. "Erik."

"Hmm?" He slid a finger under the elastic of her panty, delighting in the way she twisted and gasped again, lifting up to his hand.

"Come here." She reached out her hand to him and he took it, turning it to press a kiss to her palm, then pressed it down to the bed.

"Not yet." He chuckled as she reached for him again and took both her hands in his and lifted them over her head. He kissed the corner of her mouth, her cheek and leaned to whisper in her ear, "Stay here, stay like this. Okay?"

She whimpered but held still, her heavy-lidded eyes meeting his. She moved a bit under him but stilled. He smiled at her, watching the flush in her cheeks deepen before he turned his attention back to her body. The color in her face had blushed its way to her neck and chest and even the creamy skin of her breasts looked a delicate peach color. Without moving the fabric of her bra, he traced his tongue over the curve of her breast and closed his lips over the nipple that spiked up through the deep gold cloth. Working his way over to the other breast, he reached for the goody bag she'd let fall from her hands.

The container he wanted was easy enough to find, even without looking. It was a small, curved porcelain jar that nestled into his hand the way her breast did, as if it had been made for him. Releasing her for a moment, he sat up and back on his heels, straddling her. The cap popped off with a small sound, revealing a brush attached to the interior of the lid. She opened her eyes and looked at him as he tapped it against the jar.

"What's that?" Her words were ever-so-slightly slurred.

Before he answered, he stroked the kitten-soft brush down the centerline of her body, laying gold shimmer over the peaches and cream of her cleavage. "Honey dust."

Laughter escaped her as he stroked the brush down her belly and tickled her thighs where she pressed them together. "Stop stop stop! That tickles like crazy!"

"Well, yeah, but..." He traced his tongue over the path of powdered honey he'd just laid down her body. "It tastes really good. Almost as good as you do."

Setting aside the capped jar, he slid both hands under her back and lifted her to his mouth, licking and tasting as he unhooked her bra and lifted it off of her. The deepened peach of her nipples quivered and after a quick stroke from him, gleamed with the residue of honey dust on his fingers and mouth. "Lift your hips."

She did, without pause of hesitation, and her willingness sent another bolt through him, as electric as the feel of her flesh and the taste of her skin. Nipping at the curve of her belly again, he eased her panties off and rested his palms on her thighs, edging them apart, opening a space for him to lie. The scent of the honey on her skin mixed with the rush of arousal he felt as he pulled her closer.

"You have on too many clothes."

The chuckle he gave sounded rusty, even to him. "It's keeping me under control here."

Honest humor and wickedness lit her eyes. "Who wants you under control? Erik." Her voice deepened to throaty. "Don't you want me, too?"

It took four and a half seconds, he estimated, to undress, but another thirty to stop himself from pouncing on her again. Dumping out the rest of the contents of the gift bag bought him that time. A quick check confirmed that the batteries worked and he did a test of the vibrator's range of speed and motion. Hope's muffled groan drew his attention back to her.

She'd grabbed a pillow and pressed it over her own face. "You cannot be serious." Even through the pillow, her dismay was palpable.

Without a word, he laid the tip of the vibrator against her thigh, disappointed that her legs were pressed together again, but undeterred. The lowest speed barely registered as movement and she peeked down at herself from under the dubious protection of the pillow. "Oh. Well, that's kind of nice."

"Mmm hmm."

She wriggled a little as he traced a pattern onto her other leg. "Like a little massage."

"That's it." He felt her relax into the buzzing of the toy and took advantage, easing her legs apart. When she would have tensed again, he trailed the vibrator down to her knee. She laughed then, a quiet chuckle that called him down to her. Careful not to startle her, he leaned on his elbow and tugged away the pillow still covering most of her face.

She was flushed and a little breathless, and his leaning forward to kiss her dragged the toy in his hand further up her inner thigh. He ignored the halfhearted protest she murmured into his mouth and stroked her tongue with his as he rubbed the back of his hand against her wetness, as if by accident, as if his only intent was to trail the gently vibrating sex toy against the soft skin of her inner thighs. Moving down her neck to her breasts with kisses and tastes allowed him more access to her and she let her legs fall farther apart, let his press more firmly against her labia, wet and swollen, let him bring the vibrator closer and closer. When he set his teeth gently to her nipple, she cried out and he flipped the toy over in his hand, guiding it to enter her vagina and rest on her clitoris.

He let her cry out and clutch at him, but controlled the entry of the toy, keeping it pressed to her without penetrating past its tip. Her cries grew more frantic and her hands more insistent, but he held her there until she crested and came.

There was only the gentle hum of the vibrator and her gasps for breath for a moment, until he switched off the toy and set it down, and stretched out next to her. It took a couple of soft nudges to turn her away from him so he could cuddle her for a moment, like spoons in a drawer. "You okay?"

"Uh huh."

"Sleepy?"

"Uh huh."

"Mmm." Letting her drift for a moment, he hooked his hand under her thigh and pulled her leg forward a bit, bent at the knee, then mirrored the position with his own leg. Without any more warning than that, he thrust into her from behind, returning the vibrator to her clitoris, clicking it up to middle speed with his thumb.

Her body bowed up, all the tension that had been released returning with a vengeance. "Oh, my God! Erik!"

He held her in place with the vibrator, pumping his hips into her, his mouth at her neck and her ear. When she came again, she came screaming. The rhythmic pulses of her orgasm pulled him to the edge; he gritted his teeth and tossed aside the toy, wrapping his arms around her and holding her tightly until she quieted again.

When she turned her face to his, lifted it for his kiss, he felt the threads of his tattered self-control slipping through his fingers. "Hope, I need--" He cut off his own words, clenching his jaw as she shifted and in doing so, pulled him to her and into her, more tightly than he would have imagined possible.

Then she smiled. Sweaty and flushed, her eyes liquid with the satisfaction he'd given her, she said, "You can have it."

"Have what?"

"Whatever you need."

And with that, his control broke. He rolled the rest of the way onto her stomach, canting her rear end up with one arm around her hips, the other wrapped around her shoulders and started thrusting again. "I need this! Can I have this? Can I have you, like this?" He thrust harder, nearly mindless as she grabbed his arm with both hands.

"Yes! Yes! Erik!"

They came together the last time and when he emptied into her, he felt like she'd wrung him out and flattened him, that there was nothing left inside of him, not breath, not air, not sound. And when he collected himself enough to turn to look at her, she'd already fallen asleep, cuddled in his arms, still holding onto his wrist. He closed his eyes and tumbled after her.

Chapter Fifteen

The scent of coffee woke her, better than an alarm clock. Rolling from bed, Hope realized that she was naked and froze mid-roll. What the--

Oh, that's right, she thought. Wild monkey sex with Erik. Last night. In my bed. And again this morning. Twice. Twice!

Feeling less anti-morning than usual, she pulled the robe from her open closet and made a mental note to refinish the door on her next full day off. Shuffling into her slippers, she scuffed down the hall to find the coffee Erik'd obviously been kind enough to make before heading off to work.

What a man.

Every woman should have this kind of thing, she decided. A spectacular lover in the body of god. So what if it was temporary? He was amazing and she was having a blast.

She was humming a happy little tune when she danced into her kitchen and stopped dead at the doorway. Erik stood at her sink, washing something.

"Hi."

He glanced over his shoulder and smiled at her. "Good morning. Thought I heard movement in there."

Relieved he hadn't actually caught her dancing, she sidled up to him. "Whatcha doing? And what are you still doing here? Aren't you late for work?"

He kissed her lightly and bumped her nose with his. "Meeting got canceled. And I'm washing some grapes. Hungry?"

"Yeah, I am." She turned to the coffee maker and saw that he'd set one of her cups next to it. "I slept a lot later than I planned."

"Weird. Can't imagine why." He chuckled as she batted at him. He'd woken her twice in the night and made love to her as if they hadn't been tearing up the sheets all evening, pausing only to order pizza and fall on it like savages. "You don't have to work today, right?"

Too relaxed to spar with him, she sipped her coffee. "No, Caitlyn's watching the store. Did I have grapes? Or did you go grocery shopping this morning?"

"Neither." He carried the bowl to her kitchen table and added it to the spread. Coffee cake and a quiche had already been sliced and plates were stacked neatly to the side.

"Then where did all of this...oh, no."

Like the countdown of a timer strapped to dynamite, she turned to face...

...Her mother.

"Well, it's about time you decided to join the land of the living, young lady."

"Mom. Hi." Hope straightened the lapels of her robe in what she hoped was a casual gesture and sipped her coffee to avoid those eyes. Not to mention, that smile.

Oh, perfect. The *smile.*

Her mother clucked her tongue. "You still have that robe, Hope? It's as old as the hills, sweetheart, and twice as ratty. Here, Erik. Wash these, too, dear."

Erik accepted the strawberries and started rinsing. "What do you want me to put them in?"

Before her mother could answer, a thump sounded at the back door, followed by giggles. Miriam and the children burst through the door, hauled inside by Ruger.

"Doggie pee! Doggie pee!" shrieked Lene, bouncing on her tiny tennis shoes while her brothers chattered at Erik about the puppy's outdoor antics. Miriam leaned over to press a kiss to Hope's cheek.

"Good morning!" Mischief sparkled off of her, nearly blinding Hope, contrasting with the demure dusty pink silk and creamy beige lace of her chemise-style dress. Typical mom-wear, Hope supposed. In Miriam's world.

"Wow, what a surprise to see you all." She sent Miriam a speaking glance. "Hey, guys! No school today?"

"Teachers Inservice day." Miriam blithely accepted the freshly-washed fruit from Erik and added it to the small feast on the table. "We decided to surprise you since we knew you had the day off." She sat and crossed her mile-long legs, wiggling her eyebrows as she took in Hope's bare feet and robe.

"Great!" Hope edged toward the doorway. "I'll get dress —I mean changed and be right back."

"Yes, sweetheart," her mother agreed. "That might be best."

Erik looked over her mother's head and winked. "Who wants juice?"

Over the cacophony of replies, Miriam spoke firmly. "We all need to wash our hands first. Yes, yes, we do. And then we'll all sit down...."

Hope escaped down the hallway and into her bedroom, yanking on clean underwear and the jeans that had been tossed aside the previous evening. Her bra and sweatshirt took only moments more and she was tugging on fresh socks as she hopped back out into the hallway. She skidded back to the kitchen in time to overhear her mother's delighted tones.

"Oh, Erik! That sounds wonderful. Where will it be?"

"Columbia Towers."

"Where will what be?" She sat in the chair next to Erik that had miraculously stayed empty and he topped off her coffee mug.

"Work party. It's just networking, but a good excuse to meet someplace and drink." He flashed his killer grin at her. "Seven o'clock. Can you be ready at six-thirty?"

"Are you kidding?"

"No." He looked at her quizzically. "Why would I be kidding?"

"It—I—you..." She turned to Miriam for help.

Her sister-in-law smiled at Erik. "It's a little last-minute, darling. Is it a dressy affair?"

"I guess." Erik took a bite of the generous slice of quiche Hope's mother had handed him. "Wow, Mrs. Lindstrom, this is really good."

She preened a bit. "Thank you, dear. And please call me Rebecca. You did the last time you were here."

Hope nudged Miriam with her elbow while reaching for the bowl of strawberries. "Help me!" she hissed.

"Yes, ah. Dressy party, you say?" Miriam flashed her own killer smile. "All the men in suits?"

"Tuxes." He savored a bite of the coffee cake. "I picked mine up from the cleaners last night. Mmmmm, good."

Hope felt herself doing a fair impression of a beached codfish but caught Miriam's slight head shake. "Isn't it? I get them from a little bakery in Ballard. Tuxes and cocktail dresses, then, is it?"

"Yes, and--"

"And networking for your company."

He winced a little. "Yeah, that part won't be--"

"And you think Hope should go?"

Hope looked back and forth between Erik and her sister-in-law, trying to keep up with the verbal tennis match. Was Miriam actually helping her and this point?

"Well, yeah." He looked surprised. "Of course she should go. All the wives and girlfriends go."

"Girlfriends?" ask Miriam, a smile dawning.

"Wives and girlfriends," breathed Hope's mother, her hands clasped to her chest, her eyes sparkling.

She sputtered but no one seemed to notice. Erik just kept on talking. "Yeah, it's not the most exciting night for them, but we can always go out for a good meal before."

With a flip of her hair, Miriam smiled and elbowed her mother-in-law. "We know the trade-off, don't we?"

"Oh, yes, we do." The older woman chuckled. "Just keep in mind, dear, we tend to add to the honey-do lists after something like this."

"Oh, hey! It's not going to be that boring." He covered the hand Hope had fisted on the table with his own. "You might really like some of the people who're there. You know, you might know a few of them, too. I bet a lot of them come to Home Again."

"But I don't--"

"Have anything to wear?" Miriam interrupted smoothly. "Don't worry, I'm on it. Don't you worry, either, Erik. Fancy cocktail, I know."

He grinned at the woman formerly known as Hope's best friend. "I would never question that. Hey, I've got to run. See me out?" He squeezed her clenched fist gently.

She held herself in check as she shoved her feet into tennis shoes and waited until they were outside, on the front porch, the cozy kitchen a house and a closed door away. "What the hell are you thinking?"

"Babe." He braced his hands on either side of her on the porch railing and leaned down, resting his forehead to hers. "It's not going to be that bad."

"It's already that bad!" she hissed. "You basically implied that we—we--"

"What?" He drew back, nonplussed.

"You said girlfriends! And oh my God, wives!! You know they're going to think--" She waved her hands madly.

"That we're together?"

"Yes! And to my mother!"

"We are together."

Her mouth flapped, she could feel it flapping like laundry on the clothesline. "And you just...what? Decided this? Unilaterally?"

He straightened up and looked thoughtful for a moment, then brightened. "Yeah."

"You can't--"

"Oh, yeah. I can." Now the smile turned cocky and sly. "What are you going to do about it?"

She bristled. "Um, okay. Here's an idea, *boyfriend*. How about I break up with you? Huh? How about that?"

She could do cocky, too. Dammit.

He laughed. Actually laughed. "Yeah, that's a good one."

Folding her arms across her chest, she smirked. "Uh huh, I thought so."

"Too bad you can't do that."

Now he lost her. "What?"

"It's too soon." He mirrored her pose and grinned down at her. "After all, I'm such a nice boy, and I love your mother's cooking. So good with the kids, too. If you tell your mother now...."

She groaned.

"Well, I figure Rebecca will make your life hell for, what? A month? Six weeks?"

"Six months to a year. Conservatively. Unless I bring home someone they like better...." she finished glumly and tipped her head back to look at him. Every glorious, ridiculously handsome, absurdly successful inch of him. "I am so screwed. You jerk."

He cupped her cheeks in his hands and kissed her, hot enough to fry a few key circuits, tender enough to make her wish...wish for what wasn't.

It couldn't be.

"You're a jerk," she whispered, looking into those gorgeous ice blue eyes.

"You were a jerk, first." He gave her hair a friendly tug and jogged to his car. A grin and a wink, and he was gone.

"Jerk."

She stood on the porch, feeling the stupid smile tickling her lips until the door opened behind. "What are you doing out there?" Miriam demanded. "Hurry up! We don't have much time!"

"Huh?" She watched her sister-in-law dart back inside, heard the muffled chatter between the women. When

Miriam returned, she had pulled on her trendy cream-colored pea coat. "Cute coat, sis."

"Thanks." Flipping her golden mane out of the collar, Miriam studied Hope, anxiety creasing her perfect brow. "We need to hurry, darling. I don't know if he gave us enough time, I really don't. And oh! You need your coat."

She whirled on her strappy heels and reached for the front door, only to be met by Rebecca, holding Hope's hoodie and new purse, Lene on her hip.

"Mama shop! Mama go shop!" chirped the toddler.

Miriam beamed at her daughter and made nonsense noises while kissing her small face.

"Mirrie, sweetheart. You have to hurry." Rebecca looked at her daughter with dismay. "Oh, heavens. You have less than nine hours."

"I know, darling." Miriam included her daughter and mother-in-law in a comforting hug. "But you know what I can make happen in a short amount of time."

"But she needs so much work!"

"Hey!" Hope said indignantly.

"And Mirrie, I know I should have worked harder on her." Rebecca was almost in tears. "If only I'd pushed her more--"

"Excuse me!" Hope propped her hands on her hips. "I'm standing right here!"

"Of course you are, darling. We see you." Love and sympathy tinged Miriam's soft words. "We just want to help you."

"Help me do what?" She drew back as her mother and best friend exchanged silent communication.

"Sweetheart..." her mother began. "It's not that we don't love you--"

"And you know you're beautiful, darling. Beautiful," Miriam interjected.

"Oh, yes. So lovely. And you have a lovely personality," continued Rebecca.

"So much more important," Miriam agreed, nodding. Lene watched her mother and grandmother and started nodding, too.

"But you will be out tonight."

"The Columbia Towers events are always very elegant." Miriam gestured to Hope's tired jeans and sweatshirt. "You cannot wear this, darling."

"I wasn't going to wear this!" Hope rolled her eyes and snatched her coat and purse away from them. "I have a dress."

"What dress?" Rebecca demanded.

"That ghastly floral thing that goes to your ankles?" added Miriam. "The one that makes you look like you're a drunken librarian?"

"Nooo," Hope ground out. "I'll wear my black dress."

The other women groaned.

"What? There's nothing wrong with it."

Miriam clutched her head as if to keep it from flying off. "No, nothing wrong with it. At all." She dropped her hands. "For a *funeral*."

"A funeral for someone you don't like," Rebecca agreed. "Please don't wear it to mine."

"Oh, darling," Miriam cooed at her mother-in-law. "You will never die. We won't let you."

"And nobody else would take you," Hope muttered.

"What was--"

Miriam spoke quickly. "The black dress makes you look lumpy. You cannot look lumpy tonight."

Hope groaned.

Miriam plowed on, undeterred by Hope's lack of enthusiasm. "And Lars is going to fit us in at two, so we must be done before then."

"Lars?" Real alarm shivered down Hope's spine. "No. No. I'm not going to see Lars."

"Yes, you are," retorted her mother.

"Yes, you are." Miriam turned to her daughter again and kissed her goodbye. "Be good now."

"I am good!" protested Hope. "Oh, you meant—see, I'm all upset now. Why don't you two just go on home and I'll--"

"NO!" Rebecca and Miriam half-shouted.

"You're coming with me." Miriam grabbed her hand and hustled to Hope's truck. "We're finding you a dress. And some decent shoes."

"I have plenty of shoes."

Miriam stopped at the door of the vehicle, turned slowly and spoke distinctly. "Do not blaspheme in my presence."

Hope pulled her keys out of her purse and unlocked the truck. "Sorry."

"I swear, I wonder sometimes if you're really a girl."

She snorted at Miriam's prim tone. "I'm a woman who has what she needs for her own life."

"Well, Erik's in your life now." Flipping down the visor, Miriam gave her makeup a quick check. "And this is something you need and you don't have."

Hope groaned again. "You can't fight City Hall, I guess."

"We're not going to City Hall, darling. Nordstroms. And quickly." Folding up the mirrored visor, she gave Hope a blinding smile. "I've been waiting for this for years."

Chapter Sixteen

"Wow."

Erik stepped back from Hope's front door to get the whole picture of her. The copper colored dress, what there was of it, made her skin glow. All of it. He frowned.

"What?" she asked.

He dragged his eyes up from examining the length of her legs and caught her worried expression. "It's not right, is it?" She fussed with her hair and tugged at the hem of her dress.

"Not right?" he asked blankly.

"For the party. I told Miriam I should wear my black dress." She glanced at the slim gold bracelet on her wrist and he realized it was a watch.

"You don't have to change. You look great. You look..." He searched for something to say that had nothing to do with dragging her into her bedroom and ripping off what little she was wearing. Keeping his eyes above her neck, he caught another change. "You look really blonde."

"Highlights."

"Okay, tell me the highlights."

"No. Erik." She batted lightly at his arm. "They're highlights. In my hair. Miriam and Lars made me."

"They look great. You look great. Who's Lars?"

She clicked back inside to pick up a tiny gold purse and a dark chocolate colored wrap. "He's Miriam's stylist. He's scary."

"Huh. Okay. Is he single?"

"Who, Lars?" She paused to think about it and shrugged. "No, I don't think so. No, he mentioned his boyfriend. Why?"

"No reason. Here." Clearing his throat, he took the shawl from her and draped it around her bare shoulders. "Is that going to be warm enough for you?"

"I think so. It's not like we're going to a baseball game. Do I look okay for this?" She ran her hand through the streaky cap of her hair.

"You look beautiful. I should have said that before. I was just distracted by some very sexy legs." He grinned at her and pretended to cower as she swatted at him again. "Hey, cut that out. C'mere."

"What? No, Erik, we have to--"

He yanked her to him and wrapped his arms around her, trapping her with her shawl. As she laughed and struggled, for form's sake, he leaned in. "If I kiss you, will I get in trouble?"

"Why would you get in trouble?"

He trailed his lips over her cheek and down her neck, careful not to press too hard. "Your face is all done up. Will it mess with your shiny stuff if I kiss you?"

"Nope. Lars used something that's supposed to last all night, or the rest of my life. I'm going to need paint thinner to get it off." She flushed and lifted her face. "I'm not supposed to say stuff like that, am I? You better kiss me and stop me from talking."

An hour later, he could still feel the heat of that kiss on his lips. At least, he hoped it was the heat of her kiss. Having her lipstick smeared across his mouth might not project the image of rising young professional he was trying to cultivate.

Colleagues, acquaintances and even a few competitors greeted him as he led Hope across the stylish banquet room to the bar. He scanned the crowd quickly, one hand on her back, trying not to be distracted by the feel of her through thin copper silk. Now was not the time to pull her into the restroom and have his way with her.

Damn. Why did he have to think of that?

In a valiant—or maybe vain—effort to be the well-mannered individual his parents had raised, he asked Hope what she wanted to drink.

She looked around the room herself and pointed. "They have coffee on the table over there."

"Well, yeah, but don't you want a real drink?" He smoothed back the much-blonder strand of hair that still liked to cling to the side of her face.

"Not if I want to stay on top of these stilts."

They both looked down at the chocolate-colored stilettos she wore. He swallowed a laugh when he heard her mutter.

"What was that?"

"I said, barbaric devices of torture," she answered clearly.

A familiar voice spoke up behind him. "Yoriksson, you're not supposed to torture your dates."

Erik turned to face his boss and grinned. "Really, sir? I could have sworn that was the way to go."

Peter Fischer grinned back. He wore his tuxedo like a man well-versed in executive hobnobbing and moved with the remembered grace of college sports and weekly tennis. Silver-haired and tan in a way that didn't happen naturally in Seattle, he patted the hand resting on his arm, belonging to the scarlet-clad, needle-thin Botox victim beside him. "No, you wait until they're your wife, then you torture them."

"Oh, Petey!" the woman laughed. The warm sound of her humor made the immobility of her face oddly frightening. "How could you possibly be torturing me?"

"Have you met my bride, Erik?" The older man turned to his wife. "Angelface, this is the boy at I told you about. Erik Yoriksson. Erik, this is my wife, Lauren."

"It's a pleasure to meet you, Mrs. Fischer." Erik reached for Hope's hand, drawing her forward. "Let me introduce to my--"

"Oh, Erik. Call me Lauren!" Again, warm laughter emitted from the frozen face.

"Thank you, Lauren. This is--"

"And I do remember this name, Petey! Your 'rising star?'" Lauren Fischer planted her bony frame between the two men, placing a deceptively thin hand on the arm of each and tugged them closer. It wasn't until he leaned in to catch the joke Lauren murmured that he realized how smoothly Hope had been shut out of the conversation.

He stepped back and placed an arm around Hope's waist, ignoring the stiffness in her body that rivaled Lauren's face. "Mr. Fischer, I didn't get a chance to introduce you to my girlfriend."

"Oh, I--" Hope began.

"Well, hello!"

Erik saw Hope flinch as Fischer grasped her hand and shook it. He'd been on the receiving end of the older man's handshake a time of two and knew it wasn't for the weak.

"Of course! I remember your Brittany! For some crazy reason, I thought you were a redhead!" Peter chortled.

"Sir, this is Hope Lin--"

"But I know better than that! I know you ladies like to mix it up a little with your hair. My bride could tell you a thing or two about that, Brittany."

"Mr. Fischer." The urgency in his tone cut through. "This is Hope. Hope Lindstrom."

Peter laughed again and pressed the hand he still had clamped in his. "Oh, my dear. I apologize. Hope, this is my wife, Lauren."

Hope smiled at the pair and nodded at the other woman. "It's nice to meet you, Mrs. Fischer."

Erik couldn't tell if Lauren Fischer's return smile was really that chilly or just another aspect on her unchangeable features. He did catch, however, that she didn't entreat Hope to use her first name.

Peter Fischer took over the conversation again. "How did you two meet? Hope? It's Hope?"

"Yes, Hope Lindstrom."

"Of course, it is." He beamed at her and finally let go of her hand as his wife plucked at his arm.

"I think Petey's embarrassed! Don't be embarrassed, Petey." She fluttered her false eyelashes at him. "Isn't this the boy with all the girls? How could you possibly keep up with them all?"

Before Mr. Fischer could answer, Erik spoke. Quickly. "We actually met on the side of Highway 2, sir. Hope had car trouble and had to pull over."

"Oh." Fischer waggled his eyebrows. "The white knight. He gave you a lift?"

"No, he gave me a concussion."

Erik barely suppressed a shout of laughter. "I did not." The Fischers stared at him with a combination of doubt and horror. At least, Pete Fischer did. Lauren Fischer continued to look as if her face were pressed against glass.

"You did, too."

"You gave yourself the concussion. Remember?" He leaned down and touched her nose with his. "Or did slamming your own head against the undercarriage of your truck scramble your brain?"

Pete Fischer cleared his throat. "Well. We'll just leave you two to work this out. Won't we?" Tucking Lauren's hand under his arm again, he led her away.

"So nice to meet you both," Hope called after them, then waited until they were a safe distance before giggling.

"You little brat." He gave her sunny hair a tug.

She just stared after the Fischers, absently shaking her head. "Wow. Did you see that?"

"See what?" Erik feigned innocence until she bumped him with her hip, then laughed. "Her plastic surgery gone wrong or his oblivion?"

"Either. Both. Jeeze." She let him lead her to the buffet table and accepted the coffee he poured for her with murmured thanks. Nibbling on her lip, she hummed a little as she tapped the side of the cup.

"What?" he asked.

"Huh?" She blinked and refocused on him. "What, what?"

"What are you worrying about? And stop chewing on your lip." He stole a quick kiss. "That's my job."

She batted at his chest, pushing him back an inch or two. "Stop it. People are staring."

"No, they aren't. What's making your brain spin?"

"My brain isn't spinning." She made a scoffing sound and tried her coffee again. "This isn't bad."

"Hope. What's going on?"

"It's just---look. Look around you." She waited until her did and leaned in a bit, nearly whispering. "How many people here have had...you know. 'Work' done."

He laughed out loud, taking another scan of the people closest to them. "A lot. Why?"

"Well, aside from what's her frozen face, most of them look really beautiful. Is this what we're all going to end up doing?" She stole another look around. "Shooting our faces full of stuff and making our boobs bigger and going blonde and wearing stupid shoes and clothes we can barely breathe in?"

He shrugged and nudged her toward the buffet line. "Sure. It's common. It's going to get more common. Why?"

She took the plate he handed her and moved to the long, food-laden table, looking at her coffee cup in the other hand. "My hands are full. How am I going to do this?"

He picked up a serving spoon and piled a small mountain of tiny red potatoes on her plate, then traded plates with her when she protested. "Give me that. Just tell me what you want. No potatoes?"

"A few. Not an acre's worth."

"There. Happy?"

"Yes." She nodded when he pointed to the salmon in a chafing dish. "Thank you."

"You're welcome." He added a few spears of grilled asparagus and drizzled some of the hollandaise sauce over them. "Why does plastic surgery freak you out?"

"Do you think it's getting so normal that pretty soon, we're all going to do it?"

"All?"

"Yeah, like...is my mom going to get implants? Will Miriam have to have her face lifted? No, thank you," she grimaced when he offered her some beet salad. "Am I going to be running off to the salon to have my roots done every other week?"

Ah.

"Good questions." He added a few rolls to their plates and escorted her to an empty table. "Are you?"

She contemplated her food for a moment before shaking her head. "I don't think so. It looks nice and all, but I just don't get it. All that time and effort and money." She toyed with her food, poking the salmon with her fork.

He grunted and ate a few bites. "This is pretty good. Did you try the chicken stuff?"

"No, I didn't. Erik, do you—never mind." She stabbed her potatoes with enough force to chime her fork against her plate.

"Hey. Look at me."

She lifted her head; all the fun that had brightened her eyes had drained away. Her lush mouth settled into something suspiciously like a pout.

"You look really nice. No, listen to me." He caught her chin as she turned away and pulled her close to him. "You look really, really nice. The hair and stuff on your face looks nice. But the way you look, when it's just you and me, is incredible."

A tiny smile tugged at her sulky lips and worked its way to her eyes. "Really?"

"Really."

"So if I never get my highlights done again--"

He spoke around a mouthful of food. "Don't care."

"Or get my face all done up--"

"Whatever."

"Or wear this outfit and these shoes again...?"

He paused. "No, I think I'd like you to wear those again."

Looking down at her dress, she smoothed a hand over the copper silk. "You want me to strap myself into this thing again? I can barely breathe as it is."

"No, just the shoes." He tipped his chair back a bit to study her crossed legs. "Just the shoes."

"You're insane." She nibbled on her roll before setting it down. "Are you sure, though? About what you said?"

"About the shoes? Oh, yeah. Maybe with the underwear you wore the night at my house. You could do that. I'd be fine with it." He chuckled as she rolled her eyes and shook her head.

"Fine. I'll stop obsessing."

"Good. Because we have to talk about something serious." He covered her hand with his and bit back a smile as panic widened her eyes. "Hope. I need to know...are you...."

"What?" she whispered.

He leaned in again. "Are you going to finish your salmon?"

Hope turned another corner in the maze around the banquet hall. Surely there had to be a ladies room somewhere in this beautiful building that didn't have forty-five perfect-looking women crowded into it. She walked as swiftly as her stilettos would allow until she reached the next corner.

Another dead end.

Considering the usefulness of a hand-held GPS unit, she turned around and started to retrace her steps. It was only one building, after all. There was only so lost she could get.

Fortunately, Hope ran into one of the white-jacketed servers before she could test her theory. Within moments, she was outside the door demurely marked "ladies" in gold script. She pushed open the dark wooden door that she coveted and entered a little slice of heaven.

The sitting lounge before the actual sink-and-stall area of the restroom seemed to call to her to do just that. The carpet was plush and soft, the chairs and chaises deeply upholstered in cushiony padding and fabric. She admired the modern lines of the room even as she recognized the style would never be something she'd be able to live with.

The cool, silvery sage green of the walls allowed the richer colors of the wood and fabric to reach out and invite her in.

With a sigh, she sank onto a modern version of a fainting couch and slipped her feet out of her shoes. No matter what Miriam said about the length of heel and sexiness of leg, there wasn't enough vanity in the world to make these bearable again. How did she do it every single day?

The voices drifted to her from the hallway; she was about to be invaded. Clutching her shoes, she darted to the corner where one high-backed chair faced another. A few tugs and she was all but invisible.

"Did you see the bimbo Clarence brought with him tonight?" the first woman snickered.

"So tacky. Couldn't he just get a sports car like the rest of the middle-aged men in the room?" another answered, well-practiced boredom in her well-modulated voice.

"Well, ever since his mail-order bride left him, he's been trying to prove something." A nasty delight colored the voice of the next woman, and the whole group giggled like a catty schoolgirl clique when a familiar voice responded.

"Oh, he's proving something, all right." Lauren Fischer sat down in the chair right behind Hope. The sweet, warm sound of her voice belied the meanness of her words. Hope could just imagine the strange frozen expression of the woman's face as she proceeded to annihilate a man's character with a voice like melted honey. She shrank further back into her chair.

The first woman was speaking again. "Well, he's absurd, but he's Clarence, for God's sake. Does anyone expect better of him?"

A chorus assured her that no one, in fact, did. "And who would want to have that man around, anyway? He's a disaster."

"I heard you were interested in that disaster for yourself, Tiffany."

Tiffany snapped back, "No, Aimee. A few dates doesn't mean 'interested.' It also doesn't mean 'sleeping with,' but that's not something you understand, is it?"

A brief pause stopped the room, then Aimee said, "Excuse me? You're one to--"

"Ladies." Lauren Fischer laughed with saccharine sweetness. "A joke's a joke, but let's not take it too far. And speaking of...I finally met Peter's new protege."

"And he's a joke?" asked Tiffany.

"No, he's a dream." Lauren sighed dramatically, with enough heat around the edges to raise Hope's hackles.

"Who is he?" the quieter woman spoke plaintively. "I never know who's who around here."

"His name is *Erik*." Lauren paused again. "Erik Something. I don't know. But he's divine and--"

"Oh!" The other woman squealed. "Erik Yoriksson! I know him! I met him!"

"When did you meet him, Dara?" Aimee's voice held a wealth of derision and doubt, but Dara seemed happily unaware of it.

"At the company picnic last summer. He was so charming, but very polite." Dara's voice grew positively smug. "I think it's because he knows who Tanner is."

"We all know who Tanner is," Tiffany interjected. "What I want to know is, who's this Erik?"

"Well, he's the guy who was mingling by the stage. Very tall," Dara began.

"And very blonde. And very..." Lauren trailed off. She must have done something suggestive because the women burst into bawdy laughter.

Hope gritted her teeth. She didn't know how much longer she could sit still and wait for these four women to leave. Trying the stretch and shift without being spotted was getting harder, and she wondered why she cared if they saw her or not.

"I think I did see him," said Aimee slowly. "Very buff, very hot? And some little mouse clutching at him the whole night?"

Mouse? Hope narrowed her eyes as if the glare she felt on her face would somehow travel around the blockading furniture and smack the vicious cat on the back of her head.

"That's the one. And the mouse?" Lauren's laugh grated down Hope's every nerve. "He introduced her as his *girlfriend* if you can believe it."

"Oh, please!"

"You're kidding."

"He could do so much better."

The chorus of chatter and criticism swirled into a blur of sound and mockery in Hope's ears. The vicious quartet continued to criticize her looks and body, to mock the clothes so lovingly selected by Miriam's fashionable eye.

"...Reaching for more than she deserves—or can handle!"

"I wonder if she's looking for a golden ticket..."

"Plain girls always have to work so hard, and you know they want to be the trophy."

She felt herself shrinking back, smaller and smaller until she no longer struggled to stay hidden in her chair. There were exclamations and rustling and then the quiet she'd searched for when the women exited the lounge for the bathroom.

Moving stiffly, as if she'd been curled up in that spot for days, she pushed her feet into her shoes and walked out the ladies' room door.

Getting back to the party took less time than she'd imagined it would, less time than she could have used. The rush of sound and swirls of color seemed unreal. People shoved past her.

A hand on her arm stopped her. Dulled to feeling, she turned and saw a familiar face peering down at her.

"Hope? Are you all right?"

Rory. It was Rory and for a moment the relief of seeing someone who was a pal, who liked her, who didn't judge her on her hair or her clothes or her unsuitability for Erik brought tears to her eyes.

"Hey, what's wrong?" Rory Evans rubbed a hand along her arm and frowned, obviously concerned. She hadn't realized how cold she felt until she felt the human contact.

"Nothing. Nothing at all." She blinked hard and then looked at his freckled face. Worry still creased his brow, making him look like a fretful four-year-old. Despite herself, she smiled.

"You sure? You look..." he paused. "A little tense."

"Wow, you are good. Very diplomatic." Pulling herself together, she tipped her head at the bar area. "Just for that, I'll let you buy me a drink."

"Lucky me." He studied her face for another second or two and must have been satisfied with what he saw. Slinging his arm around her shoulders, they walked toward the crowded end of the room. "You do know it's an open bar, right?"

"See? You just got luckier." As they waited in line, she scanned the crowd. Not a blonde Viking god in sight. Suppressing a sigh, she turned her focus back to the young man beside her, placing their order with the bartender. "What are you doing here?"

He laughed. "Cousin needed a date. This is a work thing for her and she just dumped the loser she'd been dating. See? Over there." He waved at a pretty brunette, whose quelling look could be spotted from across the room. "She owes me big now."

"Excellent. Leverage on family." Striving for normalcy, she smiled as the young man. "How are you? How's the dog? And hey, look at you."

"Bond. James Bond," he quipped, straightening the cuffs of his tux jacket. "About time you said something."

She gasped and laughed. "Hello! You didn't say a word about me! Or my hair!"

He looked at the top of her head as if he just discovered she had hair. "What about it?"

"Jesus." Hope accepted the white wine spritzer from the bartender with a smile and turned back to Rory. "Are you serious?"

"What?" He dropped a bill into the tip jar and led her away from the crowd. "Your hair? It's different?"

"You really are my little brother, aren't you? No wonder you don't meet girls." Chuckling for real now, she tapped her glass to his bottle. "Cheers."

"What's that supposed to mean?"

"It's a means of salutation used when people share a beverage."

"Funny." He glowered at her a little, looking as fierce as his big, gentle dog. "What did you mean about meeting girls?"

"I mean, if you don't pay attention to stuff like a change in hair color, the girls aren't going to want to play with you." She nodded to his dapper attire as she sipped her drink.

"No way." He shook his head and gestured with his beer bottle. "You're just saying that to scare me."

"Oh, come on, would I do that? Even I know this stuff, and I work in a home center."

He nodded and looked a little depressed. "That's true. Hey, aren't you required to be a guy for that job?"

"No." She hooked her hand in his arm and strolled toward the windows overlooking the city lights. "The penis is very rarely used as a management tool at Home Again. And no matter what anyone says, it's not a good substitute for the tape measure."

"That's good to know." He chuckled and drank more of his beer. "Back to the noticing-stuff thing. How much leeway do I have there?"

She thought about it for a moment. "Not a lot, no matter how hot and sexy you look."

"Really."

She pursed her lips and shook her head. "No. Not really. You look good enough, you can pretty much get away with murder."

They looked at each other and started to laugh. "Oh, man," he sighed. "I am screwed."

"Welcome to my world." She tapped her glass to his bottle again.

"Yeah, but I don't mean in the fun way." Rory smirked and waggled his eyebrows at her.

Before she could come back to that sly comment, a hand touched her shoulder. "There you are. I thought you left."

"Erik. Hi." She looked up in surprise as his hand slid up to her neck and he pressed a firm kiss to her mouth, scattering coherent thought. She shivered.

"Where'd you go?" he murmured. "Missed you."

"I went--" Hope realized Rory was still standing there. "Oh, I'm sorry. Rory, this is Erik Yoriksson."

"Her date." Erik smiled with a lot of teeth.

Not deigning to respond to that, she plowed on. "Erik, this is Rory Evans."

"Her doctor." Mischief gleamed in his wide green eyes as he gave Hope a mocking impression of an intimate gaze then laughed when she would have punched him in the shoulder, stopped only by a swift half embrace from Erik, locking her arm to her side. The young doctor nodded approvingly. "Thanks, man."

"Don't mention it."

Rory grinned again. "Actually, Hope, we've already met."

"You can let go of me now," she said to Erik then looked between the two of them. "How did you meet?"

"Ruger introduced us."

Erik coughed over a laugh and shook his head. "Yeah. We're still working on the jumping."

Rory laughed outright. "What happens at the dog park, stays at the dog park. It's their zone."

"Fair enough."

Hope watched the two men as they flanked her. Something was happening between there, but for the life of her, she couldn't figure out what.

"Well, I'm getting the high sign from my cousin. Good to see you again, Erik." Rory leaned forward and pecked Hope's cheek. "You still owe me dinner, remember."

"Whenever you're free from the E.R."

She watched Rory thread his way through the crowd before facing Erik.

"Where did you go?" he asked again.

"Ladies' lounge." Hope drank deeply from her wine glass, shoving away the memory of the women who'd bashed her.

"You okay?"

"Yeah." She set her empty glass on the tray of a passing waiter. "Can we go home now?"

"Absolutely."

Chapter Seventeen

Erik crashed into the wall of the racquetball court. "Nice shot," he managed as he pushed himself to his feet.

"Thanks."

He fielded the bottle Daniel tossed to him and gulped the icy water. Daniel swigged at his own bottle and examined the strings on his racquet.

"This damn thing better not be fraying on me," Daniel swore. "Look. Does that look like it's coming loose?"

Erik squinted at the edge of the racquet and shook his head. "Looks okay to me."

"Should be more than okay for what I paid for the piece of shit."

Erik snorted. "Get it restrung or send it back, if it's not working for you. But...." He bounced his own racquet off the heel of his hand.

Daniel paused, water bottle midway to his lips. "But what?"

Erik grinned, sly and quick. "It's always good to be able to blame your racquet."

"Ohhh..." Daniel shouted a laugh. "Blame, nothing. Me and the racquet are good enough to be kicking your ass today. What's the matter, young'un? You playing tired today?"

Erik's response was short and succinct. And despite the ribbing, he knew they both saw it. "Takes more than a late night to make me tired, old man."

"Late night, huh?" Daniel went back to examining his racquet. "Miriam said you had a thing you went to, last night."

Erik slid down the wall to sit on the floor and took another drink of water. "She did, huh?"

Daniel squatted on his haunches and fiddled with the strings again. "Yup. And with Hope. She said."

Oh, boy.

"That's right," he said evenly. "Problem?"

Daniel shrugged and set his racquet aside, then sat the rest of the way on the floor, holding his own water bottle and looping his arms around bent knees. With his long arms and legs, he looked like a gawky heron, crouching there. "No problem. Not really."

He waited. After another swallow of water, Daniel continued.

"It's just a little weird, you know? You and Hope."

Frowning, Erik set his bottle down. "What's weird about it? You don't think I'm good enough for her? I won't treat her right?"

"Shit. Please." Daniel grinned, then laughed. "No, it's just...she's this dorky little girl, still trying to do whatever the boys are doing."

"Dan, she's not a little girl anymore, dorky or otherwise."

His girlfriend's brother snorted and rolled his eyes. "She may be taller, but she's still the same dork. Not that I don't love her, and she's got some really good qualities, but...she's no supermodel."

"Not like Miriam."

"Ah, nobody's like Miriam, man." His grin all but split his face then faded. "But Hope's still my sister. I don't want to see her get hurt when you're done."

Erik stood and walked to his gym bag, tucking away his water bottle and racquet, breathing in through his nose and out his mouth. "You think I'm going to finish with her and toss her aside? Like trash?"

Some of the anger he'd thought he clamped down must have escaped because Daniel didn't answer right away.

"Is that what you think of me?" he asked the older man.

"Erik, come on. I'm not saying anything about you." Daniel walked over to him and he gritted his teeth to see laughter in other man's eyes. "It's just Hope. She's just not in your league. You know?"

"Not in my league." He stepped back and studied Daniel.

"No, and it's not her fault. It's not your fault. I'm just saying that everyone needs to be realistic about that."

"You mean..." he said slowly. "The way you were realistic when you married Miriam? Hell, when you had the nerve to ask Miriam out." A tap at the glass over the court had them both looking up; their reserved time was over. The next players were waiting none too patiently for them to exit.

Daniel grimaced and picked up his sports bag. "You know, most of the first few weeks with Miriam are still a blur."

Picking up his own duffle, Erik opened the door out of the court, holding it open for Daniel to follow. "A blur, huh?"

"Yeah. I know I was in a bar in Oslo. I know I was having a good time with my friends. And there she was." They walked down the corridor of the sports center and entered the locker room.

"And she just fell for you? She couldn't pass you up?"

Daniel laughed hard enough to make other men walking to the shower make a wide berth around them. "Yeah, right. I have no idea how I got so lucky."

Erik set his bag on the bench and pulled out street clothes. "The contradiction has completely escaped you, hasn't it?"

"What contradiction?" Daniel stripped off his sweaty t-shirt and grabbed a towel from the shelf on the wall. The club dues were fierce, but the amenities were good and reliable.

"You were totally out of Miriam's league and look where you two ended up."

Daniel paused and wrinkled his brow. "Yeah, but it's different for us."

"How?"

"It just is."

The same bone-deep stubborn look that he'd seen set Hope's face seemed to coat Daniel in concrete. "That's ridiculous."

"Ridiculous or not, which it's not, it doesn't change anything." Daniel opened a locker with a metallic clang and stuffed his gear inside. Slamming it shut, he faced Erik again. "It's not going to work with you two, and nobody expects it to. Just don't screw over my sister in the process."

"Hope? There you are!"

The headache that was performing intricate karate moves inside her skull executed a flying kick on her right eye. "Hi, Miriam. How are you?"

Her sister-in-law danced in front of her and set her enormous purse on the pallet of bagged manure just delivered. Even reading through the invoice twice hadn't given her a clue why this shipment had been doubled.

"How am I?" Miriam crowed. "How are you? More importantly, how is Erik?"

"I'm fine except for this shipment." She pulled out her walkie-talkie and spoke into it. "Caitlyn, are you there?"

A tinny voice screeched out of the small speaker. "I'm here, boss! What's up?"

The headache erupted into a full-fledged kung fu movie. "Cait, you don't have to yell."

"Sorry. Better?"

"Yes." She pressed her thumb and forefinger to the bridge of her nose. "Could you double check the order on chicken manure? We've got twice what we need here."

"Ew!" Miriam snatched her purse off the pile.

Ignoring her, Hope waited until Caitlyn confirmed the order that had been placed. "Oh, no. It looks like it was ordered twice."

She sighed. "Okay, add that to the ad information for the sale. We're going to have to move this stuff."

That settled, she hooked the walkie-talkie to her belt and turned back to Miriam, who was still cradling her handbag as if the manure might attack. If deference to the weather that had changed to its usual rainy mess, Miriam had pulled on a silver raincoat over a dangerously short, fire engine red dress. "You look nice, " she said, trying not to compare her own attire. Not even halfway through the day, and the khakis and chambray shirt already felt grubby.

She paused, letting Miriam's chatter float past her. When had she started comparing herself to her sister-in-law again? Cursing herself silently, she turned back into to what Miriam was saying.

"--And since you're so close to that little bistro, I made reservations for lunch, because they're so busy on the weekends."

"Miriam. Look around."

She did. "What?"

Hope waved her hand at the people milling around the gardening section of Home Again, the distant beeping of an electronic lift that moved the pallets of supplies, the rows upon rows of annuals and bedding plants. "This. All of this. This is my job, Miriam. I can't just go trotting off for lunch out on a Saturday."

The other woman pouted and Hope cringed as two men crashed their carts into each other. "But darling, you have to eat. You can take a break to eat?"

Just then an elderly woman in a lavender track suit approached. "Excuse me, can you help—oh, I'm interrupting, aren't I?"

"Oh, no, ma'am." Hope nearly lunged at her in desperation and delight. She tossed a pointed look at Miriam over her shoulder. "We always have time for our customers."

Miriam sighed and folded her arms across her chest and Hope winced as the eruption of cleavage from Mount Miriam caused another collision.

"But this young lady was here first." A sweet smile turned the elder's face into a mass of wrinkles and she patted Hope's arm with a surprisingly strong hand.

"It's all right, ma'am. This is my sister-in-law. You aren't cutting in front of her." Hope covered the older lady's hand with her own.

"Oh!" The customer looked back at Miriam with a smile then returned to Hope's face, only to glance down at her work clothes. A few darting glances between the two had her patting Hope's arm again. "Oh," she said sympathetically.

Hope gritted her teeth and bared her teeth in a smile that strained the edges of genuine. "How can I help you, ma'am?"

"Oh. Well. Yes, you see, I ordered some plants a little while back and I received a call that they had arrived."

"Oh, wonderful! Let me get someone to get them for you. Aaron!" She motioned to the young man who was skulking around the bags of beauty bark. "What was your last name, ma'am?"

"It's Smythe, dear."

"Thank you. Aaron." She turned to him as he worked a winning grin at Miriam. "Would you escort Mrs. Smythe to the bench near customer service, so she can be comfortable while you get her order? She was called and told it had arrived."

"Oh, but I was going to help this lady," he indicated Miriam, whose lips were quivering a little. Hope stepped forward before actual laughter escaped.

"Aaron."

"Okay, okay. I was just--" he stopped and swallowed hard as he looked at her face, then pivoted to the elderly customer. "Mrs. Smythe, how are you today?"

In a gallant move Hope didn't see coming, Aaron offered his arm to the older lady and escorted her away. Miriam laughed softly. "Darling, that was impressive."

She glanced over and retrieved the clipboard that she'd left on the pallet of compost. "What was?"

"The *look*." The leggy blonde shivered dramatically and held out one leather clad foot. "You had me shaking in my boots."

They both paused to admire the sleek charcoal leather boots Miriam wore. "Nice," Hope observed. "New?"

"I saw them when we were shopping for you yesterday and had to go back and get them."

Hope clucked her tongue and made more notes on her clipboard. The sale next weekend was going to be a doozy.

"Oh, stop being that way. You can borrow them sometime."

Now she stopped and looked at her sister-in-law, mouth half open. "Where would I wear those ridiculous things?"

"They're not ridiculous. They'd be perfect for your next date with Erik. Speaking of...."

She groaned. "Miriam. Please."

"Please, what? He said you two were dating. And you didn't argue." Miriam started ticking off salient points as Hope walked away, trying in vain to do her job. "Your parents love him. He's good with the children. He's employed, and darling, after...oh, what was his name? The one who sat on your couch for months?"

"Robbie."

"Yes, Robbie! After Robbie, gainful employment cannot be emphasized too much."

"Yes, Miriam, I know." Leading the way to her office, she held up a hand to stop Caitlyn from joining them. "Cait, take a couple of the boys and get them to reset the annuals. They're starting to look picked over."

"You got it, boss." Shooting a glance between the two women, Caitlyn scrambled to get out of the office area.

Miriam continued on, undeterred. "He's nice to his own family and Daniel thinks very highly of him."

"And this is a good thing?" she muttered.

"He has a nice car and you saw his apartment, yes?"

"Condo. Yes. It's a nice condominium." She dropped into the chair behind her desk and pressed the heels of her hands to her eyes. She heard Miriam settle into the other seat.

"And he's tall and handsome and really quite delicious. What's the problem? Why are you so upset? Did you not have fun last night?" Rustling noise told her that Miriam was digging around in her purse for something.

"No. I didn't have fun last night."

Silence.

"All right," Miriam said slowly. "Why not?"

Hope opened her eyes. Miriam sat across from her, freshening her lipstick in a tiny mirror.

"Listen, Miriam. He's a nice guy. He's a good guy. But like you said, he's a seriously hot guy and guys like that don't go out with women like me." She picked up a paperclip and fiddled with it. "They don't go out with me."

Miriam closed her compact with a snap. "I see. Was he not at your house to take you to the party last night?"

"Yes, of course."

"And did he not drive you to the party?"

"Miriam."

"Answer me, please."

She blew out her breath. "Yes, he drove me to the party."

"Did he talk to you at the party? Stand next to you at the party? Introduce you to people at the party?"

"Yes."

A cat-in-cream smile lit up Miriam's face. "Then I would say a guy like that <u>did</u> take out a woman like you."

She tossed the paper clip into a small dish. "I hate it when you do that."

"When I'm right, you mean?"

"No, when you twist things to make me look like an idiot. I'm not an idiot, you know."

"Darling." Miriam stood and walked around the desk and leaned against it. "I twisted nothing. I merely pointed out the facts. Come, let's get you a coffee."

"No, I don't want any coffee."

"Of course, you do. You always want coffee." Miriam walked back to the other chair and picked up her purse. "We'll go to the place you like, with the really good coffee."

"I don't feel like coffee."

Miriam's purse thumped into the chair. "What did you say?"

"I don't feel like coffee." Sighing as Miriam slid onto the tiny space left on the seat, her hand pressed to her heart, Hope shook her head. "Don't be such a drama queen. It's no big deal."

"No big deal?" her sister-in-law repeated. "Most people breathe air. You drink coffee. This is a very big deal."

Hope lifted her eyes up and to the left.

"Darling. What happened last night?"

"Nothing. It's nothing. I know we're not really together. And I know it's not going to last, whatever the hell this is. But those women!" she exploded.

"What women?"

"The mean ones in the bathroom. They didn't know I was there and they were talking about Erik. And me. About how gorgeous he is and how gorgeous I'm not."

"Oh, darling. You are gorgeous! And for once you showed that off last night. Your dress was fabulous."

Her laugh was watery at best. "You picked it out, it should be. But it doesn't matter what I was wearing. It was pretty damn clear that everyone thought it was a joke that he was with me. That he could do so much better."

"J'vla hore."

Recognizing the Norwegian, she shrugged. "I can't really blame them, I guess. It was a joke that we were there together."

Miriam made a sound that was half groan, half scream. "I hate it when you say...*shit* like that!"

"You can hate it all you want." She slumped in her chair, tired. Tired of the conversation and the subject and feeling. "It doesn't change anything. There are people in this world who don't make sense together. Pretty people go with pretty people."

"Well, I'm one of the pretty people." Miriam smiled blandly. "What about your brother and me? Do we not fit? Shall I call a lawyer now?"

"It's different. It is!" she forestalled any argument Miriam might have presented. "It just is."

Chapter Eighteen

"I hope it's okay that I'm here."

Miriam's laugh was as dangerously sexy as the rest of her, Erik thought and grinned. No wonder Daniel acted like the king of the world all the time.

"Oh, darling, you are always welcome. With my children, you and your dog are particularly welcome." With a quick glance at Daniel and the children in the backyard, she arranged herself on one of the barstools. How she managed to cross one booted leg over the other, keeping the skirt of her red dress in place by some magical feat that defied gravity and fabric length alike, was beyond him.

"Yeah, you say that, but I know how it is with married people. You're going to read Daniel the riot act when I leave, aren't you?"

Miriam made a scoffing sound. "Don't be silly. I shall do no such thing. How dull!"

"Uh huh."

She laughed again. "Do you want a drink, darling?"

"Yeah, thanks, that'd be great."

"Beer?"

"You read my mind."

"One of my many talents," she replied, batting her eyelashes. "Refrigerator, bottom shelf. While you're up, you could pour a glass of the juice drink for me."

He snickered. "Walked into that one, didn't I?"

"Oh, yes. You did."

He could only laugh again. "Glasses?" He opened a cupboard near the fridge and pulled out a bottle of beer and a clear glass pitcher filled with a deep orange liquid. Filling the glass, he offered it to Miriam with a shallow bow. "Madam?"

"Oh, thank you." She accepted the glass and sipped. "I have the best sister-in-law."

"Yes, you do." He tapped his beer bottle to her glass. "To Hope."

"To Hope," she echoed. "And what's going to happen there."

He choked a little on his beer. "What was that?"

"Well, darling. You know how..." She paused and Erik could all but see her flipping through mental files for the right words. "How strong-willed she can be."

"Well, yeah. She is Norwegian." He pretended to duck as she threw a napkin at him.

"You think you are funny, but you are not." A smile belied Miriam's scolding. "And you miss my point. Hope is very determined and certain she is right."

"Okay."

She sipped again and recrossed her legs. "Do you think she'll marry you?"

He choked again.

"Oh, stop that." She flipped her long gold hair back and examined her nails. "She thinks you're too handsome for her."

"Miriam, come on." He waited for her laugh or a punchline. "What are you really saying here?"

"What I've said, darling. There is no hidden message." The humor faded from her face. "She thinks you are a temporary pleasure and you will leave. She thinks others think the same."

The conversation he'd had with Daniel replayed in his mind. "Yeah, like her own family." He took another swig of beer to wash that down.

"Who in her family said that? Rebecca?"

"No, it was--"

The door burst open and Daniel ducked under the lintel of the door, one hand covering his daughter's head. Paul thundered past him, shrieking, and Hope brought up the rear of the makeshift parade, carrying Sebastian piggyback and Ruger's leash around her wrist.

"Hey! Hi. Here!" She thrust the leash at him and let her nephew slide to his feet.

"Sanks, Auntie Hope!" hollered the small boy as he pelted after his brother.

"I'm right behind you guys! Start washing faces, please!" Hope turned to her brother and held out her arms for Lene. "Come on, prettiest girl."

The tiny blonde girl made the transfer of arms without a murmur and smiled sleepily at Erik over her aunt's shoulder. He gave her a wink and Hope whisked her upstairs, with Daniel and Miriam calling promises for good night kisses in a moment. Miriam turned back to Erik. "Who else said that Hope isn't pretty enough for you?"

"I—it--it doesn't matter, Miriam. Because it's crap." Erik kept his eyes fixed on hers.

"It isn't crap," Daniel protested and Erik closed his eyes. "I told you that this morning."

"You told him that?"

Even Erik caught the warning in Miriam's voice, but Daniel plowed on. "Yes, I let him know that it wasn't a good idea to mess around with Hope because of that. See? I'm a good big brother."

"How can you say that?" Miriam protested. "That is simply horrible to say about your sister."

"I agree," Erik interjected. "But you just said it, too, Miriam."

"I didn't say it because I think it, I said that Hope thinks it. And she's stubborn as a mule." Miriam set down her drink with an angry clink.

Daniel busied himself at the sink. "And in this case, she's right. It's a nice idea, like a story we'd read to the kids, but it's not reality. Erik's out of her league."

"Man, do you even hear yourself?" Erik demanded.

"Yeah, I do." Daniel pulled out a platter of meat from the fridge. "Babe, has this already been marinated?"

"You will be marinated in a moment!" Miriam stalked past her husband and wrenched open the fridge, refilling her glass from the pitcher. "You know how I hate this talk of leagues!"

Daniel snorted. "Yeah, when your friends made fun of you for dating me. It's different."

"How is it different?"

Erik finished his beer. "Yeah, I'd like to hear this one. How is it different, Dan?"

"Because it is!" Slamming around the kitchen, the other man gathered the things he needed for grilling their dinner. "I may not be as hot as my wife, but I bring a lot to the table, so it works out. And girls have to be pretty or that's what people notice. That's not just me saying that. That's everybody."

Miriam set her glass on the kitchen island with careful precision. "Then you are saying that a woman's value is in her appearance. Yes?"

"That's right." Daniel thumped a bag on the counter and dumped potatoes into the sink. Water splashed and stopped as he slapped the handle of the faucet, and silence rushed back into the room. He turned around, mouth open, ready to rumble until he saw his wife's face.

Erik shook his head and whispered, *"Dude."*

Miriam smoothed the front of her dress. "How fortunate for me. I have some value because I'm pretty."

"Babe, that's not--" her husband began.

Behind Erik, Hope clattered into the room. "The boys are washed up and I told them to play a little until you go up. Lene is out like a light. Although, Sebastian's yawning a little, too, so he...what's going on?"

Erik shook his head.

"Your brother is an asshole, that's what's going on." Miriam glared at Daniel.

"Uh oh." Hope sidled up next to Erik and tipped her head at the door that led to freedom.

"Oh, I'm the asshole now?" Daniel replied hotly.

Erik contemplated the kitchen door. Sure, it was close enough, but he'd have to step between the feuding couple. He wasn't really sure he was that brave.

"What will be my value, darling husband, when my looks fade?" Miriam demanded, stepping closer to her spouse, who stood his ground.

Brave, Erik thought. Stupid. But brave.

"It won't matter because we're married," Dan retorted. "And you know I don't just love you because of the way you look."

"Oh, such a relief for me. How fortunate I am that I was attractive enough to hook you while I was single."

"Aw, come on..." Daniel turned away in disgust.

The puppy barked sharply and bounced a little.

"Even the dog knows I am right. You know, I can only hope that Lene grows into a beautiful woman," Miriam folded her arms as sham concern and sarcasm dripped from her tone. "Otherwise, she'll have to make do with whatever man she can get."

"Now *that's* crap." Daniel snapped on the water faucet again.

"Yes! It is crap! And it is the kind of crap I do not want my daughter to grow up hearing!" Miriam stormed out of the kitchen and Daniel stomped after her.

"It's not the same thing! You're just mad because--"

The furious couple cleared the doorway into the living room, still squabbling, leaving a clear path to the outside door. "Run for it," Erik said to Hope, a firm grip on Ruger's leash. She nodded and grabbed her purse off the back of a bar stool.

They ran.

"Wow." Hope slumped in the passenger seat of Erik's car. Daniel had parked behind her truck and there was no way she was going back into that house to ask her brother anything.

"That was...what was that?" Erik backed the car out of the driveway and headed out of the neighborhood.

"That was a really big fight." She watched the neighborhood zip past them as he drove toward downtown. "And—oh, no."

"What?" She could feel his eyes on her as she scrambled for the phone in her bag. "What happened?"

She held up her hand as she spoke into the phone. "Miriam. Kids. Still awake. Okay." She paused, listening. "Uh huh. Okay, bye."

He glanced over. "Well?"

"Kids are fine. She's tucking them in, Daniel's banished to the back yard and the barbecue. She said they're done." She dropped the phone back into her purse.

"Done? As in...done?" His alarmed expression startled her and she replayed what Miriam had just said.

"No. No." She shook her head against the niggle of doubt. "No. Done with the fight. I'm sure that's what she meant."

Erik reached over and squeezed her hand, keeping his eyes on the traffic as it thickened. "Don't worry. Miriam will kick Dan's ass and they'll move on."

She blinked. "You think so?"

"I know so." He laced his fingers through her and rested their joined hands on his thigh. "Dan's not usually an idiot. She'll straighten him out."

From his carrier in the back seat, Ruger barked in agreement.

"Oh, is that so?" Hope asked the puppy, ignoring the smothered laughter from the man next to her. Erik's building came into view and she stirred. "Wait, I thought you were taking me home."

Erik hit a remote that opened the gate to the parking area below the steel and glass tower. "Do you have to work tomorrow?"

"Yes. So?" She could hear the petulance in her own voice, but he said nothing about it.

"Then I'll get you up in time to get your car and go home to change before work." He grinned as Ruger yapped again. "If you have a problem with that, take it up with the dog."

She huffed out a breath. "Yeah, like I'll win an argument with him." An unwilling smile teased her lips as he laughed. "You'll get me there on time?"

"Absolutely," he agreed. "When do you start?"

"Six AM."

He groaned. "You're lucky I love--" He stopped, cleared his throat.

She froze, heart pounding, staring straight ahead, hoping and fearing what he'd say next, what she'd say back. He cleared his throat again.

"--Pizza. I love pizza. We're not getting barbecue for dinner," he finished. "You feel like pizza?"

She let the breath she'd been holding out slowly. "Pizza's fine."

After ordering pizza and feeding the dog, Erik excused himself to his office. Fifteen minutes of computer time would free him up to spend the rest of the evening with Hope.

Hope.

He paused, hands on the keyboard. What the hell had he been about to say in the car? And had she caught it?

Pushing away from his desk, he paced back and forth a bit. Was he falling for her? He couldn't be. She was snotty and moody. And she wasn't even a dog person. There was no way he was going through what Marty went through.

The sounds from the living room drew him. From the hallway, he could see Ruger bracing his small paws on the area rug, jaws locked on the end of a knotted rope, tail wagging and mock growling at Hope.

Hope.

She knelt opposite him, a firm grip on the other end of the rope, laughing and talking softly. With her free hand, she tickled Ruger's ear, sending him dancing away, rope still firmly held in his mouth. Erik leaned closer to catch what she was saying.

"Oh, who's so fierce? Who's a big, fierce dog?"

Delighted growling and muffled yips answered her.

"Oh, so scary! So tough! Big dog!"

Erik eased back to his office, smiling until his gaze fell on the display on his wall. Framed certificates of merit and medals in shadow boxes that his sister assembled after he was discharged from the Army filled half the space and for once, he looked at the platoon picture. Man and dog alternated in stiff rows, the precision of their arrangement belied by the grins on every face, human and canine. Magnus sat to his right that day, ears erect and alert, his K-9 vest clean and new.

It had only been a week later that the sniper targeted the unit.

He walked to the window. All the years between, he'd avoided every dog, especially shepherds. He'd kept busy. He dated women who like *cats,* for God's sake. And now, a small white and black puppy had wriggled his way into his life.

Hope and a puppy.

Was he crazy? Was this the way he wanted to go down?

Hell, yes.

He grinned and reached for the phone. With luck, the florist down the road would remember him.

Hope placed the sleeping puppy into his carrier and waited for him to rearrange himself before closing the latch. A bit of fluff pushed through the bars and she stroked it with her forefinger. "I don't like you, you know," she whispered. "I don't like dogs at all."

"Yeah, he can tell."

She looked up with a smile already growing. "I blame you for this."

He shifted the pizza box he held. "I can handle that. Hungry?"

"Yes." She scrambled to her feet and followed him, pausing in confusion as he walked past the dining room. "Where are you going?"

"Bedroom."

"But...but it's pizza. There might be crumbs." She trailed after him and stopped short in the doorway.

Candles lit and softened the stark modern lines of his bedroom. Red, pink, yellow and orange rose petals were scattered across the pristine white sheets and made a trail across the floor. Erik walked over to the long dresser and set the pizza down. With a click on the remote, soft, bluesy music drifted into the nearly silent room.

He walked to her silently and she realized he was barefoot. Without a word, he pulled off his t-shirt and tossed it without looking into the hamper in the corner. A nervous and unwilling giggle welled up in her throat.

He was so damned tidy.

Placing his hands on her waist, he leaned down to murmur in her ear, "It's not dinner at your brother's place, but I'll try to make it up to you."

Another giggle welled up and she squelched it firmly. "You don't have to make up anything."

"Are you kidding?" Moving behind her, he massaged her shoulders firmly. "Did you see the steaks Dan pulled out of the fridge? If I were any kind of man, I would have grabbed the platter on the way out."

She laughed outright. "Well, since you put it that way...oh, yes. Right there. Why are my shoulders so tight?"

"You work too hard." He pressed a kiss to the back of her neck and she shivered.

"This is really pretty."

"Hm?" He'd moved to the side of her neck and she struggled to stay focused.

"It's pretty, with the candles—oh!" She swayed as he nipped her ear. "I'm not ready for this."

He turned her a bit. "Not ready for what?"

"The flowers and the music and everything. Pizza in the bedroom." She waved a vague hand at all of it.

He smoothed a wisp of her hair back. "How are you not ready for it?"

"I should be dressed up, like on the party night." Restless and feeling more ridiculous than usual around him, she pulled away and walked to the night table, touched the riot of roses he put there, their colors echoing the petals on the sheets. "I was dressed up then. And you didn't touch me."

"Did you want me to touch you?"

"Well, yeah!" She folded her arms over her middle as he raised an eyebrow. "Okay, no."

He crossed to her and framed her face in his hands. "How about now? Do you want me to touch you now?"

Not trusting herself to speak, she nodded.

And he did.

With deft fingers, he unbuttoned her shirt and eased it down her arms, revealing the bright pink bra with lavender daisies on it. A few swift tugs and pulls sent her khakis to the floor and showed off the matching panties. "Hope, I gotta say, you have the best underwear."

Her cheeks turned the color of her panties. "I needed a little pick-me-up."

"Hey, yeah. I'm completely picked up now.."

She laughed and gasped as he lifted her up and out of the fabric puddled on the ground. As if she was as fragile as glass, he laid her on his bed, the coolness of the sheets and the silkiness of rose petals pressed to her skin. "You don't have to do all of this."

He paused in the act of pulling off her thick work socks. "All what?"

"All the seduction stuff." She shifted a little. "You're going to get whatever you want."

A wicked light sparked in his eyes. "Whatever I want?"

She snorted and batted at his arm as he braced them on either side of her. "Cut it out."

"Uh uh. I get whatever I want?" He rubbed his lips on hers, their eyes open and locked.

"Depends." She tilted her chin as he trailed his mouth down her throat and pressed to the pulse pounding there. "What do you want?"

The laughter she felt rumble against her breast was dark enough to make her feel her temperature rise, light enough to make her feel happy as he eased down the strap of her bra. He traced a fine, damp line along the edge of her breast that pressed out of the silky fabric.

"You know..." he slid his finger under the cup of her bra to toy with her nipple, "...You said that before."

"What?" The soft, tested flicks against the hardening peak of her breast had her gasping and struggling to understand him.

"You said before I could have whatever I needed."

She laughed, a little breathlessly. "When?"

"Last time." Unhooking her bra and pulling it off, he dropped the pink swatch of fabric to the side of the bed then stood to remove his pants. Leaning over her again, he pressed a kiss to each nipple as he eased her panties down her thighs. "God. Look at you."

She blinked then reflexively started to cover herself only to be stopped by him as he caught her hands and pressed them to his shoulders. "Erik."

"Hope. Please. Look at yourself like I do."

She looked down at herself and flinched a little, at the less-than-perfect breasts and roll on her belly that was still visible, even lying down.

"You're so beautiful. Look." He caught her nipple in his mouth and suckled hard, making her clutch his head and cry out before he released her and leaned back to admire the deep peach flush to the hard tip. With a low growl of pleasure, he switched to other side and performed the same task. "See? You are so sexy."

"Erik, I'm not." She met his eyes and saw the frustration there that turned to determination.

"Really? Then how did this happen?" he caught her hand and dragged it to his penis, rock-hard and throbbing against her palm.

What was better, she wondered. The feel of the man's obvious hunger for her, right there in her hand or the groan he gave as she tightened her grip slightly and explored his length? She watched him, unable to look away as he gritted his teeth and held himself still and poised over her, allowing her the freedom to explore his body. "Oh, God. Hope!"

With a firm shove, she pushed him onto his back. Longing like she'd never felt before filled her and she bent down to him, holding the shaft of his cock between both hands and bringing the bulbous head to her mouth. Using the same method he had on her breasts, she sucked hard, feeling him arch under her.

Whether it was the pleasure of pleasing him or the power of knowing he was thinking of nothing but her, she couldn't have said at that moment. She only knew that holding him that way, in her hands and her mouth satisfied her as nothing else ever had. Nothing else but him.

"Hope," he gasped. "Wait. Baby."

She paused. "What? You don't like it?" The disbelief on his face made her laugh out loud and she started to bend toward him again.

"No, not this way. Not this time. Please." His chest heaved as he fought for breath and, she imagined, self-control.

She had done that, she thought smugly. She had brought a strong man to his knees—okay, his back and made him beg. She was the one who--

She shrieked as he sat up and grabbed her, pulling her to him, her legs straddling him as he shoved into her. Now it was her turn to gasp and clutch at him.

"So tight," he gritted. "God, you're wet."

He sat back on his heels, grasping her hips, moving them back and forth as she squeezed her eyes shut and gripped the hard muscle of his shoulders, trying to balance as he set the pace. "Erik, I can't...I can't..."

"Just let go," he urged her. "I have you. I won't let you go. I won't let you fall."

She opened her eyes to lose herself in him, in the clear, light blue of his eyes and let go. Leaning back on her hands, she let him support her body and as he did, she felt sweet tension build in her. Crying out, she pressed herself to him, feeling his heat and heartbeat inside of her. The bed shook beneath her with every thrust.

"Not yet. Don't come yet," he rasped. "Want this to last. Make it last. Hope. God, Hope. You feel so good. You feel so good."

"Can't wait," she sobbed out. "Can't! Erik, yes! Yes!" She let her head fall back to the bed, arching up into a bridge between his lap, where his cock held and lifted her to the bed. Tremors shook her and as she fell into the climax, plummeting down, she felt him press kisses to her belly and breast, then tighten inside her. Calling her name, he shook and caved in on top of her.

Gasping for breath, they lay still until she recovered enough to place her hand on his head, running her fingers through his hair. He covered her hand with his and turned into her palm, pressing another kiss there.

It might have been an hour or a minute before he stirred further. Easing her off of him, he pulled her to his side. "Pizza's cold by now," he murmured against her temple.

"That's okay." She snuggled closer but her stomach had heard the word pizza and let out an angry rumble.

His eyes popped open and he lifted his head, grinning at her. "Wow."

Mortified, she covered her face. "Oh, shut up."

Laughing, he disentangled himself from her and retrieved the pizza box. "Come on, don't do that," he cajoled her. "You can't eat like that."

She sat up and wrapped a sheet around her, ignoring his amusement and protests, and took a slice of pizza. When he continued to chuckle, she growled at him. "Watch it, Thor."

The smile fell away from his face. "Low."

She smirked and chewed the pizza, which was still warm. "Why do you hate that so much? Being called Thor? You know what you look like."

He shrugged and polished off his first piece, reaching for another. "I just hate it. I've always hated it."

"Always."

He looked at her sourly. "It's my name."

She choked. "Seriously?"

He nodded, tossing the pizza he held back in the box. "The T? It's Thorleif. Thorleif Erik Yoriksson."

Her mouth hung open. She could feel it but for the life of her, couldn't close it.

"I shouldn't have told you."

That snapped her back. "Of course you should have! Why shouldn't you have told me?"

"Because now you're never going to let me forget it." He set the box aside and rose. "Want something to drink?"

"Water, please," she replied absently. A smile played around her lips as she thought about what he'd just told her.

"What?"

His disgruntled voice snapped her out of her reverie and she took the bottle he handed her. "I was just thinking."

He watched her warily as he settled back on the bed, placing a pillow against his back. She curled up beside him, pleased when he wrapped his arm around her, despite his barely restrained irritation. "I think your parents were smart to name you that."

"How do you figure?" He hissed as her water bottle slipped and rested against the bare skin of his side.

"Sorry." She righted the bottle and opened it. "They were smart but I can't think of how they knew to name you Thor."

"Oh, God. I'm going to regret asking." He tipped his head back and closed his eyes. "What do you mean?"

"Well..." she traced a finger up and down his chest. "If what we just did doesn't qualify you as 'Thor, God of Thunder,' I don't know what would."

This time, it was their laughter that shook the bed.

Chapter Nineteen

The office was silent when Erik walked through the doors. Of course, the fact that it was just shy of 5:30 probably had something to do with that. Ruger's carrier bumped his leg and the little dog gave a sleepy, half-hearted bark and Erik set him in the corner of the office.

The garment bag holding his suit for the day fit neatly into his office closet. Before leaving the office, he pulled out the shoes he'd tucked into the bottom of the bag and set them neatly on the closet floor. He'd have enough time to run a few miles, shower, dress and get ahead of anything that was going on at work before the rest of the staff even arrived.

He took a quick look the carrier; Ruger was already asleep again. Dropping a light drape over the front of the mini kennel to block light and muffle sound, he left the puppy to snooze through his run.

Sliding his key into a small pouch attached to his shoe, Erik hit the stairs as a warm up. Today wasn't going to be unmanageable; he just had to stay ahead of everything and everyone. No problem.

The streets of downtown Seattle were still quiet, the buses and cars few and far between, compared to the morning rush he was used to. To amuse himself, he started counting coffee shops as he ran.

An extremely sleepy looking teenager ambled down the hill Erik was running up, waking up long enough to say something rude about Erik's questionable sanity. With a casual wave, Erik kept running.

The kid wasn't a morning person, he thought. Just like Hope. Well, just like Hope, unless he woke her up just right, he thought with a grin. He'd have to accept that if they were going to be together.

Together. The thought slowed him down more than the thirty-degree angle of the hill he was taking. What had he been thinking these last few days? He knew he wanted her. He knew she turned him on. He knew he liked her as a person, once he got past the bitchiness she used as a shield.

Hell, who was he kidding? He even liked that snotty attitude. Was it the way she challenged him? What the hell was wrong with him?

Kicking up his speed again, he considered what he knew he wanted. He wanted his life in Seattle. He loved the city and being close to his family. He wanted to keep moving forward in his work, maybe start his own business one day. He wanted....

Oh, he might as well admit it. He wanted what Daniel had. A kid or two. A nice house, with room for the dog. He grinned as he realized how foolish he'd been ignoring that want for so long. And he wanted a good marriage, even if that meant a screaming fight now and then. Nothing wrong with a good fight with the right person, if it cleared the air. And made way for make-up sex. He wanted that.

He wanted Hope.

The reality of it punched him in the gut. He wanted Hope. He slowed again, approaching the office building of Western Telecomm. All this time and this is what he really wanted. Hope.

Bracing his foot against a bus bench, he pulled out his key and opened the side door to the lobby, punching in his code for the security panel. As he walked through the marble and glass entryway toward the elevators, the shops that he usually breezed past caught his eye. He paused, staring through the plate glass window at the display of diamonds.

And started to smile.

"Hope, pick up line two, please."

She checked her watch. Still shy of eight o'clock. Who the hell would be calling now?

Visions of owners and natural disasters in other time zones danced in her head as she hustled to the store phone in the garden center. She had the boys resetting the annuals and perennials in prep for Mother's Day. The store would be flooded with gardeners, they would host the first of their annual how-to gardening shows and to top it all off, she would have her yearly argument with her own mother about daughterly duty and her lack of appreciation for the woman who gave her life.

God. Talk about pending natural disasters.

Shaking it off, she picked up the discreetly placed handset and pressed the blinking light. "Thank you for holding. This is Hope, may I help you?"

"Hey."

Erik's voice was low and warm in her ear and she firmly squelched the silly grin it provoked. "Hey, yourself. What are you doing, calling me now?"

"I missed talking to you."

She laughed. "In less than three hours?"

"Well, you're not very conversant in the mornings. You might not have noticed."

"Thanks," she laughed again and leaned down on the counter.

"But you're much more awake now."

"That would be because of the jet fuel you put into my coffee cup this morning—Kyle!" she yelled.

"Actually, it's Erik. We've covered this, haven't we?"

"Very funny, Thor. Hang on." Without hitting the hold button, she set the phone on the counter as Kyle came skidding up to her.

"Yeah, boss?" He sounded slightly breathless, as if he'd been caught racing in late. Which, in fact, he had. "What's up?"

"The first thing that's up is the time. Look with me at the clock on the wall, my boy."

Kyle dutifully turned and looked at the huge clock mounted over the doorway. "Twenty-seven minutes late."

"That's correct. Seven-thirty means seven-thirty. And you will give me twenty-seven minutes sometime this week."

"Aw, Hope..." he whined.

"Pardon me?" She rotated slowly to face him. "Was that complaining? Whining, even?"

"No, ma'am."

"Thank you." Then she pointed at the jumble of binders and tape, notes and stickers under the cash register. "Second, did I not ask you to organize this mess three days ago?"

"Oh, man." Kyle scratched the side of his head. "Yes, and I totally forgot."

"Well, now you're totally going to do it." She rummaged through the mess and pulled out a notepad and a pen. "Go to Interiors and pull the supplies you'll need to do it right. Then see Caitlyn for the requisitions form for everything you pull."

"Okay."

"And I mean everything, Kyle. We're not going through the same nightmare on inventory night this month that we did last month."

"Yes, ma'am."

She held him pinned with her gaze for another moment, then nodded. "Go, and sin no more."

He went and she picked up the phone again. "Hey, I'm back. You still there?"

"Yes. I am." Erik cleared his throat. "Hope...do you have any of your fancy panties and bras in black? Shiny black?"

The blush started around her knees and crept slowly up and over her face. "Erik!"

"Do you?"

She glanced around. "Yes. Why?"

"Hm. Think you can wear them and give me a scolding like that sometime?"

She laughed. "Depends. What have you done to deserve it?"

"Oh, well, I don't know. Were you in the bedroom with me last night?"

She laughed again, helplessly. "Erik."

"Because I think I definitely deserve it."

"Oh, my God." She covered her face. "I'm at work. I'm at work! I cannot be having this conversation here. Not here, not now. Why did you call? Do you know why you called?"

"I have no idea." There was a small silence. "Yeah, having a hard time getting past the image of you. Black underwear. Maybe some boots. You got boots?"

"Oh, lord."

He chuckled. "Yes, I know why I called you. Ruger and I would like to meet you this evening. Would you take a walk with us?"

"Okay." She twisted a piece of twine left on the register around her fingers. "What time?"

"What time are you done?"

"I'm out of here at four today."

"Then we'll pick you up at five, at your house."

"Okay," she said again. "See you then."

She hung up the phone and smiled at it, replaying the fun she'd just had. Fun. During a stupid phone call. What was going on with her?

Humming under her breath, she turned and stopped short. Caitlyn stood in the aisle, arms folded over a clipboard.

Grinning.

"So that was him, right?"

This much blushing couldn't be good for her, she thought. "Yes, that was Erik."

Caitlyn sighed. "And you're in love! Finally!"

Hope gave her a disbelieving look and started back toward the office. "I am not. And what do mean, finally?"

Caitlyn trailed after her. "Oh, come on. If you were any redder, we could use you as a sale tag."

She snorted and kept walking. "So I need a tan. Like that's going to happen in Seattle."

"And you smile when you talk about him or to him," her assistant continued doggedly. She was starting to sound a bit breathless keeping Hope's pace through the store.

"Well, I tried hitting him with a bat, but everyone got mad at me. So now I'm smiling." She took the stairs quicker than usual, but Caitlyn kept up.

"And all of a sudden, you're a girl."

Hope stopped and spun around, catching Caitlyn by the arms before she could crash into her. "What is that supposed to mean? What was I before, a platypus?"

"Nooooo. Well, now that you mention it, when you get irritated, you do get a little--" Caitlyn mimed a duck's bill in front of her mouth. "You know, I never put the platypus thing together until now."

"Caitlyn."

"Weird, huh?"

"Caitlyn!"

"What?"

"What did you mean, I'm suddenly a girl?"

"Oh! Well." Caitlyn paused, chewing her upper lip wrinkling her brow. "It's like, we always knew you were straight and all because you know." She giggled. "The guys."

"Caitlyn."

The younger woman cleared her throat. "Sorry. But you're the boss. You're—okay, don't take this wrong, but you're The Man."

"Pardon me?"

Caitlyn hurried on. "But now, even though you're still totally in charge, you're acting like a girl. You're excited about this guy."

"So what!" She turned and stomped into her office, Caitlyn training behind again. "That's nothing new. I got excited about guys before."

Caitlyn wrinkled her nose and shook her head. "No, you didn't. You were super nice to your guys, which is why they walked all over you. But it's different with this one."

"Yes, it is different, because we're just dating. There's no--" Hope began.

"And you're nicer to him now and all, but you did act like yourself, even the not nice part of you, which is super important because if a guy doesn't know who you are, like inside of you, then he doesn't really know you--"

Hope sat on her desk, staring at her assistant manager. "I don't think I've ever heard you say this much when you're sober." She narrowed her eyes. "You are sober, aren't you?"

"Yes, and stop changing the subject." Caitlyn huffed and folded her arms. "I know about this stuff."

"Ha! You're half my age!" Hope laughed.

"I'm twenty-four!" Cait protested.

"You're a baby." Hope stood and walked around her desk and turned on her computer.

"Excuse me, I am not a baby. I have a baby. And while you're being all smarty-pants, answer this: which one of us is married?" Caitlyn planted her fists on her hips, clipboard and all. "Heck, which one of us can stay in a relationship longer than six months?"

Hope froze. "Hey. Ouch."

"You deserve it."

"Okay, I'm sorry about the baby comment."

"You should be. And I know why you're doing that. You don't want to think about it. You don't want to ask yourself if you really do love Erik or not. You don't want to count up the number of times you think about him in a day, or the way you feel when you're with him, or how the sex with him is better and not just because he can do it better." Caitlyn took a deep breath. "Why don't you ask yourself how you feel when you introduce him to your friends? To family?"

Caitlyn paused as Hope thought about this, letting her chew that over. Something on her face must have pleased Cait, because she nodded sharply.

"That's what I thought." Caitlyn checked her watch. "Store opens in a few minutes. I'll get the tills up and going."

Hope stayed behind her desk, the computer humming, and saw nothing.

In love? With Erik?

"Oh, dear God."

Ruger attacked a fly that had foolishly landed on a clump of grass. Growling like the fierce hunter he was, he shredded the grass as a warning to all other flies. And sod everywhere.

"Ruger, do not eat that grass. If you barf while we're proposing to Hope, I'm going to be really pissed."

Erik flipped open the ring box again. The platinum bezel setting of the diamond would allow Hope to do her job without getting the stone caught on everything. Not that he expected her to wear it all the time; hell, rings could be dangerous when working with power tools. Even he knew that.

They'd pick out a chain to hold her rings later.

"This assumes she says yes." He crouched down and scrubbed a hand over Ruger's head, delighting the puppy. "But who could resist us, huh? Nobody, that's who!"

He stood and looked around the park, and checked his watch again. Hope had called a couple hours earlier to let him know that she was running late and would meet him at the park.

So he'd shifted to Plan B. The picnic was easy enough to assemble; the fancy grocery store near his condo had even supplied the cooler for the champagne.

He grinned at the set-up. It was unlikely the same thing would happen when he and Hope had champagne this time as it did when they finished the bathroom, but he'd never look at a bottle of champagne the same way again. But that was for later. For now, he just needed her to show up.

Ruger started jumping and leaping at the end of his leash again, making a sound that could only be described as squealing. Erik spotted Hope crossing the rich green of the park lawn and lifted a hand. She waved back and continued toward them. "Remember," Erik said to the small dog, "We want her to be your new mommy. Be cool."

The puppy looked up with green strands hanging from his mouth. Erik sighed and swiped away the mess. "And quit chewing on the grass. No barfing. No barking. Be cool." He picked up the insulated travel cup and straightened up.

"Hey." She made it up the small hill and spotted the picnic behind him. "Oh. Wow, okay. I thought this was just a walk."

He smoothed her hair back from the side of her face. "You had to work. We walked already. Hi." He leaned down and pressed his lips to hers, letting them cling as she softened against him. Before he could lose himself in her and her magical mouth, he eased back.

"Hi," he said again and handed her the cup of coffee.

With a small sigh, she opened the lid of the cup and inhaled the steam. "Oh, yes. Yes. This is what I needed. And it's still hot."

"Yeah, seemed appropriate." He waggled his eyebrows at her as she groaned.

"I'll let that go since you brought me coffee."

"I'm relieved." He gestured to the picnic blanket. "Your table is ready, madam."

"Oh, I don't think so." Hope shook her head and remained standing as she sipped her coffee.

He saw Plan B crumble before his very eyes. "Why not?"

"It's May." She ran her sensibly-booted foot over the bright grass. "The ground is going to be seriously wet."

He crouched again and flipped up the corner of the blanket, showing her its waterproof backing.

"Oh. Cool. Where did you get that?" She sank down to the ground, setting her purse aside. "And the hell-beast isn't going to chew my purse again, is he?"

He glanced over at the hell-beast in question. "I don't think so because he keeps eating the grass. Hey! Cut it out! I said no grass!"

"Obviously, that meant a lot to him, too."

"Yeah, thanks." He chuckled. "You're a big help."

She sipped her coffee again. "This is nice." She fiddled with the cap of her travel mug again.

"Are you hungry?" He opened the basket. "I got some snacks to hold us until dinner."

After spreading out the small sandwiches, a cheese platter and some fruit, food took precedence over conversation. "What a beautiful day." She sighed and he watched some of the stiffness work out of her shoulders.

"Rough one at work?"

She laughed and shook her head. "It's May. Mother's Day will be horrible and Memorial Day will be worse."

"You mentioned that before." He picked another sandwich and bit into it. "Why is that?"

"Mother's Day is a big planting weekend. Oh, thanks." She looked over the fruit tray he held out and selected some melon. "And then Memorial Day is the first long weekend of summer. There's a lot of home repair and yard work done that weekend, too. So much can't be done outside until the weather gets a little more reliable, like painting, but if you're a big gardener, you want to get things in the ground at the time that will give you the best use of the growing season."

"Makes sense. So I can count on not seeing you at all that weekend, huh?"

"Memorial Day? No, not likely." She leaned back on her hands and tilted her face to the sunshine. "How was your day?"

"It was okay. Put out some fires, lit a few underneath some people who needed it." He took a deep breath. "This is good, isn't it?"

"Mmm."

"We should do this more." He glanced over and watched the sunlight gild the curve of her cheek, the lush line of her mouth. Her eyes were closed.

"Okay. We'll do this more."

"What are you doing, say, for the rest of your life?"

Her eyes flew open. "Pardon me?"

He sat up a bit straighter, chuckling at the look of shock on her face, and caught her hand. "Hope, will you marry me?"

Chapter Twenty

"What?" Hope felt like someone had grabbed the skin on her face and twisted it in opposite directions. "What did you say?"

Erik laughed. Laughed! Like this was some big joke, like it was funny? "Marry me, Hope. Please. We'd have a great time."

"Is this a joke?" She jumped to her feet, furious with him, furious with herself for believing, even for a split second, that he really wanted to marry her.

Tears stung her eyes and she looked up and to the left to stop them. No way was this man going to make her cry!

"Hey, hold on." He placed his hands on her arms, rubbing up and down slowly, soothingly. "I would never joke about something like this. I've never asked anyone to marry me before. Hope. Look at me." He gave her a gentle shake. "Look at me."

She met his eyes, teeth gritted, waiting for the knockout punch. She could feel it, oh, just feel it coming.

"I love you."

And there it was. She shook her head.

"How can you say that to me?" she whispered. "How can you say you love me? You don't even know me."

He dropped his hands and took a step back. "I know you."

She laughed, a sound devoid of real humor. "You don't know me. You don't know anything about me. What is this, some sort of bet?"

He took a deep breath in through his nose. "I know you can make me crazier than anyone else on the planet. I know you lash out when you're scared or feel stupid, and that's probably what's going on now."

Heat rushed to her face and she felt the tears press against her eyes again.

"I know you love your family. I know they make you crazy, too, which makes the fact that you love them even more impressive."

She turned her back to him, not walking away, just unable to face him. His voice gentled.

"I know they don't always see who you are, how amazing you are. And I know you forgive them for that. I think it's because you don't have a clue how amazing you are, either."

A small sound escaped her and he wrapped his arms around her from behind and pressed a kiss to the top of her head. "I know you're nice to people like my family, even though they show up at inconvenient times. I know you treat your employees like another part of your family. I know you try to be fair and you don't tolerate a lot of crap."

She gave a watery giggle and he leaned down to rest his cheek against hers. "I know you hate the mornings, but making love in the morning makes life a little bit better for you. I know you drink way too much coffee, and we are going to talk about that."

She snorted and started to pull away.

"I know that we will have that conversation because I do love you. I know you'll listen, even if you don't want to, to what I have to say. Not because you'll agree with me, but because that's who you are. And maybe it'll be because you love me, too. A little."

The ground was suddenly the most interesting thing in the world to look at, and heat rushed up her neck again.

"I know that I want to spend the rest of my life with you, Hope Lindstrom, and I know that every day, every single day I want to learn something about you that I didn't know before. Because I love you."

She shook her head and his arms tightened around her.

"Let me love you, Hope. Let me in. You've opened the door a little for me, let me all the way in now."

She stiffened and for the first time since he'd started talking, found her voice. "Let you in?"

"Yes." He smiled at her, not the smile she hated, but close enough. It was happy and just the tiniest bit triumphant. "Please," he added.

"Because, of course, I've been so closed off."

He laughed. "Well, you're not exactly an open book--"

"Because you've been so open with me."

Loosening his hold, he stepped back from her, studied her face. "I've been pretty open," he started, cautious now.

"Um, not really." She folded her arms and faced him. "I found out more about you from your condo and from a few hours with your family than you ever told me."

"Oh, that's bullshit."

"Is it?" She widened her eyes. "Is it, really?"

"Yes, it is. And what did you want me to do? Say, 'Hi lady, wow, your head thumped on your truck pretty good there, let me tell you about me! I'll start at birth.'" He made a scoffing noise and walked away, then turned back. "If you wanted to know something, all you had to do was ask."

"I did ask."

"What did you ask? When have you shown the same interest in me that I have in you?"

The unfairness of the question obliterated any concern she felt for the hurt in his voice. "What did I ask? How long were you in the army? Where did you serve? Who's Magnus?"

He froze and she could see him closing in.

"That's irrelevant to anything we're discussing."

She spread her hands. "And here we are."

"And...and...that's your answer? I tell you I love you and I want to spend the rest of my life with you, and this is your response?" He turned to the horizon, where the sunset had started to color the sky.

She heard a choking sound and looked down. Ruger was at her feet, making odd, gulping noises. "Erik."

"This is perfect. The sun's going down, the sky is clear, I got a ring in my pocket and my girlfriend's just told me I don't 'share' enough for her to marry me. Goddamn perfect."

"Erik!"

"What?" he roared and spun around.

She'd crouched down to the swaying puppy and placed a hand on his heaving side, watching the vomit color the ground in hideous yellow, deep brown. And bright red.

"Oh, my God. Oh, my God. Okay," he started to reach for the pup, then grabbed the picnic blanket, tossing the plates and food aside. "Wrap him in this and meet me in the parking lot."

"But I--"

"Just do it!" He left at a sprint, flying down the hill to the parking lot, which suddenly looked miles away.

As carefully as she could, she wrapped the shivering puppy in the blanket, fabric side nest his small body. "Hang on, Ruger." Holding him the way she would have held one of her nephews or niece, she threw the strap of her purse over her shoulder and started down the hill.

The gleaming BMW roared into the upper parking lot and jumped the curb, tearing across grass and a flower bed to meet her part way. The passenger door flew open. "Get in!"

"Where are we going? Do you have a vet near here?" she asked after sliding in the car and slamming the door shut. With one arm supporting the dog, she yanked on the seat belt. Erik ripped back across the grass and sent the car jolting back onto the paved parking lot.

"GPS." He nodded at the slick device mounted to the dash and handed her his phone. "The number's there. Hit send and let them know we're coming in."

Free from the restrictive path from parking lot to road, Erik opened up the power of the car. Hope listened to the ringing of the phone. "Come on. Come on, pick up."

"Queen Anne Emergency Animal Care, may I help you?"

"Yes!" Swallowing a sob that threatened to break loose, she gritted her teeth as she spoke. "We're bringing in our dog and he's really sick and I don't know what's wrong with him. He throwing up and there's blood. There's blood in the throw up."

"He's a dog? What breed and how old?"

"I don't know. I can't-- Erik? What breed is he?" she turned to him.

"Wire hair fox terrier." Mouth set, he careened around a corner, slowing only a bit.

"He's a wire hair fox terrier, and he's just a baby."

"Six months old."

The brisk voice on the line asked, "Do you know how much he weighs?"

"How much does he weigh, Erik?" she asked again.

"About ten pounds, a little less, maybe."

"Less than ten pounds," she recited.

She heard the voice on the line muffle the phone. "Did he eat something with metal? Does he have any toys with hard pieces?"

"No, we were at the park and he'd been eating grass and Erik told him to stop, but then we were talking and we didn't pay attention--"

"We're here," Erik interrupted. He slammed the gearshift up and yanked the emergency brake.

"We're here, we're coming in now." She stopped talking and hung up the phone as Erik ran around the outside of the car and opened her door. "Here, take him."

He scooped the puppy out of her arms and ran into the building as she untangled herself and her purse from the seat belt and followed, barely remembering to shut the car door behind her. By the time she made it into the lobby, people were swarming around Erik and Ruger. Two minutes later, she and Erik stood there alone. Ruger had been taken to a treatment room. They were not invited to go along.

The murmurs from the television in the waiting area eddied around them and without thinking about it, she reached for his hand. "Let's sit down. Come on, love. Come sit down."

An old lady with a cat in a plaid carrier sat across from them. Erik stared at the wall, and all she could do was rub her hand up and down his back. What seemed like hours passed, and the elderly woman rose as her pet's name was called.

"Don't worry, dear." She smiled kindly. "Dr. Zakos is wonderful. She saved my Mr. Whiskers last year." With a sympathetic nod, she took her cat to the back office area.

They sat in silence for a while. Even the ticking of the clock seemed like screaming in the stillness of the room and staring at the clock, Hope could have sworn the hands never moved.

"This is taking too long."

She looked at the man next to her. Erik looked frozen, his eyes dull with grieving. "We don't know how long it's supposed to take, Erik."

He shook his head. "It's too long. It's over. They can't save him."

"Erik, come on."

He shook his head.

"Erik—"

"It's just like Magnus."

She waited but he stopped, just stopped and suddenly, it stopped being about what she wanted to know, needed to know. It was about what he needed to say. "Who's Magnus, love?"

He scrubbed his hands across his face and dropped them into his lap again. Watching him, the slump in his shoulders made fear and sorrow into a physical ache in her chest. "Erik. Come on. I know this was…I don't know, life-changing, I guess."

"It was." He looked at her and looked away again. "It was."

"Please. Please tell me."

The little old lady and her cat were called back and he watched them disappear into the back before he spoke. Haltingly at first, then faster. "Magnus…was my K-9 partner in Afghanistan. German Shepherd dog. Big guy. One of the biggest concerns with K-9 units is protecting the dogs from snipers." He shuddered. "The sniper got him in the neck."

"Oh, my God. Erik. Baby, no." Tears streaming down her face, she pressed her hands to her mouth.

"I got into the unit because I'd always had dogs, always trained dogs. My whole life." He gave a short, humorless laugh. "And I was good. Magnus and I were good. We did our job and we did it well."

"I'm sorry. I'm so sorry."

He didn't seem to hear her. He didn't seem to be able to stop, now that he'd started. "I was next to him when he was shot and I got to him first. I held pressure on the wound. I yelled for help. The troops guarding the unit got the sniper but..." He shook his head again. "I held him while he bled out and died. And I was done."

Erik stood and walked to the window, staring out as night raced into the city and cars streamed by. She would have bet what he saw were the eyes of his shepherd as the life ebbed out of them.

"I haven't had a dog since. I wouldn't have had a dog now if it hadn't been for Marty, my old boss from K-9. But he asked for a favor." Erik rolled his neck. "And he got me out of the unit after Magnus died. I owed him."

Silence, but for the ticking clock, fell again. She opened her mouth to say something, anything that might help and realized not only the futility of such an attempt but the insult it would be to imagine a few trite words would ease him. So she sat. She reached out and held his hand. And they waited.

Three and a half hours later, the office door opened. A tall, lanky brunette woman stood in the doorway. "Mr. Yorkson?"

"Yoriksson, yeah. That's me." Erik rose stiffly from the chair he had returned to. Hope stood too, more slowly, studying the tired eyes of the woman before them.

The vet held open the door. "If you'd like to come on back?"

Chapter Twenty-One

"They said it was probably a toadstool."

"Oh, no!" Miriam's screech vibrated the phone and Hope held it a little away from her ear. "Those are so poisonous!"

"Yeah. Totally awful. I can't even talk about how awful it was." She switched ears and held the phone in place with her shoulder. Her toolbox sat in front of her, a complete shambles, as she rummaged for the right screwdriver. "It's been three days and I still want to cry whenever I think about it."

"Darling. It's only three days. You must give yourself time. Feelings like these do not disappear overnight."

"I know, I know. Aha, there you are!" She pulled out the correct tool.

"What are you doing?"

Hope knelt in front of her kitchen cabinet and opened the sleek wooden door. "I'm putting child safety locks on my cabinets."

There was a small, humming silence. "Is there something you should tell me, darling?"

She snorted. "No."

"All right. Why the locks, then?"

"Well, when I redid the kitchen, I didn't put them in, because I don't have kids and they're ugly, you know?" She tightened a stubborn screw with a grunt. "Get in there."

"Yes, very ugly."

Hope picked up the other half of the locking mechanism and checked its position. "But after the thing with Ruger, I got to thinking about it. The kids do spend time here, and what if, God forbid, one of them got into something?"

"Oh, dear God."

"Yeah, so I looked through the catalogs at work and found some that weren't as disgusting looking." She tightened the last screw and tested the door. "There. Hey, these are pretty good."

"And yet, my cabinets have ugly locks." Miriam's voice was a perfect mixture of sadness and resignation.

Hope snickered. "I have locks that will coordinate with your cabinets on order. They'll be in next week. And I'm making a safety section in the store now."

"Well, that's very wise. And a way to make good out of this horrible event."

"Yeah, I thought so." She heard a car door shut. "I think Erik's here."

"I shall leave you to talk to him, then. Call me later."

"I will and when I do, you're going to tell me how everything worked out with you and my rotten brother."

Miriam laughed. "Don't talk about my husband that way. Only I may call him rotten."

She tossed the screwdriver into the toolbox and attempted to close it. "So you two are okay?"

"We're fine. Go see to your own man."

Hope chuckled as she set her cell phone down and studied the mess of tools. She really should ask Erik to reorganize it for her. Later, she thought. After dinner.

Going to the front of the house, she opened the door as Erik reached the porch, a large box in his arms. She held the screen door wide for him and the black and white bundle of fur and electricity that shot into the house. Ruger yapped excitedly and proceeded to race in circles from the living room to the kitchen to the dining room.

"Oh, look," she murmured. "It's the Terrier 500."

Erik leaned down and kissed her. "Hi, honey. We're home."

"You certainly are." She closed the door behind him as he set the box on the floor. "Didn't the vet say he should be quiet for a few days?"

He grunted in agreement as he took off his trench coat and hung it in the hall closet. His stone gray suit looked as immaculate as it had that morning when he left for work. She was going to have to get used to that, she supposed. "What the vet said was he would probably be quiet and not himself for a few days. That we should let him rest and recover as his body finished the healing process. We should leave him be and not worry too much if he looked mopey."

Ruger skidded to a stop in the living room, yapped at them again, then took off at top speed in the opposite direction.

"Mopey, huh?"

"Yeah. Then she opened the door to his kennel and he jumped out of it and started slamming against the door with his paws. The vet stood there for minute watching him and said, 'Or...not.'"

She laughed. "Oh, jeeze. Three days ago, he was an inch from death."

Erik nodded. "No one at the office could believe he survived. They're calling him the Little Miracle."

As they watched the puppy flew back into the room and leaped up on the couch. Butt in the air, head low, he wagged his tail madly and yapped again.

"Little demon spawn, more like." She shook her head. "Okay, let's get him out back for a while. He can run off some of that energy before he decides he needs to eat the couch."

"Is the yard secure?"

She nodded. "The fence was fine before and I did a check for toadstools earlier today."

"Okay." He didn't move from his spot, just watched the puppy tearing around for a moment.

"He's going to be fine, Daddy." She patted his arm and walked toward the back of the house, calling Ruger as she went.

As the dog raced around the backyard, barking at nothing, they watched from the deck. Clouds had rolled in and the day was dim with the coming rain. "Are you going to marry me?" Erik asked abruptly.

"Uh." She stared at the dog, unable to form words. In the days since his original proposal and the race to save Ruger's life, nothing had been said about the question she hadn't answered.

"Yes or no, it's not complicated." Ice-blue eyes roamed over her face as a small smile curved his beautiful mouth.

"It is complicated, Erik. First, where are we going to live?" She planted her hands on her hips as she faced him. Not complicated. Ha!

"Here."

"Because I love this house. I bought this house because I love it."

"I know." He nodded. "Here."

"I've a lot of work into it and I do not like moving." She folded her arms and paced away from him.

"Okay. Here."

"And it's not all pristine and fancy like your place— what did you say?"

"I know you love this place, Hope." He crossed the deck to her. "We'll live here."

"But your condo."

"I'll sell it."

"But it's so perfect and organized."

He shrugged. "I'll organize stuff here. Then you'll yell at me and we'll argue. Then we'll make up and have make-up sex."

He pulled the velvet box from his pocket and flipped open the lid. Stepping closer to her, he held the box between them.

She touched the satin lining of the box, too afraid to reach for the ring. "It's so pretty. Looks different than Miriam's ring and my mom's ring. Not so sticky-outy."

"Well, that's the technical term for it." He laughed as she whapped him on the arm. "It's a bezel setting, so it won't catch on things at work."

"I'll probably get it all banged up anyway." Glumly, she studied the perfection of the ring. He always did the perfect thing and she never would.

"It's platinum, Hope. It's pretty tough. And it's meant to be worn, not just sit in a box." He brushed the hair away from her face, cupped her cheek in his hand. "I love you, Hope. I love who you are. I love how beautiful you are even if you don't see it. I love how you think, even when I don't understand it. Will you marry me?"

She sighed. "Fine."

He tipped her face up to look her in the eye, raising an eyebrow at her. She rolled her eyes. "Yes. I'll marry you."

He smiled. "Now tell me why."

She blushed. "Because I thought you were an angel when I saw you first, even before I thought you looked like Thor. And because you're funny and you're smart, despite the way you look."

He laughed.

"And because you're nice to your family. And you know how to love. I know you mean it when you say you love me."

He took the ring from the box and slid it on her finger. "And?"

"And I love you back." Tears pricked her eyes. "Why me, Thor?"

He made a face and she laughed even as she cried. "It had to be you, Hope. I could never settle for anyone else." He kissed her and she felt like she was floating above the decking, over the yard. Ruger's bark was a distant sound.

"And we're going to live here?" she confirmed.

"We'll live here."

"And you're going to be okay with it, even though it's not quite finished."

He nodded. "I'll even help with the remodeling." Her look of horror made him roar with laughter. "Okay, okay. I won't."

"Thank God." She settled against him, wrapped in his arms. The dog was now rolling madly in the grass and the breeze picked up. "You can organize my toolbox, though."

THE END

Turn the page for a Sneak Peek at

Training Heels

Tails Of Love, Book 2

Coming Soon!

Rory Evans watched the faces of the tormented shudder and strain. Sweat dripped to the floor and someone choked back a sob. The sadist in charge barked out a command and counted down the last ten second of their hell, releasing those poor souls from the punishment. Even the strongest gasped for breath, bent double, hands resting on their knees. The weakest collapsed to the floor, too spent and abused even to cry.

Maybe Crossfit wasn't the workout for him.

A rush of cold air nudged at his back and he turned to see the monster who talked him into visiting this "gym," or third ring of hell, come in. Big, buff and blonde, the kind of guy every woman dreamed of, everything Rory wasn't. Rory eyed him with loathing. "You."

"Hey, man." Erik clapped a hand on his shoulder. "Good to see you. Ready to give this a shot?"

"No."

The Nordic-god-in-training laughed. "Come on, I'll introduce you to the trainer who's going to do our class. Tyler! Over here!"

When the man turned, Rory relaxed a little. Although obviously fit, the trainer didn't seem as terrifying as the woman who had been directing the last class. This guy had a youthful, honest-looking face, blue eyes and short-cropped hair. He walked over to them, hand outstretched. "Hey, I'm Tyler. Welcome to *Blood, Sweat & Tears.* You're Ronnie?"

"Rory, actually. Nice to meet you."

"Yeah, you, too. Erik tells me you're looking for a challenge."

Rory coughed. "Yeah, well. Erik might have been drunk when he said that." When both of the other men laughed, he shook his head. "See, no one takes me seriously."

Tyler just grinned. "Let me give you a tour and explain how this works. Erik says your work schedule varies."

The next fifteen minutes were a blur of faces and names, class schedules and training rules. Rory thought he was still on the introductory tour when he found himself standing in front of a large, wooden box. "You want me to do what?"

"Jump up on it. Let's just see where you are right now."

"I can tell you where I am. I'm standing in front of a really big box." Rory studied it a moment longer, took a deep breath and jumped. It was more luck than anything else, he thought, that he landed on top of the box, more the hand of God that he didn't splat face-first into its hard edge. But he seemed to have satisfied the two men standing by, watching.

"You've got some power there, Rory. That's good. We're going to push that, see how far we can go." Tyler made a few quick notes on the clipboard he held, then smiled again at Rory. It was reassuring and frightening at the same time. "All right. Let's get started. Don't worry,

no one expects you to hit everything on the first day.
We're going to take it slow."

Slow.

Lying in a puddle of his own sweat forty-five minutes later, hearing his breath wheeze out of his young and, he thought, relatively fit body, he questioned Tyler's understanding of the word. Then he questioned Erik's level of friendship. Lastly, he questioned his own sanity. None of the answers pleased him.

"Hey." Erik's face floated over him and he blinked away the blurriness in his vision. Damn, sweat was just everywhere.

He closed his eyes again. "What." Maybe Erik would go away. Or bring him a cold drink. Or bring him a cold drink, then go away.

"You going to get up or are you going to lie there all day?"

"Day's mostly over. I'll take option B."

"Come on. Don't make me tell Hope what a pansy you are."

He opened his eyes again to glare at the schmuck he once called friend. "Hope likes me. Hope must know by now that you're a psychopath." He took the hand Erik offered and pulled himself to his feet.

"She likes you. Not going to stop her from mocking your candyass." Erik slapped him on the shoulder and Rory didn't quite manage not to wince. "You know that.

She had brothers before she married me. Razzing is imminent."

"Blow me."

Erik laughed and rubbed Rory's head. "You're not my type, little man. And you did okay today. I didn't think you'd make it to the end, but you held on."

Rory attempted to stretch his arms overhead and groaned. "I didn't do all of the stuff."

Tyler spoke from behind them. "All of the stuff takes a while. Erik couldn't do everything right off the bat—"

"Hey, hey!" Erik made a cut-off motion with his hand. "He doesn't need to know that. That's between us, man."

A group of athletic looking teenagers surged into the main area of the gym and Tyler jerked his head to the right, pointing at the lobby area at the side of the room. The scary-looking trainer from the earlier class waded into the fray and spoke to the group. In a surprisingly short amount of time, she had the group settled down and listening to her with the fixed attention of young males who'd just figured out what made girls different.

He didn't blame them. Scary or not, the gym lady was seriously hot.

Following Erik and Tyler, Rory envisioned the perfect night to follow this descent into hell. Pizza, he thought. Pizza and some ibuprofen and a long, hot shower. Of course, he'd have to make time for Serena, too, but-- He realized that Tyler was speaking.

"And some individual work is a good idea. If we can work with you one-on-one, we can make sure you're using the right form, getting the most out of every workout."

Erik nodded. "Reduces the likelihood of injury, too."

"Which can really derail you. Speaking of," Tyler walked to the fridge by the check-in desk and grabbed three bottles of water. "Hydration is pretty critical."

Rory twisted off the cap and drained half the bottle before speaking. "No kidding. Okay, you're saying three times a week, average time in gym sixty minutes or less. And once a week, individual work with...who? You?"

Tyler scanned his clipboard. "I can work with you, sure. Or you can have Bob or Cameron."

Rory nodded and gulped some more water. "Okay."

"Or Steph. My wife. Actually," he scanned the notes on the clipboard again. "For your schedule, she might be the best choice."

Rory stretched again and bit back a whimper. "Is she nice?" He blinked as Tyler lit up like a candle.

"She's the best," he said simply.

Rory nodded, resigned. "Sign me up."

The paperwork was relatively simple. Before he had time to reconsider the madness he was undertaking, he'd already signed his life away. If he didn't like it, he told himself, he didn't have to go. If it was really awful, he could just cancel.

If he didn't mind Erik laughing at him like a Viking hyena, he could quit.

Yeah. That might happen.

Walking out to the lobby, he spotted Erik leaning against the reception desk, looking a little trapped. The sight of a pretty blonde chatting him up. Erik looked up and caught his eye, the expression of a drowning man on his handsome face. *Ah, yes*, he thought. *Revenge.*

"Okay," he grinned at his uncomfortable friend. "I'm good to go. See you later, Erik."

"Hey, Rory, wait up!" Erik tried to dodge around the blonde, but she was wily. She blocked Erik's escape and stepped over to him in one smooth, practiced moved. He had to appreciate the level of skill.

"Hi!" she chirped, holding out her hand to Rory. "I'm Sarah. Are you joining the gym?"

He found himself shaking her hand. "Uh, yeah, I—"

"Did Erik tell you about it?" She smiled at him, sweetly, without the predatory intent she'd had while gazing up at Erik. "Erik is a great example of what boys can grow into, especially if you're working out here." She paused when Erik rubbed a hand over his face. "Oh, I'm sorry! I meant...young men."

"Sarah," Erik began.

"You know, Erik's mentored quite a few of the high-schoolers here. Do you have a mentoring program at your school?"

Molly Jane Johnson took a deep breath and pushed open the doors to *Blood, Sweat & Tears*. Her hands were clammy enough to slip on the metal handles, but for once, it wasn't the pending workout that had her nerves jumping. It was the possibility of seeing *him*.

He'd been coming to BS&T for six weeks now. She knew it was stupid, and so freaking high-school to keep track of that, but even the thought of him sent her fluttering back to her years of teen-aged goofiness. And watching him work out? She was lucky her knees hadn't given out on her yet.

He was, like that pop song said, a teenage dream.

She had an advantage, she told herself as she signed in at the desk, exchanging hellos with the young man working there. She'd known him a good chunk of her life. And he was friends with her brothers. And her parents loved him.

He was the perfect son-in-law-to-be.

Humming a little, she zipped to the central part of the gym to check out the workout of the day, written up on the whiteboard. The box jumps made her grimace, but she could feel the adrenaline start as rolled her shoulders and moved towards the track for her warm-up. Stephanie was leading the work out. She loved it when Steph led the workout.

Especially when the cocky newcomers were there. That was just fun.

She moved smoothly from warm-up to mobility, the pre-workout stretching segment of her hour. Her hour. Not anyone else's. Not that begrudged her kids, as she thought of them. She loved teaching gym, especially to the elementary grades. When she'd worked with the high schoolers, it wasn't nearly as fun, but K through sixth? It was awesome.

But she loved this gym, too. One day, when she had kids of her own, she might have to give it up, but for now, this was her time. If she allowed herself to dream, maybe one day she have those little rugrats, and she and her man would dump them at their Nana's house while they escaped to the gym for a workout. And a hot shower afterward that would inevitably lead—

"Okay, people, let's line up." Steph's voice cut through her reverie and she flushed, hoping no one could guess what she was thinking about.   Bouncing up on her toes, she joined the others readying themselves for their daily challenge.

And they were off.

"Arg!" She dropped the weight she clean and jerked, stepped back as it bounced. Cheers rang out from the other participants and the smile she wanted to flash back at them trembled around her mouth. She braced a hand against the wall and fought for breath. The weight-strength challenges were always the hardest for her. Damn, she hated being short.

"A new max weight for Molly," Stephanie announced behind her. She looked over to see her name on the white board, and this time, a huge grin broke through the panting she was trying to control. She'd done it! She'd actually topped her past max!

Her gym buddies crowded around her and she laughed, accepting their congratulations. Hugs from a couple of the other women, high-fives from a few of the guys. Barry, or Gramps as they called him, rubbed the top of her head. "Proud of you, kid," he rumbled.

"Thanks." She turned back to the board, studying the stats next to her name. Even though it was just the elation from the workout, in that moment, she felt invincible.

If only he was standing here, I'd...I'd tell him everything.

She shook off the craziness of that thought and started cooling down with the others, laughing and moaning about the torture they'd endured once more. It wasn't until she was walking out that she spotted a face she never thought she'd see in BS&T. He was standing near the gym owner and the big blonde guy she'd had that one disastrous date with more than a year ago and...she frowned. That was weird. Why did he look so pained and horrified?

She shrugged. Weird or not, her past was standing there.

Rory felt the light punch just as he was about to answer the twit in front of him. He turned, a flicker of battle lit inside of him and goggled at the pixie standing there. "What are you doing here?"

"Same thing you are!" The tiny brunette beamed up at him and launched herself at him for a hug. He gave her a rib-cracking squeeze and laughed when she squealed, then spun her around. She smelled like good, healthy sweat and gumdrops. She'd always smelled like gumdrops, he thought, even when they were kids. They pulled back from each other and just grinned. "Long time, no see!"

"No kidding." He set her back on her feet and turned to the others standing there. "Molly, this is my friend Erik."

She chuckled, the low sound that always surprised him, coming from her slight form. "Yeah, we've met. Hey, Erik. How are you?"

"I'm good, thanks." The other man looked like a giant next to her. "How are you? How's your team?"

"Oh, they're so much better this year, have you been watching? I mean, they still need to beef up their defense, but you know." She rolled her eyes. "That was always their problem. I mean, come on! The goalie is the last line of—"

Rory gave her curly ponytail a tug. "Seriously? Five seconds and you're yammering on about hockey?"

She went a little pink but grinned unrepentantly. "Things you can count on."

"Weird girl." He wrapped an arm around her neck and gave her a little noogie. "I can count on that. Oh, sorry. Do you know Sandra?"

"It's Sarah." Both women corrected him in unison.

"Oh, sorry." He gave Sarah one of his professional smiles and caught Molly's look of surprise.

"We know each other," Sarah said coolly. "I'm surprised you two do, though. Are you teaching some of the older kids now, Molly?"

Molly met his chagrined look with barely contained amusement. "She thinks you're in high school!" she whispered gleefully.

The gym owner, who had turned to answer questions from one of the other trainers, returned to their little group. "Okay, Rory. You're all set up and ready to roll, man. I know your schedule is tight, and Steph's aware of the possibility of last-minute changes, so don't worry about that. You're not the first doctor we've had working out here."

Sarah's flabbergasted expression would have delighted him more if he hadn't been distracted by Molly's excited chatter. He stepped out of the way as Molly bounced up to Tyler and exploded into a stream of words and gestures about what he could only assume was her work out. Tyler shifted his focus to her and nodded, apparently understanding exactly what she was saying.

"You're a doctor?" Sarah asked, doubt like a neon sign on her face.

He drank deep from his water bottle then nodded, not bothering to answer verbally.

"—And then I did it, Tyler! I totally beat my max!" She did a little dance and made the man laugh.

"You're amazing, Moll." He held up his hand. "Up top."

She had to reach a little to smack his hand, Rory noted, but Tyler didn't adjust for her. He gave the gym owner points.

Erik caught his eye and Rory moved to the counter where he stood. "How do you know Hockey Freak?" he asked quietly.

Rory snickered at the man's nickname for his surrogate little sister. "Good one. We grew up next door to each other. We—me, her brothers and mine—were the terror of the neighborhood. Molly tagged along."

"Small world." Erik shook his head. "Well, listen, man, I got to run. Hope's family is coming over tomorrow and there's a *list*."

"Better you than me."

The blonde man grinned and shrugged. "The trade off is worth it."

Judging from the spring in his step, it was, but Rory wasn't going there. There was little too much living to do yet.

38393436R00197

Made in the USA
San Bernardino, CA
07 September 2016